THE TRUTHS THAT DECEIVE

SECRET SOCIETY OF THE OBSIDIAN KNIGHTS: BOOK FOUR

KRISTEN LUCIANI

Edited by: Elaine York of Allusion Graphics

Cover Design by: Book Cover Couture

Photo Credit: Wander Aguiar

 Created with Vellum

IMPORTANT NOTE TO READERS

This is a dark romance that contains very triggering situations such as primal play, graphic violence and gore, graphic murder, graphic language, dub con, kink, spanking, public acts of sex, description of graphic sex acts, edge play, rope play, D/s, and anal sex.

This book is not appropriate for those under the age of eighteen based on the dark themes and situations.

CHAPTER 1
SMITH

The bullet whizzes by, the whine of its flight and burn of heat scorching my head, a blast of reality that pushes my adrenaline up high as I weave across the stone floor in the old Scottish castle. Shouts and footsteps behind me get louder, heavier.

Closer.

I dive behind an overturned heavy wooden table, slide out the empty clip of my Sig, and grab a new one, slamming it into place.

One thing's for sure. I'm not about to fucking die in Scotland while on a much-needed vacation.

"Got one," a thick-accented voice yells out. "Another one of those fuckers went through here."

Shit. There's only me and Reaper inside the castle.

If I have to go back and save his sorry ass...

My pocket buzzes exactly twice.

Reaper's down, but not for long. I don't bother texting him back. There are girls in here, down in the dungeon slash sex video room. And I'd prefer to find them and pick off the Bolivian dickheads holding them captive—apart from their leader, who'll no doubt be down with the girls—without having to arrange the rescue of someone Reaper's size.

I count.

Every step.

My heart pounds, ears ringing from the cracking of bullets.

I ignore the searing pain and the blood on my arm— super glue will take care of that. Instead, I slow my breathing.

It won't take them long to work out where I am, these fucking mafia wannabes who've been making major waves in the sex slave markets.

The wrong sorts of waves.

They're upsetting UR Fantasies, one of my clients back in the States, so I'm here to take them out. And if I'm being honest, I fucking hate relaxing on vacation. I'd much prefer to let off steam by destroying the evil bastards who buy, sell, and torture innocent young women.

Reminds me of my old CIA days.

They're not shooting. Yet. There are four of them in here by the sounds of it. The room's huge, and since we caused a hell of a lot of carnage in here earlier, there are plenty of places to hide.

So either they're conserving bullets or they think I'm easy enough to find.

I wait. Unmoving, gun in my outstretched hand, ready to fire.

Glass crunches nearby and a single shot goes off. Someone hisses something in a Balto-Slavic dialect, something about being the son of a pig in shit.

Reaper will pick off the ones in the back of the castle, the ones who might still be in hiding and waiting for a chance to escape. Then he'll make his way back to me. I don't know how many are outside this room, and since this is my last clip, I wait until they get closer to take my shot.

I'm betting Reaper took a dive to play dead. An actual dive. In the moat. Because this place has a motherfucking moat.

Ragged breathing gets closer. My finger tightens around the gun handle.

I spring up from my spot and shoot the heavy breather behind me. Then I shift my arm and fire off another shot at the one directly behind him before slamming the gun's butt into a third guy's face. He groans and grapples with his gun and I turn him into a shield to take the bullet from the fourth dick-head who manages to squeeze off a couple of shots.

Dropping the bullet-torn body, I hold out my gun, my finger ready to press the trigger when a bullet rips through his skull from the back, splattering the area in front of him with bits of face and brain matter. He crashes like a block of cement, smashing against the ground.

Reaper grins at me.

Dripping wet.

"You're a psychopath," I say.

He shrugs, snatching a gun from the now faceless dead guy. "I deal in death for money." Then he stands up. "More mercenary with psychopathic tendencies."

"All clear?"

"All that I could see." Which means he cleared the grounds and rooms of human life.

I grin. "Wanna rescue some girls and torture information out of a low-life scumbag?"

"Smith." He puts a hand on his heart. "I thought you'd never ask."

∾

THE ADRENALINE LINGERS. Days after and it still lingers. Maybe it's fucked up to have a spring in my step because of a murder spree and a rescue done right.

The only thing that still bothers me is the Bolivian leader of the cell we just took out. He managed to hide with some rich fucks who were rutting the young girls while Reaper and I massacred his crew. And when we finally got to him, the bastard had little to say.

I sip my scotch and sit back in my seat at the modern low-lit bar that overlooks the glitter of new and old London.

Well, he had a lot to say. Just not about the things I wanted. I didn't go into that castle of death for my goddamn health. I went because I wanted information. And when I dropped the name of one of the assholes who was going to rape, use, and exploit my daughter after he kidnapped her, the leader clammed up fucking fast.

That man's long dead, but it makes me wonder about the sticky little threads of the Collectors.

The sex trade arm of their operation. How far reaching it actually is.

Rich, depraved assholes like the Collectors, people who are as rich as I am and even richer in some cases, they usually look for higher-end trophies. They don't tangle with low-life brutes like the Bolivians in a deserted and remote Scottish castle. They like, as their name suggests, to collect things.

Best of the best, rarest of the rare. And they're sick and twisted in ways that not even a man like Reaper could be. He's one of the few outlier Obsidian Knights. A loner. His appearances are few and far between at the Knight headquarters in New York, but he's loyal, a man who'll kill for any of his fellow Knights without blinking or asking why.

Reaper likes to kill. I don't know if he gets off on it or if he just likes the high that each contract killing gives. One thing I know is he'll carry out a kill order for anyone, as long as they're guilty by Knight standards.

And also as long as he gets his paycheck.

I'm sure a guy like Reaper has had his fair share of non-Knight ordered kills, too. He's like Mercer Vale in that way. Holds many of his secrets close to his bones.

I shift my thoughts in another direction, because Mercer makes me think of Orion, and Orion's now tangled up with my daughter.

Maybe I'll extend this vacation and miss her wedding. Not that she wants me there, anyway. I could—

The shadow that falls over me stills and I tap my hand on the glass snifter, a conceit I like when it comes to expensive liquor. I don't look up. "You're late."

"Had things to do."

"Next time I'm here, we meet at the League's club."

Enver laughs. "Can't stand that place."

Of course he can't. I knew him long before I became a Knight. Same with Reaper and Orion. Some worlds are pretty damn vast and tiny all at the same time.

Enver hates the trappings and what they represent, the type of people who give places like the League the veneer of respectability. People who never worked a day in their lives.

I like the League because it reeks of money, old money, the kind that comes drenched in with class and stained with secrets.

In places like the League, secrets are discussed and aired, and all kinds of information is there for the taking. It's a gold mine where I can find exactly what I'm looking for.

"I'm assuming this isn't a social meetup?"

He sits down, steepling his fingers as the waitress in sleek black places a glass of rum in front of him. It's white rum, artisan. Tinged with the taste of vanilla and fall apples, warming white pepper and a touch of lime.

Sipping my single malt, I wait.

Enver's a man as dark and emotionless as Mercer. Meticulous. Equally deadly. But their methods are different. Enver sells and buys secrets. Yes, he kills like all of us, but this Knight's been out in the field for a long time.

He pulls an iPad from a black leather satchel and hands it to me.

I flip it open. "Doing so well you want to farm out jobs?"

"This is up your alley."

"Yours, too."

He ignores me. "It's a simple job. An assisted trip back to the States, with all the hacker's equipment."

"What's her story?"

"Calista Hendrix is CIA. She's not in the field," he says in a hushed voice. "The girl sits behind a desk and has apparently gone AWOL after her field agent did the same. Big Daddy wants to find out who's selling what to who."

"Could be anything." I swipe the screen, continuing to read the brief.

"Big Daddy," as he refers to the CIA, is reluctant to put anything even close to worthwhile in the file so I need to rely on Enver for hidden details.

"Yeah, I know. There's more fucking black on that screen than a goth party in a blackout. But the point is... she's wanted. For questioning in Big Daddy's campgrounds."

Or in one of their prisons and holding places where, like Gitmo, people can disappear and be scrubbed from existence. Whatever this is... they think she's selling information.

"So why don't they just pick her up?"

"Not your business or mine," Enver says. "You're interested."

7

He doesn't ask. Just states the obvious because he knows me.

"I'm on vacation."

"You just went on a killing spree with Reaper in Scotland, blowing apart a Bolivian dirty little porn and slave ring. I know you, Smith. You're not in any hurry to go back."

"I let off some steam."

"You're hiding out here."

"Don't try to fucking psychoanalyze me. This job was handed to you, not me."

"I'm giving you a reason to stay here. Doing you a favor to keep you here."

I bite my tongue and tap my foot as I stare at the city outside the large floor-to-ceiling windows. The leather armchair's surprisingly comfortable, which is good. Because Enver takes his time with the next request.

He takes a sip of his drink. "And I'm asking you for one at the same time."

"So you're offering me a chance to get out of the wedding by saving your ass from whatever it needs saving from?"

"We served in the CIA together," Enver says, ignoring my question. "Got out and went into private intelligence work. We're also Knights."

"And?"

He sighs heavily and takes a swallow of his rum. "This kind of job puts me in the crosshairs of people I need to stay away from. Plus, I'm in the middle of something, and heading back stateside isn't on my agenda right now."

"You really think they're going to lock up one of their own? Fuck me, she's only twenty-four," I scoff.

Her age sits uncomfortably close to that of my own kid, Dakota. A little older, but...

It doesn't matter I became a parent before I hit eighteen, a kid's a kid and fucking babysitting in a soft kidnap job isn't high on my list.

Even if it does keep me away from the wedding.

"She's been naughty in Big Daddy's ever-seeing eye." Enver shrugs. "She's an adult."

"It's soft fucking kidnapping."

"She's computer intel, a hacker. Calista dropped off the face of the planet because she knows she's a target." He pauses, reaches over, and swipes to the next page on the iPad.

I follow the words on the page. It's boring shit about her background. Calista "Hendrix" Price. Younger brother, Henry Xavier, is in the hands of Big Da—the CIA.

"Under close protection" is their code for "watched and a prisoner at a moment's notice."

I look back at Enver. "If you're trying to tell me Calista's all soft and basement bound, I'm not going to believe you. Daddy trains well and you fucking know it."

Last sighting was in Berlin.

"She's young and she's never been in the field. There's a difference, Smith, between desk job and field agent, and you know it."

"So she's wet behind the ears, dropped off the planet, and Daddy can't find her?" I shake my head. "Not buying it."

"No one's asking you to. Just to bring her in. All you have to do," he says, reaching into his satchel and sliding a black leather folder that'll have a backstory and passports, or my name isn't Johannes Schmidt Jaeger, "is tell her she needs to report in at home and you're taking her."

"Why me?"

"Your blueblood Patrician mother had a hard-on for an American-born German man, Herr Jaeger. Live her fucking dream for her."

"My mother was not—" I stop. There's no point playing in

that pool with him. The point he's making is that I should go in because I've got a German name even though I'm very much American. I keep reading the brief. "Just bring her in, any means necessary to gain her cooperation?"

Then I flick to the last photo of the girl. Pink, blue, and purple-streaked ice-silver hair pinned up, showing an undercut.

Big eyes like looking into a stormy ocean. Gray and turbulent.

And with that soft mouth and stubborn chin, she's pretty, ridiculously so.

She also looks about fifteen here.

And yeah, it's not like she's an active field agent. She sits behind a desk for the CIA. So how fucking hard could it be to find her and bring her in?

I've got contacts in Germany, both in the Bundesnachrichtendienst federal intelligence service, also known as BND, and outside the agency.

I look at him. "When?"

He puts a burner down and on it is a first-class red-eye to Berlin.

"Tonight."

CHAPTER 2
CALISTA

The techno beat makes my bones thrum and thump in time.

Someone's out to get me. Call me paranoid, but I know the signs and I need to gather intel. As much as I can, before it's too late.

I move through the darkened coffeehouse and club. The place is old, leftover from before the wall came down decades earlier. It's cheap and fits with a punk and artist drug vibe with the feels of a speakeasy.

It's a perfect place for someone like me.

Someone who's trying to avoid Uncle Sam's reach but wants to stay close to where I worked.

Wants?

No.

Needs to.

Getting out of Germany's only half the battle. I need to get the hell out of Europe and back to the States, all without being flagged.

And I'm not sure how to do it.

First things first. If I can find Johnny, the field agent I've been handling, things will take a turn for the better. But I have a sinking feeling that if he does turn up somewhere, he won't be alive to tell the story.

That familiar queasiness hits, rocking my stomach and sending burning bile up the back of my throat, leaving a bitter taste in my mouth.

Is he dead?

Gone underground?

Working for someone else as a double agent?

I don't know. All I know is he stopped communicating and I waited too long to report it. There were reasons, like my own agenda and the fact that he asked me to hold off so he could look into Bolivia.

Now panic beats in my veins.

What I need is time I don't have to look into Bolivia myself, to find my own contacts there, to poke into chatter on the dark web, to listen for any clues about where the hell Johnny might have ended up.

And my own agenda?

I get a soda from the bar and snake my way to the back, past the people in clusters who are high past their eyeballs and swaying to the beat of electronica, past the others hunkered down at tables with their computers and phones.

The corner table's dark, close to an exit just past the restrooms that leads out to another *Straße*, or street. It's a good vantage point because I can also see who comes into the place. I'm not an idiot. The CIA or one of their sneakier subsidiaries will have people out looking for me. My time's borrowed and currently riding on a ticking bomb.

I put my personal computer down on the battered wooden table and open the lid, using the hot spot from the burner phone in my pocket. If I so much as touched my CIA-issued computer, they'd have me pinned in a hot second.

Every now and then I glance past my laptop screen, sipping from my glass. Sure, relying on my training should be enough. I should be able to read the room and people from my periphery.

But the information I have scrapes at my brain to the point where there are so many potential threats, I don't know how I'll ever be able to thwart them all.

Johnny thought the Iranians might be using Bolivia as a base of operations. Poor countries often take big chunks of money without looking too closely at where it's coming from. The fact that he's disappeared makes me wonder if he was onto something, something the Bolivians wanted to cover up.

And now I'm also sitting on information someone high up in the CIA wants. I squeeze the glass in my hand, my lips pressing tightly together.

I went deeper than I should, poked into things far above my clearance level, and now...

Well, with what I've got, I'm not sure who I can trust.

This new weapon is... scary. In the wrong hands, it'll get buried deeper than the corpse they'll turn me into if I reveal it to the wrong person.

I take a deep breath before tapping into the dark web in an attempt to gather information on CIA, and other international intelligence agencies such as Britain's MI6, Germany's BND, Russia's FSB and SVR, and other government agencies, big and small.

I don't get any hits.

Yet.

If someone from any of those agencies is actively looking for me, it's classified, even beyond my reach.

But the niggle in my hacker brain keeps catching on a group

of names, and landing on something in the illegal chatter and murk of the Obsidian Knights—whatever they are. That name's so slippery, I can't find anything beyond the odd mention.

I'd quickly dismiss something like the Obsidian Knights as just a code name, which it probably is, except for one thing that catches my attention.

The Collectors.

Sex trafficking.

Sex slave rings. Girls for sale.

Girls who suffered just like my mother did a long time ago.

She got out. In body, anyway. But her mind?

Not so lucky.

And definitely still captive to the travesties of that time in her life.

The Collectors are still around, and the reason I'm not about to turn myself in is that I'm going to ruin them all financially and then find one of their founders, Jon Trenton, who raped my mother and set her down the path of horror from age fifteen.

That was the name in her diary, anyway. All I have to go on.

He went dark, supposedly dead. Yet his accounts are active, all of the hidden ones, that is.

At least, up until the demise of the biggest wing of the Collectors.

Trenton's not a concern to the CIA. Rogue agents and clandestine groups are. But my mentor, Aaron Riley, formerly of the CIA and now a senator, warned me about rich and powerful people like Trenton, of the seemingly dead. Of people who take high profile yet shadowy positions so they can fly under the radar to continue their depraved work. The ones who hide in both dark corners and out in the open.

Like the Devil himself.

Riley has a healthy distrust of everyone. It's probably why politics suits him so well.

I shift on the uncomfortable wooden slab of a seat, trying to separate paranoia from possible real danger.

My calves tighten, as the urge to run grabs hold. But I don't. Instead, I glance around in the darkness. No one new has come in since I arrived. Yet...

A cold whisper of unease slips down my spine. I copy the information I need to a thumb drive, just in case I can't get online at some point. Then I send it to my Jane Doe cloud account where it'll be stored securely.

Switching to some mindless gossip website, I log off the hot spot but keep the page up. I stare at it, pretending to read the words when the hairs on the back of my neck prickle with fear.

Three people sit to the left of me at another table, and to my right's a man in black, his nose buried in a book.

For some reason, my gaze catches on him. He's tall and needs a shave. He's about mid to late thirties with chiseled good looks. Dark honey-brown hair, muscular, full lips. I absently twist a strand of hair around my finger as my eyes take note of every feature.

People read in places like this. He's got the look of an artist, definitely German. But...

But.

But he rubs me in a way that has my senses screaming. I pack up my laptop and walk over to the bar. The man rises from his table. He brushes into me as he passes and electricity cascades.

Penetrating blue eyes meet mine. "*Entschúldigung,*" he says. "*Das ist gut.*"

I let him know all's good, ignoring the velvet darkness of his voice that holds a carnal edge. Immediately, I decide to go to the bar for another soda. "Wolf," I say to the bartender in German, "can you do me a favor? If anyone asks—"

"I have never seen you, Hendrix."

I flash a smile, hating the miniscule exposure of even this, standing here in the shadows. "And point anyone asking about me in the opposite direction of where I go when I leave. The usual."

And I slide over a few more euros to him.

He palms them and winks.

The mystery man is gone, but I'm still unsettled, so much so I don't log back in to the dark web when I sit back down at the table. I just mindlessly surf the web for celebrity gossip and fashion trends.

This time when I pack up my laptop, the deliberately battered shell that hides state-of-the-art hardware, I leave my drink and a copy of whatever book I pull from my pack on the table. Then I slide out the back door past the bathrooms and into the gloomy Berlin day. The inkling that my life is about to become equally gloomy suffocates me like someone just stuck a plastic bag over my head.

Because in my line of work, that could easily become my reality.

THERE'S no way I'm going to be able to nap at my little hole-in-the-wall sublet apartment in Mitte, so I decide to change clothes and my look. I twist my hair into knots on my head, exposing the undercut, and I pull on my schoolgirl-on-crack outfit. Long thigh-high striped socks and chunky Mary Janes, plaid skirt with a white shirt and tie.

Then I paint on cherry-red lips, heap on lots of eyeliner and mascara, and pull on a black jacket.

I quickly cram my computer, fake ID, and all my hardware into a red and black backpack and sling it on. I glance in the mirror.

Hacker to party girl in minutes.

A perfect disguise.

I bounce from place to place through the city. In and out of gallery shows and parties, skirting the edges, scouting for anyone who doesn't belong.

The beat of unease grows deep in my gut, and I'm on edge, the needlelike teeth of that unease nibbling harder and harder.

Finally, I make my way into a club, dark and moody German industrial music playing in the background. I scout the space as my eyes adjust to the dim light. This place definitely takes in a certain type of clientele, and anyone working for the government—no matter which one—would stand out like a dick on a cake.

And field agents? They're not sending one of those assets after *me*.

It'd be men in suits with no sense of humor.

Like when I got arrested at fourteen for hacking into top government sites.

Still, I'm itching like ants are crawling all over me, and I can't stay still.

Rookie behavior, a voice in my mind screams.

I slip farther into the space. Smoke fills my lungs, stinging my eyes as I find my way to the center of the dance floor.

Although the real rookie behavior is me giving in to the emotions and physiological reactions to being followed.

Shit, it's like a beacon calling out to anyone watching.

I push through the crowd on the dance floor to the bar on the other side. I order a whiskey and down it to calm my nerves. Then another for good measure. The golden heat of it sinks into my flesh to smooth the frayed edges of my nerves. I drink just enough for that, not nearly enough to lose the sharp-ness I need to survive.

In the next room, one that smells like sweat and smoke and the sweet and cloying aromas of vapes, I find a small table. I pull out a chair when a shadow falls on me.

All of my senses burst into life.

The man grabs my arm.

His touch is electric, burning through the fabric of the jacket.

"*Bitte*," I say. "*Ich*—"

"*Nein*." The velvet is hard now, cold like steel. Wintry. "You're not as hard to find as you think."

"*Bitte*," I say again, letting out a string of German where I tell him he's got the wrong person and to let me go. The words fall over each other but he understands them perfectly, even though he's switched to English.

Dammit. I don't want to cause a scene, but I also don't want to be dragged off to a windowless room here or in the United States. So I act.

I stomp on his foot with my huge platform Mary Jane and elbow him hard in the chest.

His hand slips and I run.

Bolting out the back door, I gulp down oxygen, panic exploding into each and every cell. My lungs tighten as I pant out each constricted breath.

The alleyway behind the club takes me down and through a set of streets before I realize he's not following me. I meander around, off the beaten path, wandering in and out of small places as I continue to peek over my shoulder at anyone who dares come close.

But I'm wasting time. And as the sky above rumbles with thunder, I make my way slowly back to my street. I should have probably hunkered down back at the apartment instead of risking my safety, but I needed to know for sure that somebody was out there looking for me.

And now I do.

I need to run. I need to just grab my shit and vanish again, move out of Berlin, maybe toward Latvia, or even somewhere like Italy, a place they might not think to look.

Keeping a firm grip on my panic, I eye the street around my building and organize in my mind what I need to do.

Make sure no one's lurking.

Then fucking run.

If I pack the few things I need, I can be gone in under ten minutes. Well under. Get my stuff and run, then think.

Money, hard drives, makeup, clothes. I'm not a makeup wearer on the whole, but it works when a quick change in appearance is needed.

I look around me. No one's lurking.

I circle the block twice, then cautiously make my way into the building.

The walk down the hall to my tiny little apartment is too long, too dark, too quiet.

It doesn't matter if that's all in my head. It's how I feel, and my heart slams hard into my ribs with each step.

Outside my door, I tentatively place my hand against the wood. With extreme care and quiet, I insert my key and turn the knob.

Everything's quiet. I flick on a lamp as lightning flares outside.

I look around.

Nothing seems out of place.

So far.

I drop my pack and jacket near the door.

Some might call me overly suspicious and paranoid. Everything seems to be untouched, and though there's a shift in the air pressure, the tiny place seems empty.

But I'm way too aware of the meaning of the word "seems."

Too aware of the panic that wants freedom.

I make my way to the bedroom and push open the door.

The shape moves so fast I almost don't see it until his hands are on me and I'm slammed into the wall, face-first. My breath rushes from my lungs from the force but I still fight.

He twists my arm up, pinning me to the spot.

"If you want to fucking live, stop fucking moving. Now."

Everything turns to ice at the growl that assaults my ears for the second time tonight.

Because I know exactly who that voice belongs to.

And I've got a pretty damn good idea of what he wants.

CHAPTER 3
SMITH

Creep doesn't even begin to describe how I fucking feel right now.

Calista's stopped struggling but my hands on her feel good, too good to want to stop touching. They make me want to take things further.

Faster.

Harder.

Fuck my life.

"Let me go, you pervert," she snaps at me in German.

"Not on your fucking life."

I don't bother with the German. She's CIA, so she no doubt has a number of languages under her hat, like me. But while she's young, she's fit. I can feel that in the power that she doesn't bother to try and hold back. She hasn't learned the knack of going soft and pliant until she launches into fight.

Comes from her fucking desk job.

But that inexperience licks up along my senses and fires into my cock. There's just something about her. Her fire, her fight, her sass. Maybe all of it. And even though she's way too young for me, I was drawn in the second I deliberately bumped into her and planted the tracker on her pack.

Maybe it's the fact she's pretty, although I'm not the kind of guy who gets dumbstruck by a beautiful face. I'm also not sex deprived, so getting off isn't the reason why my cock's in such a twist right now. It's just her. The way she's prey with claws and teeth. The way she cased the room and ran from both places, the way she wants to kill me right now.

It's hot.

It's pure catnip. Fuck.

She wants to fight me and run, and I want to let her. I want to chase and tackle her down and—

I deliberately shut down those thoughts before they take hold of my hands and my mouth. "I'm going to check you for weapons," I growl against her ear.

"I don't have any, asshole." This time she speaks English, and the vibration of her muscles warms my skin. "I'm not exactly in combat gear."

I shift, pressing against her, pushing her into the wall.

Oh fuck, she smells good. Oranges and jasmine, with a hint of spice. It's an erotic scent that doesn't seem to belong on her. Or maybe it does. She's dressed like a punk version of a hooker in schoolgirl cosplay, and now she looks eighteen.

I remind myself I'm not into women below the age of thirty, but this one is shattering that and stirring the fragments into something new and compelling.

"You get your tiny rocks off by doing this? Feeling up young women? Exerting whatever bullshit control you think you have? Does that make you feel like more of a man?"

Shit, her words are poisoned aphrodisiac-dipped syllables. I love the sting of them, and I move, holding her with one hand as I pat down an arm, up along her torso, skimming the underside of soft, full tits.

She hisses air, her ribs fluttering as I deftly switch hands to pat down her other side.

I go lower, skimming along her waist, and then I drop my mouth to her ear. "I'm going to let you go. Try anything and I'll fucking shoot you. Got that?"

"Not if I shoot you first."

Laughter bubbles up as I keep a hand on her wrists and step back. She twitches, and I grab my gun, then press it against her temple. "I said I'd shoot."

"You haven't yet."

"You haven't made an escape."

"Early days," she says, her low voice full of the right mix of contempt and challenge that makes me want to tear her panties off with my teeth.

After I've tackled her to the ground.

I press the gun firmly against her, but this time she doesn't even twitch.

The safety's on, but I have to admire her "fuck you" attitude that could raise boners from the dead.

So I put the weapon away and I slide my hand up her inner thigh.

She gasps.

"Don't get your panties in a knot," I murmur. "Just checking for a weapon."

"I don't have one there, you jerkoff."

Slipping my fingers to her outer thigh, I shift up to her hip and then low at the top of her panties. Cotton from the feel.

"You, Miss Price, would be shocked at the places women hide weapons."

"Unless you're planning on giving me a pelvic exam, you can trust I'm not carrying." Her snarl's ruined by the breathy edge to it.

And now she's filled my mind with images of sinking into

her, seeing if she's as furnace hot as she seems. Testing the tightness of her, the stretch of her around my cock as I thrust into her.

I want to taste her, bury my nose and tongue in her. Suck on her clit. I want to bite and taunt until she's an utter mess of pleading offerings.

Fuck.

Slowly, I move to her other hip, trailing my fingers over her ass as I do so. If I was still in the CIA, I'd be fired for this. But I'm not and I don't give a fuck. She's warm, and don't think I didn't notice how she's pushed her ass out a little, widened her stance.

It's the kind of offering that's as loud as a moan of need.

Calista Price likes it. She'd never admit it in court or to my face, but the fucking little minx, who's young enough to be my daughter, likes it.

Her response might not even register to herself, but I'm tuned in to her and I let my fingers slide up her inner thigh, up high toward the heat that radiates, the promise of that wet, tight cunt opening for me, beckoning me...

I suck in a breath as she bites off a moan. My fingers pause at the top of her thigh and my knuckles brush the underside of her panties. Her wet fucking panties.

My cock strains against my pants.

"See? I'm not carrying a weapon," she whispers.

"I'm still checking."

Knowing that what I'm doing is so wrong barely registers as my hands slide up higher, fingertips dancing a slow waltz over the hot, wet cotton. Back and forth.

She whimpers, pushing into me, and I'm ready to peel off her panties and slip my fingers into her cunt when reality bitch-slaps me.

"Dirty, but no weapons." I pause. "Or if there are, you've

shoved them so deep you won't be able to get them back before I can cause you harm." I pause a second time. Waiting a beat. "Want to try?"

"You perverted dick." This time she yanks her arms free and spins out from me.

She slams herself against the wall, much harder than when I did it. And I take a step toward her.

We're so close, face-to-face, her tits almost brushing my chest as they heave unevenly. I let her go but she doesn't try and run. "This perverted dick is here to make sure you get back to the States and into the right hands."

"Or the wrong ones." She puts her hands on my chest, and I fucking swear my skin sizzles at her touch.

I'm on edge for so many fucking reasons right now, but being jet-lagged and sleep-deprived pales in comparison to the effect this girl has on me.

Goddammit, this isn't my job.

Feeling her up isn't my job, either, yet here I fucking am. I hold my ground. She's unarmed, but I don't know her skill set. And she looks too young, way too young, even though she's more than of age to do serious damage.

Her lips are red, parted, and I recognize the rush of color in her cheeks from excitement, from the right buttons pushed, the right switches flicked.

I throb with need.

Calista Price wants to gut me, fuck me, and she looks as confused by that as I feel. My gaze flickers to her window, the thunder outside a low rumble.

Three cars pull up to the curb.

No lights.

Fuck.

"How ready are you to go?"

"I'm not—"

"How ready?"

"Before or after I kill you?" Her eyes narrow but I've shoved my libido back in its box.

I can't hear the car doors close or footsteps along the pavement, which means it's not a raid. No, these people aren't cops, they're intelligence.

Or worse, hired killers.

"Kill me later," I say as I step away from her and head back out to where her computer is in the backpack.

"Shit." Calista doesn't look out the window, doesn't make a move to it, but she's watching me, reading me like I'm code. "Pull the flower patch off the front of the backpack."

She doesn't wait. In the soft half-light she moves quickly, unscrewing an air duct and pulling out a waterproof sealed envelope that I'm betting contains cash, papers, and her passport. Then she grabs some hardware from the stove and under the sink. She's about to open the freezer when I sling the pack over my shoulder, flick off the safety, and say, "I've got your gun."

"Fucking government grunt."

"The same government you work for."

"Bringing it down from the inside," she snarls.

I can hear the sarcasm lacing her words, but if I were an actual grunt, she'd be slapped so hard with treason she wouldn't see the sun or freedom again until well after her three-hundredth birthday.

"Watch your fucking tongue."

"Why? You've already judged me."

"Move it. Now." I gesture to the door with the gun. "If you don't, you'll have much bigger problems than me judging you. Problems that will make you wish you were dead... long before you're actually killed."

∾

GETTING AWAY FROM MITTE, the center of Berlin, was anticlimactic. By the time we slid out through the basement where the trash and recycling go, we were in the next building.

From there, darting through the streets was easy. A hot-wired car and a short drive later, we're at a building that I own in Charlottenburg.

She sits in the kitchen of my apartment, quiet and brooding, her glass of scotch untouched.

Calista's drowned rat demeanor should be a total dick deflator, but it's not. I take a swallow of scotch and turn the glass in my hands. We're both dripping wet, but there's no way I'm getting changed until I'm sure she's not going to try to make a run for it.

She's soaked to the bone, but rats are smart. They fight. And they have a nasty bite.

What's her bite like?

But honestly, there's nothing rattish about her; it just makes me feel more in control thinking that way.

"At least the rain washed that makeup off." Her eyeliner and mascara ran down her face in streaked puddles of black, but she used a tea towel to wipe her face clean. She looks older now for some reason. No longer the little girl pretending to be grown up.

"Hooray for me." Her gaze flickers from me to her glass, then she takes a swallow, grimacing. "So when are your superiors coming for me?"

I cross over to her and crouch down, boxing her in. "What the fuck are they after and where's your agent?"

There's a flicker of something that crosses her face. I'm tempted to say it's a chink in her armor, but I don't think so. This is more like... honesty.

"I don't know what the CIA wants. Or where Johnny is. All I know is he went missing and..." She stops, then drags in a breath. "I took too long to report it."

Something's missing from her story but it's not my business. All that matters is getting her to focus, to trust me enough so I can get her back to the States, and pick up the paycheck Enver doesn't want.

"Who pulled up outside that Mitte hellhole you were staying in?"

"I don't know."

"CIA? BND? FSB?"

She doesn't look happy with those options, but who the hell would in her position?

I continue to throw out names of government agencies, of big criminal groups. Then I swerve. "What about MI6?" Her eyes roll. "Or maybe the Bolivian Front?"

She jerks, a spasm that's beyond her control. It wouldn't be the Front. As a political group or intel collection agency, they're as efficient as soaked bread.

But I know there are groups in Bolivia being watched. Groups up to unsavory things, just like the ones I took out in that Scottish castle.

I cast my mind over everything big and small and eye her carefully for any telltale signs that I might have hit on something. "Bolivia." I pause, thinking of information that's trickled my way. "You've been reading the chatter about weapons. Some new type, I'm betting."

"That's classified."

Rising, I put a hand on the table and one on the chair and lean right in close. "I don't give a fuck about classified. I want to know what I'm dealing with."

It's like a light goes off. She sits up straight, looking up at me, her mouth close. Too close. Not close enough.

"You're not CIA."

My drowned rat of a jailbait throwback moves. And fast.

She slams her glass into my temple, sending me staggering backward. More from surprise than anything else. Then she runs, darting past me.

"Fuck."

I bolt after her, ignoring the streak of fire, of desire that surges through me.

Before she can make it to the door, I grab her and she turns, tugging my shirt, pulling me in, and kissing me.

Calista's lips brush mine, and I twist my hand into her wet hair, some of the strands cascading down over her undercut and I grip. Hard.

"You want to play, little doll? Because this is a big girl game and I'm not sure that you are up for the challenge."

CHAPTER 4
CALISTA

Heat coils through me. My throat closes, the inside of my mouth turning into dust like the Sahara during a drought.

What on the fucking planet Earth am I thinking?

My goal was to distract, run, hide.

But that's not what I am thinking.

I wanted to see if he tasted as sinfully good as he looks.

Thinking isn't what my brain is doing. No, it is in idiot mode.

Before I can say a word, he catches my chin, then slides his other hand down the side of my body, to my hip. "Don't even try, Calista Hendrix Price. Because I won't be a fucking gentleman."

His hand reaches under my skirt and his fingers are back between my thighs. The heat of shame morphs into heat of desire and heads south. I shift, parting my thighs.

The flare of masculine pride tells me he notices, and I get the feeling not much gets past him.

I don't even know who he is and he's slipping fingers over my wet panties that have everything to do with him. His thumb strokes my clit as his fingers slide over my covered folds, pushing the fabric up between my pussy lips.

God, I want more.

Right or wrong. Batshit crazy or mildly insane. It doesn't matter.

I want more.

Crave more.

And I want to run.

Worse. I want to run and have him chase me down.

I've had sex, done some wild things, and I know vanilla doesn't get me hot. Nothing's gotten me as hot as when his fingers touched me, felt me up. He unleashed something and I want to bound down that unexplored path. I want to flee in the opposite direction. And I partly want to stand here and just see what he'll do to me.

Something shifts in him. He stills. Just the slightest intake of breath and tilt of his head. Like he can read me. Like he's gonna go to town and tear me apart, bit by bit.

Like he knows I'm going to let him.

He still holds my chin as he slides my panties out of the way and pushes two fingers inside of me. A bolt of exquisite delight hits me, making my insides clench at his demanding touch.

He doesn't stop as those blue eyes glitter with pent-up need. He dips his head, lips brushing against my ear. "What I'll do is take that invitation."

The man pushes into me again and I gasp, trembling as another orgasm threatens to hit. He starts to stroke into me and my legs almost buckle from the sensations crashing over me.

"I'll take it," he says, "and fuck you senseless. If you try and run, I'll put a bullet between those pretty eyes and not lose a second's sleep."

Now his fingers suddenly stop moving and he pulls his hand away, the loss almost making me whimper. Then he steps away, leaving me to slide, boneless, halfway down the wall.

He turns, sucking his fingers, which is the hottest thing I've ever seen. His hard cock catches my attention through the fabric of his pants as the fire in me flares with that erotic act of tasting my juices.

"You're not going to kill me."

"I might," he says, pulling out a phone and looking at something on it. He slides it back into his pocket. "You're very annoying. Tasty, but annoying."

There's charm there beneath the surface, careless and deadly, and probably only doled out on very rare occasions. This isn't one of them. Just a savageness lurking beneath a veneer of sophistication, behind something masquerading as that careless charm.

And it makes me want to moan.

Crawl to him.

Take him in my mouth and build my own altar and hand him a dagger of my own making.

What I need is to get myself together.

Somehow, I manage to drag myself back into a standing position. "If you wanted to kill me," I say, "I'd be dead."

"As I said, you're very annoying. Consider this a warning."

"You took me, not the other way around." I cling to the barbs in his words. They bring the clarity I need to get back onto safer land. "I get to be annoying."

"You pissed off Big Daddy."

I go still because I've heard that term used before. He's

definitely CIA. Or was. Question is, why him and not someone on the legitimate payroll?

Because there's nothing legit about this man.

But I also have to play this carefully.

"Who's that?"

"Your owners? CIA?" He goes into the kitchen without another look at me.

The word run beats hard, but I don't. No way would a man this resourceful, this clever—and he's clever, it doesn't take much to see that—leave me even for a nanosecond if he thought I'd be able to get out.

Maybe I could if I left everything, but I'm not about to do that. If it comes down to me and the government, then I'll need as many weapons as I can squirrel away.

He comes out with his scotch. I watch him down it, then set the glass down on the living room table.

The lavish apartment's a mix of decorating styles, but the layout is pure modern with its open spaces. He pulls his shirt off and dumps it on the floor. My heart leaps, but he doesn't make a move toward me.

"I don't—"

His sharp look cuts off my words. "Look, cut the shit. I know your name. I know you work behind a desk for the CIA in information gathering and you've been handling a field agent who's missing. And while most of what you're doing's been redacted, the CIA wants you back."

He shoves a hand through his wet hair. I know I should get my hardware out, even though it's protected in the waterproof bag, but if I'm going to run, if I manage to have that opportunity, I have to trust that protection.

"We went through this, remember?" he asks. "You lost your agent. You took off for reasons I'm betting have to do with weapons and Bolivia, so spill."

"I haven't ever heard that term used for them. Big Daddy," I say. "That's all."

This man both riles and makes me want to drop to my knees, head down, hands behind my back. He makes me want to fight and to rip his clothes off.

What I need is to ignore those urges and focus on the real issue. I need to find out all I can, to use him, and bottom line, to save my skin. Which isn't easy when I've got no idea who exactly I'm up against.

And when I have a second agenda.

So I gaze at him, like I'm the lowest-level agent who has no idea what the term he used means.

His look calls me out on my lie, but he also can't possibly see through me that easily.

Right?

"Drink?"

He turns and pours two scotches while I try like hell to pry my eyes from his body.

Lean, muscled, scarred. Enough to make a woman drip. Hell, he's enough that I *am* dripping and—

And he knows what he's doing to me.

His back is almost completely inked, some writing in cursive and what looks like a wound except it's a tattoo, and through the open flesh of the art is a hand. Like it's the Devil reaching out to pull whoever and whatever's in its way back down into the depths.

I shiver and curl my hand because I want to touch it. When he turns around, I'm struck by the one tattoo on his chest, over his heart.

The USA. I love my country, but in my experience it's a special kind of asshole who announces it on their skin.

The tattoo's a line drawing except two states are colored red.

THE TRUTHS THAT DECEIVE

It takes me a moment for my geography to kick in, and when it does... I frown. "Are you from both North and South Dakota?"

"No."

That's it. No. Nothing else.

"Then—"

"Go take a shower and don't think you can get out. There's a bedroom to the left you can use." He hands me the drink, sipping his at the same time. "I'm going to my room to do the same. I'll meet you back here in ten minutes."

I nod but I don't move. "And if I run?"

"You can't."

With that, he leaves.

And I'm left gaping at so much more than my fugitive predicament.

∿

AFTER MY SHOWER, I wander around. I try to jimmy the door and the windows, but the door's got both a thumbprint keypad and an old-fashioned lock. Damn windows are locked, too. There's even a keypad next to each of them.

Next, I look for possible weapons. I'm in the study that's both clean and unlived in—the laptop's unfortunately dead—when his sigh makes me drop the letter opener I'm considering as a possible weapon onto the desk and whirl around.

He leans against the door and I'm in a T-shirt and jeans that are way too big. Women's jeans, belonging to someone taller and way shapelier than me.

"By all means, try to pry open the drawers, but if you damage the desk, you're going to pay for it. And I'll warn you now, it's very expensive."

He's in a charcoal suit, gold and green tie, and I nearly swoon, he's so fucking divine.

"There's nothing in the desk anyway. I don't live here, and I haven't used this place in a couple of years. Others do every now and again, but..." He shrugs. "There's not a thing here that's going to help you. Here."

He tosses me a passport and my heart thumps. With shaking fingers, I open it.

"Juniper Hunt."

"Your middle name, my last."

"So what do you know?" I say, snapping the passport shut.

"He has a name."

"Smith Hunt." His phone buzzes and he pulls it from his pocket. He sends some texts, then he looks at me like he wasn't knuckle-deep in my pussy barely an hour ago.

Shit, I don't want to be thinking about that. About what it says about him or me. I clench the letter opener and stomp toward him, wave it at him, and then stomp past. I need another drink.

More importantly, I need to get out of here.

My phone's on silent and it's down at the bottom of my computer backpack.

I finish pouring my drink when he comes up and takes it from me, having a sip, and then he hands it back. "Please don't make me handcuff you. I will."

"You're going somewhere?"

"Meeting. Getting you out's going to be slightly more difficult than I thought."

I toss my hair and my asymmetrical cut falls over one eye, so I have to blow it back from my face. "Leave me here."

"Not on your life. You're worth money, Calista Juniper Price. Where'd you get Hendrix from?" His mouth curls up into a smirk and I want to smack it off. "Henry Xavier, your twin."

Panic swoops in, clutching me by the throat. "Leave my brother alone."

Henry isn't me. He's still at school in New York. We used to hack together, but I took the fall because it was my encouragement, my rogue ways that got us caught. Henry... he has different ideas for his life, and getting locked up by the CIA or hurt by this cretin with the magic touch isn't exactly on his vision board.

"Then behave," Smith says.

"You touch him and I'll gut you."

The smirk deepens. "How about this? I'm going out and you will be good. The whole place is wired, and not even you can unlock it. But if you're going to wreck my shit, I'll handcuff you to the radiator. And then I'll order someone to shoot your brother dead. Got it?"

I stare at him with intense dislike. "Yes."

"Don't wait up."

And he's gone. I throw the letter opener and it hits the door, embedding deep in the hardwood slats because it's that sharp.

"You're a fuck, Smith," I mutter to the empty room. "And I'm going to make you pay."

CHAPTER 5
SMITH

I take the freshly rolled cigarette from its white gold case and place it between my lips before lighting it. Then, with the cigarette hanging out of my mouth, I open the umbrella and swing it up to obscure my face. Not that I really need to do that. No one's after me.

That I know of.

But this way I can keep tabs on the area in relative cover, make sure we weren't followed. I stop and stand with my back against a wall, the cigarette still in my mouth while I dial Jones's number.

He answers after two rings. "What the fuck are you doing in the rain, Smith?"

I glance around, noting the few cars, and who, if anyone, is in them. There aren't many people on the street, so that works mostly for me. "Smoking."

"Aren't you supposed to be on vacation?"

"A job came up."

"Another one?"

Of course he'd heard about the one with Reaper. And he

knows I only smoke on a job, when needed for appearance's sake. "Can we find out what the big guys are up to in Germany?"

He pauses. "CIA?"

"Can we?"

"That's your arena."

"I've got a meeting set up. But..." Fuck. My phone has so much protective shit on it I highly doubt even the CIA can listen in.

But maybe Calista could. Her resume and rap sheet suggest she could do it in her sleep, but she can't access any of her tools right now. I've got her phone, and I locked her hardware away in the safe.

Of course, if she can listen in, others can, too.

"I'll get someone on it."

Jones doesn't need to say discreetly. He doesn't have to. The Obsidian Knights deal in discreet.

He drones on about some bullshit job. A girl he's trying to find, one who was taken recently and sold into sex slavery. Probably bought and sold five times over from what he's saying. My heart might not be much, but it squeezes tight.

I'm incredibly aware we could be discussing Dakota, my daughter. And I should be furious at one of my closest friends and fellow Knight, Orion, for sleeping with her after rescuing her from the Collectors. But I also know Orion genuinely loves her and he'll keep her safe.

Not that I get a say. I lost that right long before I even knew I had a child.

Jones flips the conversation to some contract killing that Eva, aka the Black Widow, completed, and I finish my walk up and down the street, as the rain comes down, thunder rolling loud overhead.

The rain right now is so heavy that I'm the only idiot out

here wandering around. But I haven't seen anyone casing my place, not from the lobby across the Straße at the apartment building opposite. Not at the restaurant or bar. And not in any of the cars parked along the street.

"Are you taking on this job to avoid a certain upcoming wedding?"

I take a final drag, drop the butt, and grind it out while scowling at nothing. "Fuck you, Jones."

I hang up on his sharp laughter and head down to the exclusive bar where I'm meeting my contact.

Marta is still as beautiful as I remember when I catch her walking into the bar, long ice-blond hair falling around her face in thick waves with plump red lips. She's wearing the kind of dress in a matching red that takes all the attention away from her stunning face.

Her glass of Krug is waiting for her as I sip my scotch. I don't mind bourbon or whiskey, but for some reason I'm into scotch right now. It's a good drink for Europe, and it fits with the moneyed man I'm playing.

I'm also fucking beyond loaded, but it's not something I tend to flash around unless it suits me. Here and now, it suits.

"Schmidt," she says, kissing both cheeks and leaving a cloud of perfumed air as she settles onto the stool. She's one of the only people who calls me that, from a decade ago when we'd burn down places with the hot sex we had, along with the hotter intel we gathered together. "I assume this isn't a booty call."

"Nope."

I slide a piece of paper over to her and she looks at the word on it. "You're not with the agency anymore. Last I heard you were out of freelance intelligence."

"Humor me."

Marta sighs. "I'm BND, Schmidt."

"I'll get you a medal." I nod at the piece of paper with Hendrix written on it.

"I've heard of the hacker. Supposedly with the CIA. But that's all I know. There's talk of something else being up, but everyone is jumpy about it."

"A weapon?"

Her mouth thins and she nods, then sips her champagne. My eye catches for a second on the red lipstick stain on the crystal flute when she sets it back down. "I don't know much, just parts of a new weapon turned up. I only know that because my government's unhappy since some of them showed up on black market sites, and together, they enhance other ones. And some of those weapons are German made."

She tips her wrist to look at her slender watch and a diamond ring glitters on her finger.

"Congratulations."

She smirks. "It's for show. I'm like you. Not the marrying kind." She toys with the ring. "If this is about a girl, play it smooth and low-key, okay?"

Once upon a time, I'd have talked her into coming back to my place. Or to meet me in the bathrooms here, or even a hotel room, and she'd have said yes in a heartbeat. The invite is there in her eyes. But even though I'm interested on a base level, I'm not.

Because there's a girl with rainbow hair in the way. Rainbow hair and a tongue that spits acid. I want to chase Calista down in the fucking rain.

So I don't take her up on the silent offer. "Okay."

After Marta leaves, I order another drink. There's a part of me that wants Calista to break out of the apartment. Her fight and fire have stirred the primal part of me, the hunter that's in my name, in my being. I want to stalk her, chase her. I want to fight her down to the ground and fuck her hard in the mud and rain and come inside her, biting her, marking her, staking my claim.

All because of this unexpected and sudden rush of desire that burst free of floodgates the moment she shifted and parted her thighs wider for me when I frisked her.

She wants all of that, too.

"Got some info."

Years of training are the only reason I don't jump a mile at the sound of Reaper's voice behind me.

The dark-haired man slides into Marta's vacant seat. "You didn't want to hit that?"

"I've hit it plenty."

"I know, so have I. Marta's a hot number and she wanted you." He grins as he takes my drink. "Of course, that's only because she didn't fucking see me there in the shadows."

"Stick to murder, man, because you're not going to make it as a Casanova."

He finishes the drink and orders two more. I'm not even sure if they're both for him or if one's for me. "Jones called. Did some digging."

"Weren't you in Scotland?"

"I was," he says, "and I've got business here. Some of us don't take vacations."

"I take it you have something?"

The drinks arrive and I grab one before he can suck them both down.

"There's nothing on any radars about the girl or the agent," he says.

"Weapons?" I ask.

"Seems like the CIA's been trying to get info on who has blueprints to new weapons of ours that are being quietly shopped around on the black market. They don't want to just stop the sales. They want to trace back to the source."

"That's—"

"No, ground zero source."

I look at him. "As in how the fuck did they even get out to be sold?" I frown. "It shouldn't be hard."

"No, it shouldn't. What's weird is, this is all so hush-hush, people working on it don't even have the full picture of what they have. Everything gets handed in and assembled at some upper level." He shrugs.

I wrap my fingers around the glass. "You think the girl's a key or a traitor?"

"No fucking idea. But I'm going to see Jones about that job. I'll be in New York for a while. Do you want me to keep an eye on things there?"

As in her brother? He hasn't given me anything. But it's hard to give information if you don't have anything. So I'm going to need to play this by ear. Get her back, hand her over, collect my money.

I'm just interested in all the whys and other details because I can't help myself. And the brother and my bargaining chip works. "Yeah, I do."

"And?"

I meet his eye, knowing what he's asking. "If I give the order, you know what to do."

He grins. "Gotcha."

We shoot the shit for a while and it's late when we leave and part ways on the street. The rain's stopped for now so I keep the umbrella shut, using the would-be weapon as a walking stick just in case.

Calista's asleep when I get back, and the letter opener spitefully stuck in the wooden door should piss me off, but it makes me smile. I leave it and check in on her. She's passed out on the sofa in the study, the computer on her lap, and I'm guessing she's been trying to get the thing to wake up.

Except the battery charger is under lock and key in the safe, too.

I pull the computer from her lap, and she mutters something but doesn't wake up. Scooping her up, I carry her to her room. She's not big, but even like this, with one arm flung in the air, I can see the toned muscles. And she's warm. She fits.

I should never have fucking fingered her because my brain's still whispering about pulling her panties off with my teeth and licking her deep. I already know what she tastes like and fuck, I want more.

I lay her on the mattress, pull the duvet over her, and go to my room to undress. My fucking cock's half-erect as I fall into my bed. A deep sigh escapes my mouth. It wouldn't take much to get completely hard, wouldn't take much more to jack off.

My mind trips back to Calista splayed out on the mattress a few doors down.

And I realize I don't want my hand.

I want her pussy.

Which means I'm very close to being completely fucked.

CHAPTER 6
CALISTA

Fuck Smith. And fuck his stupid event.

This morning after I woke up in his guest room, he told me he wants me to pose as his daughter at some event. What a fucking joke that is when he can't even keep his hands off me. He didn't give me any details about where we're going, why, or who's going to be there, just that I needed something appropriate to wear.

And then he told me about his own daughter. Nothing beyond her name and age, though. He must've been really young when she was born since she's close to my age.

Dakota's her name.

My mind flashes back on his map tattoo and curiosity knots my brain. I want to know more but dammit, I hate myself for even letting that thought percolate.

I heave a deep sigh while he leads me through store after store. Shopping's not one of my favorite things, and the red wig he basically threw at me back in his apartment itches. Red hair should be sexy, but this thing is a pageboy and I think it was made before I was born. What I need is the internet, but he only hands me a burner phone with one number programmed in.

If I could get online, I'd order clothes, make him pay.

The man's obviously got plenty of money and he didn't make it on CIA wages.

Also... shopping? Like, what the fuck?

I blow out a breath and stare at my reflection in a shop window and troubled gray-blue eyes look back.

Yes, I need to get back home, but not until my ducks are in a row. Not until I have everything I need and know what I'm up against.

Someone somewhere just might be out to get me or pin shit on me. And with Johnny missing, I...

I'm stuck.

With a Smith-shaped problem.

What he doesn't know is I've got a spare SIM card I can slide into any phone. It has numbers on it I might need so I'll swap out the cards as soon as I get the chance. It won't do much, but it'll make me feel better, give me a little more control.

And I have information, a copy of everything hidden away. Close enough that I can grab it quickly and run if need be.

One of the stores we go to is exclusive and the dresses are beautiful. He steers me toward the dressing rooms. "Strip."

The word filters in through the red velvet curtain and I glare at the top of his head, clenching my fingers and making no move to do anything he asks. "I'm not your toy."

"And I'm not fucking in there getting an eyeful," he says.

He disappears and I switch the cards in the phone. The SIM is simple, a set of emergency numbers I need, like Henry's CIA HQ and some other contacts. I come up on the name Johnny and run a finger over the screen.

It remains like it's been for the past week. Silent. No texts. Nothing from my brother.

I slide the phone away and pace in the small space. Smith is... argh. Smith gets under my skin. I want to label him a disease, a virus. Fast-moving, probably deadly. I already know he's CIA. And based on some of the things said, he's about as in the dark as I am. Except that I'm wanted.

This is a government kidnap job. I've heard CIA "water cooler gossip" about how they go down. I'd never know otherwise. Those jobs are way above my pay grade. I also have a guillotine blade hanging over me for my past teenage crimes, the type that are harmless but things those in power don't forgive and forget. I was spared because of my knowledge and skill set, bribed to work for the CIA and offered a chance to have my slate wiped clean if I agreed to their terms.

I broke into unbreakable governmental sites. Left my stupid footprint, a digital graffiti tag. Fourteen-year-olds are idiots.

So are twenty-four-year-olds, judging by the position I'm in. Under some kind of lock and key with a man I inexplicably want and don't trust.

A man who got into my sealed documents and is willing to throw past crimes in my face.

The curtain yanks back, the rings scraping the top of the metal bar.

Smith steps into the small space as the assistant hangs up a pile of clothes. Then with a longing look at him, she disappears. I roll my eyes.

"I could have been naked."

He pulls the curtain shut and crowds me against the soft pile of clothes. "Could've been, but you're not. How the fuck did you get to be in the CIA if you can't follow simple instructions?"

I poke his chest, trying to push him back, too aware of him, his strength, his presence. The scent of him is earthy and dark, a hint of spice like a desecrated church. Like sin. Dark and boozy and sex and cigarettes.

And that scent coils down in me, stroking over me, down into my pussy and I struggle to drag in breath, keep hold of some semblance of reality.

I'm a fugitive. And his captive.

"It depends on who gives me the instruction," I say.

He moves in a little closer, his mouth against the column of my throat as he whispers, "I like a challenge. Why does the CIA want you?"

"I don't know." I push the words out. It's true, I don't. I have my suspicions but I'm not going anywhere near one of their strongholds until I have the cards. "But I don't answer to you."

"No," he says, lifting his head. "You don't, Calista. But I need you to work with me until I can hand you over."

"I'm more than capable of heading into the Berlin HQ. I don't need your help. And I don't need to help *you*."

"You're mistaking me for someone who gives a fuck. I don't. But I'm not tasked with that. I'm tasked with a handover in the United States. So—"

"Do as you say, or you'll hurt my brother?"

"Something like that, but no. I need what you have. It'll help your case and possibly save your ass."

He has the face of a killer. Not the psychos who'll do anything for the thrill or the payout, but a man who's killed and will kill again without remorse or regret.

Smith might have a tattoo that represents his daughter, but I'm betting he'd sell his loved ones.

So I need to go along with him until I can make sure

Henry's safe. I'll be compliant and hide behind the snark until I can make my escape.

"I don't have anything." I shove my hands against his chest. He steps back and I know it's only because he chose to.

Smith doesn't say anything, but it's clear from the way he's studying me that he doesn't believe a word.

I chew on the inside of my mouth. The new passport will get me back home, and then—

"Stop plotting," he says, all soft menace, "because I will break all your shit. All of it. People, things, freedoms. Just because you'll piss me off. *Know* you can't get away. I'm excellent at everything I do, and the chase?"

Smith tips up my chin a little too harshly.

"The chase, Calista, is my fucking jam. You'll either love it or hate it. Depending."

I swallow over the sudden lump in my throat and try to breathe with the tightness in my chest. "On?"

"On whether it's a chase for fun or one where you try and get away." He steps back and opens the curtain. "The only reason I want what you have is to find out exactly how short to keep the leash and who else might be after you. I'm getting you back stateside as tasked, whether you like it or not."

"I'm not a traitor."

He remains emotionless. "I'll be waiting. Show me the outfits."

I slide down the wall after he leaves as the tight band holding me hostage loosens and my head spins. "Breathe. Just breathe."

I do, deep and slow, and then I push up, my legs a little shaky.

Toeing lines doesn't come easy to me. One thing that appealed to me with the CIA is how I could find freedom within the perimeter of rules, how it taught me so much, got me an education on a grand scale.

But this Smith character floors me with his quicksilver rule adjustments, the tightening and releasing of freedoms.

Who am I kidding? He floors me because if he's on my radar, everything is on the fritz. From common sense to libido. And I don't understand it. One bit.

I strip down to my underwear and put on the first outfit, a dress that makes me look twelve and wearing my grandmother's finest. It makes me look completely out of touch. But I hold my head up and stomp out.

His blue gaze shifts from an assistant standing nearby then back to me, and though not one thing changes in his expression, I can almost feel the inner wince.

"Stunning, isn't it?" he says to the assistant.

I whirl and stomp off. Each outfit's worse than the last. From skirts to pants to dresses and back again. The casual things make me look like I've escaped from the last century and the party clothes, if you can even call them that, are Madison Avenue matron conservative chic.

All wrong, all horrible, and that wince grows more pronounced in the air.

I'm in a twinset with a knee-length boxy skirt when something inside of me snaps. I shove my hands on my hips. "What's the deal with this event? Are you ever going to give me details? Why do I need to look like a fucking hoity-toity country club grandma? And why are we taking a weird-ass break by going? Aren't you on a schedule?"

"You're in some kind of rush to get back to the States and face whatever might be waiting for you there?"

No, I'm definitely not, but I swallow down those words.

I put a hand on either side of him. "I'm not a traitor. I have nothing to fear by going back."

"Sometimes it's the fear you don't realize that gets you in trouble."

"Because someone's after me?"

"Always operate by thinking that way." He doesn't answer me and he might not know for sure, but it makes sense.

But I know if I'm too eager and question him more, he'll dig into everything, dig into me, personally and with gusto. If I'm too unwilling... that's a can of worms, too. "Why go out, then?"

"Because I have a business reason to attend this event. And If I'm going to keep you safe until the handoff, we need to put on a front and disguise you so nobody asks questions or raises eyebrows."

"I'm not your daughter."

"No," he says, "you're not. But you'll play that part. We're rich, attending the Klein Art fundraiser tonight. Dinner, dancing, and we'll be seen together."

"Make a splash and get dismissed that way, in plain sight?"

"This one." He gestures at what I'm wearing, and it's a clear command for me to step back, and for some reason I do.

"This outfit?" I frown. "It's horrible."

He grins slowly. "I know.

A quiet buzz breaks through the insufferable soft music, the kind designed to be so inoffensive that it offends. He pulls out his phone.

"Get that and some other things." He hands me a credit card. My eyes drop to the name. JJ Smith. Probably an alias. "I need to take this call."

With that, Smith gets up and heads for the front entrance. He pushes through the glass doors. I watch him lounge against the window, so self-assured, so infuriatingly cocky in his movements and facial expressions.

For a split second, I think of asking the assistant where the back exit is, but he just spent the last few minutes charming her, so she won't help me. Instead, I slap down the card on the counter.

He said to get anything I want. "For a fee, can you have some things delivered here?"

Her eyes light up. She knows I mean a private fee for her. "*Ja, das kann ich machen,*" she says. "*Was brauchen sie?*"

Of course she can do that. And what is it I want? That's easy. I describe the items to her, each of them in detail, and then I move around the shop, leaving some of the outfits he said to get and choosing some others.

If I'm going, I'm not pretending to be his daughter.

After everything's paid for and wrapped, and my other purchases arrive, I take the packages and step outside in one of the ghastly dresses he chose.

I expected Smith to be outside the door, but he isn't. And he's not on the street.

Heart thumping hard, I find a tiny side street and duck in. My mind works quickly to process scenarios. If I thought I could run, I would. But this dress makes it impossible. I also want my computer and one of the passports. Fake ones can be bought, but I'd need to use his card, which would track me. Besides, they take time to make. And I'm betting the one he got me circumvents all the biometric rules where it's going to be a problem for me if I use another fake one.

So I do the next best thing. I pull out the burner phone to call my brother when my hand starts to tremble because of what I'm seeing on the screen.

A contact, a hacker from Estonia I'd befriended, sent me a message to contact her. I'm about to call when everything in me goes on full alert.

And Smith grabs my wrist.

"I wanted to see just how stupid you were." He snatches the phone right out of my hand. "I'm thinking you're up there with world-class level of stupid. Who does this Estonian number belong to, and what the fuck do you know about the Collectors?"

CHAPTER 7
SMITH

Calista's still a little too wet behind the ears to notice someone like me waiting for her. She never spotted me while I was on the other side of the Straße, having coffee and getting information from Jones.

Her bones are delicate, but strength radiates through her.

I want to sink my teeth down into her throat, bite my way up to her ear.

This pull to her on such a visceral level is something I don't really understand at all. I figured putting her firmly in the daughter box as we get the fuck out of Dodge would help me keep it in my pants, but her looks still burn into me.

They're complicated ones that hold both longing and dislike. The ones where her eyes tell me she clearly wants to run, but also hold the fire to fight.

And even now, the alternating push and pull commands her where she's both trying to snatch her hand back and tilt her hips toward me.

But I keep my brain on the question. "I knew you'd have a fucking SIM card. Fuck, I hate stupid."

"I'm not stupid. I graduated Oxford at seventeen, thank you very much."

Shit. I hadn't read over the education of Ms. Price. But the similarities eat at my brain. I graduated Cambridge at eighteen. Smart enough to go, and a way to isolate from others older than me. Fuck the CIA. They must have sent her even earlier than me.

Then again, I hadn't hacked anything. I was actively recruited, and when I wanted to turn it down because of Sylvie, I was pushed.

I shut that shit right down because I can't get caught up in my past. Not now.

But the pain isn't something that goes away.

Not Sylvie. I'd loved her. We were fucking teenagers; of course, I did. But the pain of losing her has been dulled by life, by time. I doubt we'd have made it more than another year or so, anyway. Maybe a little longer because of Dakota but...

The Dakota pain. Those lost years. That gulf between us.

It doesn't go away.

I let pretty, young Calista go and step back, scooping up the packages.

From there, I get us a car back to the apartment. Not a word's exchanged between us. But there will be.

I'm biding my fucking time.

Who the fuck in Estonia is texting her about the Collectors?

My apartment building has state-of-the-art security built in. No one gets in or out without me knowing, not even if I don't come back here for years. I don't keep close tabs on the building, but I keep enough to know it's uncompromised. Once we're inside, I toss the bags down and ask the question I held off on spewing at her.

"Why did you run from the CIA if you weren't guilty?"

She swallows. "Someone got into my work. I received a threat."

"And you didn't report it?"

"They were looking at me funny, Smith. Questions started coming up about my agent. And what could I say? That he asked me to keep his going deep a secret? I know how that looks and—"

"What was the threat?"

"Just like the one you made... it was against my brother." Her voice drips with dislike. But behind that dislike is fear. "A photo."

That's a threat all right.

"And what about Estonia? The Collectors?"

She's quiet. Then she breathes out, pulling off the ugly wig that failed epically to make her less attractive. "A source and I don't know. You snatched the phone before I could investigate."

Calista's lying. It permeates the air. But lying about what and why is the intriguing part. Is there someone the government's interested in who was a Collector? *Is* a Collector?

I'm guessing yes, because there were plenty before we decimated them, and there are enclaves now. Rich people who think they can do anything, who want more than they should, are dangerous, and always watched on some level.

But the Collectors operated for years without being torn apart. Until the Knights. Until they dared touch my daughter.

I study Calista, how she swallows like her nerves are picking and poking away at her throat. How she moves like her limbs aren't her own.

She's nervous. Scared. And angry.

"So you just decide to fuck around like you can do anything?" I say, poking the bear. "This isn't a game. Anyone could follow you."

"No one is."

She never saw me, so doubtful she's even aware who is out there. I shrug, noting the thread of panic in her tone. "We've been lucky. The earlier rain cleared the streets. Made anyone following either disappear or easier to spot."

"I know," she says. "I'm not an idiot. Just let me go. I'll—"

"What? Turn up at a designated time and place as long as I let you do your thing?" I ask.

Because the thing is, the Collectors, or someone involved with them, might be at the center of this. I don't need to know what the weapon does. I can guess at the usual suspects interested in it.

And maybe she's the one who got her agent snatched so she could sell blueprints, or just information. It's not a far stretch for someone like her to put all the scattered pieces together—scattered pieces the CIA uses to protect—and sell to the highest bidder.

Like someone in the Collectors. Someone who escaped our big purge.

Calista Price with her skills and youth would be perfect to carry that out.

Throw in the brother as the reason why she did it if she's caught?

Perfection.

I cross over to her. She flinches but stands strong. The air crackles as I get close, a pull to each other that neither wants. A pull we both want to dive into.

"Tell me," I say, capturing her chin and tilting it. There's more than one way to pursue prey. I bring my mouth close, skimming over hers. "Tell me what you know."

"Even if I knew something," she whispers, her lips seeking mine. I don't even think she's aware of it. "Telling you the tiniest thing amounts to treason."

I slip an arm low on her waist and she flows up into me. I'm fucking hard. This girl makes me beyond hard. She's like a fucking walking ball of freshly minted hormones masquerading as human.

Fuck, do I remember that feeling.

Right now, it's a living nightmare.

But I slide my tongue up her throat anyway, loving how she arches for me, an offering and a submissive move that makes my blood burn.

Everything about her is hedonistic. "Withholding's treason."

"You're no longer part of the government."

"Neither are you. Not since you ran. Also treason, by the way."

She shudders a breath and her fingers close on my lapels. I'm not sure if she's clinging or trying to push me away, or if it even matters. What I do know is she'll be wet if I head down south.

I stay above the border of her because we're not even close to finished.

"You're taking me in. So why not just do it?"

I lift my head, rubbing a thumb over her mouth and she shudders, the tip of her tongue touching my flesh. "Before that message today, you weren't in a rush, and now you are."

I slip my thumb into her mouth, and her lips close around me. She licks and sucks and makes me harder than I've ever been, something I didn't think was possible.

"I just—"

I press down, cutting off her words, opening her mouth and pushing in deep. Her eyes are a wild storm.

"Think hard about what you're going to say."

In and out, in and out. I thrust slow and deep into the wet, sucking depths of her mouth, basking in the way her tongue slides against my invading thumb.

"Because here's the thing. And we've touched on it, but it bears repeating," I say. Something made her not want to go back, and I've got to fucking say, a place like Gitmo is not high on my list of tourist attractions. "In all honesty, I don't care what you did or why. Curious, but not really a burning need to find out the truth. Money's my motivation. And that makes me dangerous for you to cross. I'm not a zealot, I don't have an agenda, and there's no one I'm loyal to."

I move in and dip my tongue into her mouth. She trembles.

"You're selling secrets? You'll pay. You're working with some group for other reasons? You'll pay for that, too. But we're going to this fucking event because someone was watching you. I don't care if it's the Germans or Russians— you'll do better in their hands than you will some unstable new country or with a rich fuck who wants to rule the world."

I bite her, just at her ear, and place my mouth at the canal's opening. "You're lucky that you being handed over means I get paid. So we'll work together. We'll look like the Hunts, father and daughter. I'll do my business, and then we'll get the fuck out and back on US soil. Behave and your brother lives."

Releasing her mouth, I raise my head.

Truth and lies.

Manipulation and temptation.

I tell her just enough. But this event will give me insight about what I'm up against. That's the "business" I'll be conducting. Reconnaissance. Even with her wig and new passport, things can still go very wrong. It all depends on who's lurking. And how much she wants to run.

"Let me go."

"You and I will get along a lot better if you play nice. The Collectors?"

Calista goes still, then she turns, her movements jerky. "I don't know them. Just... I've seen the name show up."

"In the papers?"

Her eyes flick to me as she moves around the room and gets herself a drink. She wants out more than she wants that drink. But I let that slide. "Chatter. Just... chatter, and then that text message I received."

I know from what I've read that her agent was deep undercover because his identity and his handler's identity are redacted from the case file. Everything except Calista's name.

There's something not right about this whole thing. Maybe it's how her role is so redacted on paper or the crimes of her youth. Or else it's just my nose for trouble warning me.

"Wouldn't be enough. You're CIA and you got scared enough or suspicious enough to run when you knew how it would make you look."

"I can't trust you."

"No one else is here, Calista."

"I need my phone."

"Not happening." Last night, I went through everything, but getting into her phone or computer is impossible. For me. Probably for most.

"I need yours. I..." She takes one step toward me. "Please."

The phone isn't my personal one, but it's set up like it is. Anyone getting their hands on it has a whole lot of rich asshole crap. Calls and conversations. I don't think she can do much damage with me standing here. So I unlock it and hand it to her.

She makes quick work of opening something and hands it to me. A cloud storage with screenshots.

The type of screenshots that are enough to land her in the kind of hot water that burns down to bone.

"Fuck." The threats like the picture she got of her brother. Gossamer thin and innocent until you think about it.

Pictures of her working. Lunch. Dinner. Going out. Coffee. Or statements like "I hope you enjoyed your caramel latte."

Tiny things no one would take seriously. Tiny things that make her look incompetent and the cause of a leak.

And the thing is, maybe it is Calista. She's clever enough.

Not my problem. I need to get her home and collect my pay.

I close down the cloud and pocket the phone. "Good thing we're leaving as father and daughter—"

Suddenly, she shoves me and darts for the door. I grab at her, dragging her away from the lock as she tries to pry it open. Calista can't get out, but it pisses me off, lights the fires of the chase in me, and I tackle her down to the ground.

She struggles, fighting me, inviting me, her thighs parting, hips thrusting up. I coil my fingers in the silk of her colorful hair, wrenching her head back so her jugular's exposed, and I've got her pinned.

The weight of me presses into one of her thighs and I thrust against that inviting softness there. Her breath comes in panting sounds. I glare down at her.

Her eyes glitter, the mother of storms coming. I scrape down on her pounding pulse, my teeth exposed, my touch light. I don't want to mark her. Yet. I want to feel the reined-in power, the violence of response in her.

"I told you," I murmur, "I'll take and not give a shit. Calista, that means one fucking thing."

"That you're a pervert out to make money off me?"

I flash her a smile and lick her jugular, making her moan. This time when I lift my head, everything goes still.

"It means," I say, "that there will be consequences."

"Like?"

"This."

CHAPTER 8
CALISTA

He's off me in a blink. Then he flips me onto my stomach so hard and so suddenly, the air whooshes from my lungs. It's like carpet burn, scraping on all my senses and lighting them in the wrong way, the kind of way that'll pull and stick with me for days to come.

If I even have days.

He uses a zip tie to restrain my wrists, then sits on the back of my upper thighs, my clit mashing into my panties, pushed against the floorboards.

And my heart beats wild and fast.

I'm uncomfortable but humming at the same time.

It's a low-level buzz that inflames all my nerve endings. The dislike and want for this man moves through in viscous, equal measures.

He hasn't kissed me, but he's touched me, felt me up, and performed lewd acts that on paper don't amount to much at all. On paper, they could be construed as wrong. But how can it be nothing much, and how can it be wrong when it shakes me to the core, when it sets off a heavy beat of need and longing in me?

I don't know. I don't know anything right now other than the fact that I like his little power play games. "Get off me."

"How come I think you want more?" He strokes my hair, the lightness of his touch sinking down into my depths.

"I don't."

He leans in. "You like to be hunted, chased. But, little girl, you've found the wrong predator. Because I won't stop. If you manage to get away, you better be willing to hide the rest of your days because I'll track you, find you, and destroy you."

My head spins.

I don't think he's talking about killing me or me escaping. Or if he is, it's on another level completely. A place of sex and bones and teeth and blood. Somewhere I can revel in lust and—

"Get off me." I can't go there. Because I'm shaking.

The chase. Running. Fighting. Going down with him.

This is so new. It's frightening. Exhilarating. It's coming home.

I try to breathe. Calm down the beating center of me. Stop the heat that rises from my pussy.

"This is how it's going to go. You're going to do what I say, when I say it, or you're going to wish—"

"What?" I snarl the word. "That I'd met you sooner?"

"I'm your worst nightmare, Calista. No, you'll wish you'd made more of an effort in toeing the line. For your brother."

"You bastard."

He just laughs softly and gets off me, leaving me there.

It takes a while to realize he's not coming back. It takes longer to get that he's leaving me here, on the floor.

One polished shoe lands near my face, and the fine wool of his dark suit pants falls in perfect lines.

He crouches over me and fingers of one hand with silver rings brushes hair from my face, a gentle touch that riles every inch of me.

"I'm going out now. Punishment and reward, Calista. We can get you back and into the right hands the easy way or the hard way. It's up to you. I get paid either fucking way."

And then he's up, and his shoes move to the door. It opens and he's gone.

"Fucking bastard!" I say. Then I pause. And I scream. "Fucking perverted asshole!"

And the sound echoes throughout the room as I'm left completely alone.

GETTING free's no easy feat. I can't shake the feeling that it's nothing more than a warning, a test.

If a man like Smith doesn't want me free, there'll be no way I can do it. Even though I kept my wrists loose, but fists pumped, the slack is only in the length between the wrists, not in how the plastic wraps my flesh.

Getting up is less than dignified, as is finding a knife, but at least I'm free now. I'm in the middle of systematically pulling the place apart when someone speaks behind me. I jump and twist around.

My heart sinks. Blond and gorgeous. I'm pretty sure she's Marta Krause, high up in German intelligence, the BND. I always made it a point to know discreet international operatives because they can be the most dangerous.

She's effortlessly cool, one of those ageless types who could be late twenties to forties, and she oozes sophistication.

"Marta Krause?" I ask.

A cool smile plays over her perfectly painted lips. "You should know Schmidt knows everyone there is to know."

Something dark and sharp-edged spins through me. "How did you get in?"

"It was unlocked, so claws back in. I'm your escort, so dress up. Seems Schmidt doesn't trust you."

I'm not close enough to the knife, and the black dress she wears is so tight, there's no way she's packing under it.

Then again, what did Smith tell me? I'd be surprised by where a woman can hide a weapon.

And the cool smile shifts up a degree in warmth. "I do the boring work now. Desk, liaise, and learn all kinds of interesting things. You weren't really on the radar of the BND until Schmidt met up with me. All I heard was something about a hacker named Hendrix. Did you steal the blueprints to this weapon?"

"No."

She blows out a breath and looks at a diamond-encrusted watch on her wrist. "You wouldn't tell me, anyway. Does the CIA do a high school program?"

I almost snap my age at her, but I hold it in. I don't even have to look at the door as she turns her back on me and goes to the living room.

"Run, by all means, Baby CIA, but I have people on the ready, and from what I can piece together, you're going to be safer with Schmidt. There are people with a real hard-on for that weapon and the blueprints."

I flash her a look of dislike, then shower and do my makeup. Subtle like a grown-up with taste would wear. That's what this is.

That is, if she's taking me to the event at all.

I shimmy on the dress and unpack the new wig. Then I

edge to the door. Because if he let her in, but her agenda is something else entirely, then I'm screwed.

But she's speaking German into her phone. "She's quite the handful, Schmidt," she says. "Not your type at all. But she's in one piece. And you owe me."

When I'm ready, I walk out, and I note she leaves two plane tickets under an empty glass. I don't ask but assume they're for me and Smith. "Let's go," Marta Krause says.

She also locks the door with a key, one she hands to me, and I slide it into the hidden pocket on the dress.

It's a nice ride out to the estate where I assume the fundraiser is being held. At the front door, Marta melts away, and I'm not ashamed to admit I'm thinking of making a run for it when a hand comes around my arm and I'm pulled in tight next to the heat and intoxicating scent of Smith.

"That's a small taste of what I can do and who I know. Eyes are everywhere. Here and in the States."

I swallow, a bitter taste in my mouth. Henry. He means my brother.

"Leave him alone, Smith, or I'll—"

"What?" he says against my ear, "stomp your foot? Run? I'll give you a safe word for when we play properly, Calista. You're into hacking. I'm tempted to go for back door, but that might be playing with fire. How about Code?"

"I don't want a safe word."

"Like to live on the edge?" he asks, his hand slipping down the silk of the gown, to the low dip in the back, and I look up. His eyes are blazing blue, locked on to my nipples pushing against the fabric. "Maybe you do."

"They always do that," I say, lying. My nipples don't. It's taken the cold and a guy's mouth sucking and tugging to make them like this.

Smith?

He just has to look, and they're so hard, it's ridiculous.

"Soft, wet, and hard in all the right places. And hot. Mouth and cunt, Calista."

"You're such a bully."

"No, I just like to play with my food before I devour it. Safe word, no safe word, it's up to you, but when you run and I chase, when we're down in the dirt, I see no and yes. The only time I'll stop is your safe word."

"I'm not playing with you."

"You will."

"Fine," I say, pushing the word out through gritted teeth, "Code. So... Code times a thousand."

He laughs against the wig. "Good girl. Now, you want to tell me what the fuck you're wearing."

I scowl up at him. "Considering I had to escape your... consequences, I think I look pretty good."

"I didn't comment on that looking good or not. I'm fucking talking about how you don't look like my daughter."

"You and your fetish."

Before he can come back on me, a matronly lady comes up to shake his hand. "Herr Hunt. Is this the lovely Juniper...?" She trails off, more an American move than German, but I slide an arm around his waist.

"Frau Hunt, his wife," I say with a demure smile.

They make small talk as I take my leave to find a drink and check the place out. I could walk out the door. Or through the service entrance. It wouldn't take much to find my way upstairs to steal a different set of clothes. Or considering the staff are in black, find one of their outfits, either a spare work one or someone's clothes they wore here.

But I don't.

And not because his eyes are on me. It doesn't matter I can't catch him looking. It certainly doesn't matter he doesn't follow as I slip to the door where a garden is artfully lit in twinkling fairy lights.

The man is watching. Stalking.

Always.

He's waiting to see if I'll make a break for it, and I'm tempted. I'm so tempted I'm quivering. The light music tinkles with the gurgle of voices in conversation. And I've counted all the exits.

But he waits. He wants me to make that move.

And I'm not going to get away.

He's not about to leave me to explore if he knows I can break out.

Maybe, with someone else, I'd risk it. But I'm not a field agent, and though I have skills that were drilled into me, this man drips the quiet confidence of the best of the best I've seen.

I'm not sure if I want to see what will happen if I run.

I don't know if I want to find out exactly how much I'll like it.

I start to turn to go back inside when a small gate catches my eye.

Maybe I—

"Don't."

One word. Quiet. No emotion.

Yet it lacerates.

"I just wanted to see."

He moves then, backing me into the stone wall, and my heels sink into the dirt as I cross the border of the pavement into the flowers.

Smith doesn't touch me, but his expression is utterly feral, the kind that makes my knees weak and me wet between the thighs. "You wanted to see if you could escape? Or how far, exactly, it'll take for you to push me into the hunt?"

I swallow over the burning, sudden lump in my throat. "No, I..."

This man's taking me home. He's going to hand me over to someone. I'm pretty sure that someone's high up with the CIA, but it doesn't mean that that someone's on the up-and-up.

I'm in the dark as all the information I've collected is shards, things I haven't put together. All I know is somehow, some way, the Collectors name has shown up in all the chatter. And that makes me uneasy.

Not to mention my agent's gone.

I also have my private mission. Revenge. And...

I'm in big trouble.

And I might not be able to sort it out before I'm handed over.

Right here and now, I make a decision. I'll use Smith to get home. And by then I'll work out how to run. I need to see if there's a double agent, if everything's connected.

I need to make sure my brother's safe.

Smith's an enemy.

I know this.

He puts a hand next to my head and leans in. "No, I, what, Juniper?"

My middle name caresses my skin with his low voice.

"No. I'm thinking..." I'm thinking I need to get to the bottom of this. I'm thinking how I can turn my enemy into my asset. I'm thinking I don't know what's worse, this man or whatever waits at the CIA or out in the wild. "I'm thinking I need my brother safe. He's innocent."

He nudges my thighs apart with one of his. "So that makes you guilty?"

"I thought you didn't care about anything but getting paid?"

"I don't have to care to like answers."

Our gazes meet. Those blue eyes are pools of deception. Cleverness and barbs. Ice and heat I want to touch and melt into.

I don't really think when I put my hand on his lean cheek, but the moment I do, the world lights up. And then I rise up and press my mouth to his.

For a moment he doesn't move, and then he kisses me.

It's a slow, devastating kiss, one that could floor a city to rubble. It makes my blood sing and my brain fog, and in those blissful seconds, all reasoning's lost.

Slowly, he lifts his head. "Just remember," he whispers, thumb rubbing on my lower lip, "you started this."

CHAPTER 9
SMITH

Calista is exactly what I thought and utterly unexpected.

I take her mouth, hard. And she gives back just as brutally. Hot and wet, her tongue spars and teases and it's a tango of a kiss. One where we work together, stoking the fires, building and fighting for dominance. But hers is a game, a subconscious one giving me what I want and need. She fights just enough to make each slide and push of my tongue a micro victory.

She rocks against me and offers me her throat as I kiss my way down. What I want is to sink my teeth into her soft flesh, to slip a hand under her slinky skirt, and plunge into her hot pussy because I'm pretty fucking sure she's not wearing panties.

No bra either.

I want to fuck my fingers into her beneath the dress, I want to tear it to shreds and bite down on her jugular so hard she shrieks. So hard she comes. So fucking hard that no one can be mistaken about just who she belongs to.

I want to turn her and push her into the wall, unzip her dress and fuck her from behind. I want to suck and bite and pull on those luscious tits with the nipples that always push and tease and seem to beg for my mouth.

And I want to sink teeth into the soft smoothness of her ass and send her racing off naked across the grounds so I can chase and tackle her down.

Last, I want her to fight me, to come at me with everything she is and draw blood right as I overpower her and take her hard.

My primal play kink is way stronger than any simple D/s play, stronger than sharing a woman, or anything else I can do at the clubs.

Marta was fun at this. A handful of others, too.

But right or wrong, I think Calista will blow them all out of the water.

I lick a path down her throat, then come back to her mouth and feather kisses over it, the kind of kisses that make her set free tiny moans, both of need and frustration.

She wants it rough more than she wants the sweetness of this little moment.

I lift my head as her hand comes down to cup me and her eyes widen the instant she touches.

I push her hand into me, holding it there against my hard cock.

"Is this all you've got?" she asks, voice a little thick and a lot bitchy.

"I can get someone else in to fuck your cunt at the same time if this doesn't work for you."

Somewhere in the back of my head, I know I'm playing with fire.

"No. I don't even want you in there."

"Really? You kissed me. You started this. Now you have to play it through."

"I'm pretty sure there are some laws about that."

"Do I look like a man who gives a fuck?"

She looks at me. And then very deliberately, she says, "Code."

I release her and step back.

Riling her up and taunting her on all the levels I am isn't really in the money-making brief of soft kidnap back to the States.

I offer her my arm. "You decided you're my wife, Juniper. So let's go back inside and see what the rest of the evening has to offer."

Her eyes narrow but she loops her hand through my arm because she knows there's nothing she can say to that.

DANCING slow with Calista was torture, she played reckless little games, plastering herself against me, rubbing against my cock.

Stupid, tiny games that will have huge repercussions for her. Very soon.

Her saving grace was the shift into young chic sophisticate, sliding easily into the role as my wife. How she arrived, even without the kiss or the dancing or innuendo that flowed, both spoken and silent between us, placed her slightly too old to be my daughter. Even my own daughter borders on the too old by virtue of when I got Sylvie pregnant. Way too young and—

I stop, staring out the window as we're driven back to my Charlottenburg apartment.

Calista doesn't say a word, hasn't since I dropped the veneer of genial rich man the minute we set foot inside the car.

Marta would have had the place searched after she left, an unspoken deal between us since I let her collect Calista.

Low-level BND search, under the ruse to see what I have, if I'm who I say I am. The details will go on, and they bore me. Nothing will have been found but clothes and the airline tickets.

By having it searched by someone I know means the other vultures—if they're out there, circling—have had no chance to get in.

I unlock the door and Calista's gaze sweeps the room, eyes landing on the tickets. "Someone's been here."

"They have." I close the door, take off shoes and jacket, and pick up items to pack. Behind the sofa's a suitcase. I open it on the floor and start to add some things when I go still.

It's a soft sound, but I know what it is.

Dropping the clothes into the bag, I walk out into the living room and start to undo my tie.

She's got the door open.

I grin.

"Step back from the fucking door, Calista."

"You left it unlocked." Her voice is breathy, a knot of something akin to excitement running through it.

"I know."

Her hand tightens on the knob. "What are you going to do? Chase me down?"

I take another step. "Yes."

And so much more.

Fuck, she's actually vibrating, turning electric. It isn't fear. No, it's excitement, and it zings between us.

I know what I should do.

Grab her, haul her inside, and lock her in her room until it's time to get out of here. I should keep my hands to myself and not ask all the internal questions bubbling up.

Or I should, on the flight to New York, question the shit out of her. Get all the information she's piecemealed together. Find out what she knows about the Collectors and why she's got a bug up her ass about them. See what she knows about the Bolivian connection and if Estonia has anything to do with this.

I have questions.

Normally, I wouldn't ask.

Normally, stars don't align.

"I don't believe you." There's defiance in her tone. A dare and it hooks me deep, drawing blood, making me hard.

"You don't think I'll chase you down."

She flicks a glance over her shoulder to look at me, to judge my mood and the distance and how far she can get.

It dawns on me. Calista wants to play. She wants the chase.

Because she fought hard to keep her computer and hardware with her. She won't leave it behind.

And she doesn't have it now as she stares me down, daring me to follow through on my threat.

Her fingers tighten, then loosen. She lets go of the knob, and then she's out the door.

I fly after her, fingers grabbing at her wig, pulling it off. She hisses with a bite of pain and triumph, and she hits the landing... one more half flight and she's out the door.

Which isn't happening. I grab hold of the thick, glossy wooden balustrade and slide as I vault over it at the turn, landing in front of her.

Calista lets out a little shriek and I grab her by the waist and toss her over my shoulder. My heart thumps hard and she struggles, but I ignore her. Just like I ignore a door that opens and shuts above us, on the floor above.

She takes a breath.

"I wouldn't," I say, "not unless you don't want to sit without pain for the next week."

"You're sick in the head. Don't touch me."

At my apartment, I slam the door and hit the keypad, locking us in, and then I dump her on the couch.

She scrambles back, tits heaving, one of them exposed from the struggle, and if I didn't want her before, I sure as fuck do now.

Pale and pink with a beaded tight bud. It's a tit men would write sonnets over, a perfect fucking breast they'd try to capture in paint and pastel.

I want to suck on it, but I do the next best thing. "Your truth's showing. You want me to touch you. Very fucking badly." I flick her nipple with my thumb, and she moans low.

"You're—"

"If you're going to call me a pervert, I can be one. Would you like that?"

I take hold of both sides of the thin silk dress and wrench it hard. It rips right down the middle and I'm greeted by perfection.

She's sleek, long-legged, narrow-waisted, and those fucking tits are just the right side of big. Soft and plump and decadent. I shift my gaze down.

Her pussy is bare, the hair waxed away, and my dick throbs at the tiny tattoo on the left side of her pubis, a little close to her clit for my liking. It's an electric blue, a mess of lines and shapes of a microchip's insides.

Most women would have a fucking flower or a heart. Maybe an initial or a butterfly. If she's really edgy, it'll be a skull and crossbones.

Calista?

A fucking computer chip.

And it's one phenomenal pussy. Puffy lips, clit roused—made for my mouth and cock.

I duck as she throws a punch.

Grabbing her wrist, I back her into the wall. My gaze drops to that spot on her throat, where her jugular beats hard, erratic.

I bite and suck, hard. And she cries out, a moan of need and want. When I look at her, the sweet, lightly salty taste of her moving through me, she scowls. "Fuck off."

"Not code?"

Her neck is red, a bruise already forming, and I wait. A sullen darkness shifts over her. "I said fuck off."

"You are fucking sweet, Calista. So fucking sweet."

I don't give her a chance to feel the form of her "yes" moving through me and I wrap my hand around her throat and squeeze, cutting off her air as I haul her in and kiss her slow. She struggles, whimpers, and her mouth flows open, desperately seeking my kiss.

The harder I squeeze, the softer the kiss. I'm right at the edge because when she can't breathe, she's so fucking giving, all the turbulent thoughts and arguments are shut down and it's just feeling.

And when she's just feeling, she's almost divinity itself.

But I let her go, pushing her into the wall and she coughs, splutters, and shakes. I shove her against it, my hand now on the back of her neck as I free my aching cock.

I want to jack it, but I don't because the ache that borders on pain needs to go without any relief as I trace a finger down her spine and gather up the remnants of her dress.

"Just so we're clear," she says, pushing out the words, "I don't like you."

"Like's got shit to do with anything, Calista. I caught you, and now I'm going to devour you, collect on the retribution you owe."

Slipping a finger between her thighs, I slide into her. She's right, but so wet, her pussy's already prepped. And her low moan is an aphrodisiac in the air.

I use that hand to pull her hips back and I push her down the wall, holding her head there so she can't move. Then I kick apart her legs, and fuck, she's perfection. Her wet cunt on display, a little spread from where I just invaded.

I line myself up. And wait.

Not a single fucking word from her.

Not a hint of her way out, of *code*.

I wait another beat.

"Your little dick stopped working?" she snarls.

And I laugh, slamming into her.

Oh fuck, she's tight.

"Oh... oh God... Oh hell..." Her words come out with each thrust and soon she stops.

Her hands are spread on the wall, and I move mine to hook my fingers in her mouth. She tongues me and sucks at my fingers until I pull down, making her keep her mouth open, making her drool.

It's fucking filthy hot and my balls climb, tighten, the urge to spill into her thrumming hard as I thrust deep.

I bring my other hand around to pull at her cunt lips, pressing on her clit as I make everything almost impossibly tight. Calista rubs herself against me, shoves back onto me, and she starts to shake and convulse, her pussy clenching down on me, pulling me deep.

It's too much. That one step I can control as she milks my cock and I slam into her hard and come deep.

And when I'm done, I pull my hand from her mouth, rocking into her.

"Happy you got some?" she asks, her snark in place and it licks against me.

"You think that was the end?" I grin and thrust again because I'm still hard. "Little girl, we just got started."

CHAPTER 10
CALISTA

I can't stand. The orgasm that hit me still rolls through my body, still ringing bells deep inside. And his cock's still buried in my pussy. That thing is big, fucking huge even, and apparently can just keep going.

I'd think at his age, he'd been popping little blue pills except there weren't any in his toiletries when I went through his things. I found the gun but no clips. And I seriously doubt he keeps performance pills with his bullets.

I think this is just him.

And I want to sink to the ground.

Like Smith can read my mind, he pulls out of me and lets me do just that.

I collapse on the floor, my torn dress surrounding me, my inner thighs slick with remnants of both of our orgasms. I'm hot and cold. Overdressed and humiliatingly naked.

He touches my cheek. I smack it away.

His soft laughter settles like a blanket over me. I turn my face up and he's dressed, cock out. He should look ridiculous.

He doesn't.

With his hard cock and the severe look on his face, he's dangerous, masculine, and God help me, he makes my motor rev and hum.

Smith chased me down, leaped over the damn railing to get me, and then he dragged me back up in here. He choked me, ripped off my dress, and fucked me hard and fast against the wall.

Every moment is something I want to hate.

But I loved each one.

I want to do it again.

He's ignited something in me, and I need it again. The fight, the chase, the devouring.

All of it.

"Jesus." Smith lowers himself down onto the floor next to me. "You're supposed to look at me with fucking disgust, not like you need more. Like you want more."

"Stop being so full of yourself."

He crawls over me, his mouth on mine, his tongue a welcome invasion. Then he breaks the kiss and flips us. And though I'm on top of him, his cock getting harder and at full fucking attention between my thighs, it feels like it's the other way. That I'm caught in his web. Trapped in his arms.

But I'm on him, my fingers in his shirt, and he's looking at me like I'm his favorite science experiment.

"You liked it. Being my prey, being chased, the roughness. You can try and kill me now." He offers that slow grin that makes my toes curl. "If you like."

"Maybe," I say, coming right into his face, our lips a smidge apart, "I pretended."

"Maybe, but I don't think so. Why don't you sit on my face and try and smother me? I'll let you suck my cock."

"What if I bite it off?"

He slides a hand down my spine and then moves it to the

front and I lift my hips, letting him place the head at my entrance and I slide down on him, stretching, taking him in deep until I hit home. I think my eyes roll back.

"Yeah, I don't think you'll do that, but when you do suck me off, it's a risk I'm willing to take." He pulls me forward and kisses me. "Ride me, Calista. Hard."

This should be slow, but it's not. It's a hard, rough, fast fuck, but he flips the script and flips us right when I'm flying fast into my orgasm. He's on me now, plundering my pussy in the most delicious way possible. My orgasm threatens to slip away with the change in position, but he hooks my legs up over his shoulders so he can hammer hard and deep, making it hurt in the best ways, making it feel even better as I stretch. I light up like my insides are aflame.

He fits perfectly, and every time he pulls almost out, it's like he's stealing a part of me only to slam back, balls deep like he's rebuilding me from the inside out.

The intensity overtakes, consuming every cell, and I go along for his ride, offering myself, taking him as deep as I can, a greedy desperation raking over the fires inside.

Smith looks down, watching his cock split me open, watching as it pistons into me. It's hot, proprietary, like he's branding me as his. Then he looks at me.

The orgasm rips forward and he starts to hammer in to hit me in a certain way, making me suddenly cry out as I come apart once again.

He pulls out and my legs flop apart, missing him between them. But he's not done. He pulls me onto him, and he starts sucking my clit. He slides three fingers inside of me and it's too much. Everything's overly sensitive, and I scream a little, trying to get free, but he doesn't let me. He's relentless. Pushing, eating, licking. It's a feast and he's eating me alive.

I want to yell my safe word, but I can't get my breath. I

can't let myself because things are changing. What's too much becomes nice, good, and then fucking incredible.

But Smith still isn't done.

He continues his oral assault, and suddenly I don't even know where I am. Everywhere at once. I can feel it thunder up inside of me, something I've never felt. It's an orgasm, but it puts every other one I've ever had to shame. And I feel it *everywhere*.

Even my mind buzzes and burns.

My entire being contracts and expands, the pleasure overwhelming, everywhere, and it's the only thing, my entire world for those blissful minutes.

It's almost religious.

Slowly, I come down from the euphoric high, and I'm wet. So is his face. And humiliation suddenly hits. Christ, I'm easy.

He rolls off me with a self-satisfied grin on his gorgeous face and gets up, tucking himself away. "Get up and get ready. We're heading out in two hours. I'll pack."

I'M TORN between his lack of acknowledgement with what happened and annoyance as we drive out to some remote field. I should be marking it all off in my head. How we circumnavigate the Autobahn and take a variety of small roads.

But I can't think.

Smith looks good, which only pisses me off more. His hair's rumpled and the rings are on. I eye them. Apart from those, he's the epitome of urbane European with a classy, understated edge. Except for the rings.

I don't know why I'm fixating on them.

They pick up the light on his phone as he sits behind the driver's wheel. The only other jewelry—if you can call it that—

is an expensive watch. I'm not up on my watches, but it's a cut above a Rolex. Black face and strap and...

A man into jewelry wouldn't just wear them to an art show or event. He'd wear them all the time. And a man fitting into the European style his clothes suggest would wear a chunky watch. Maybe a bracelet.

"Are you sitting there silently judging me?"

"I'm admiring your jewelry," I snap.

I turn away and stare out the window. He left an outfit for me, and I wouldn't have put it on after my shower except everything else was gone, and I'm not about to go naked for anyone. Not even him. No, wait, especially not him.

So I pick at the dark-blue stretch denim that ends at my ankles. The chunky-heeled slender boots beneath it are comfortable enough, the oversize long-sleeve black top, too. I'm just not a fan of the pretty bra under that.

Modest in the way it covers, but the lace netting is see-through, and the silk flowers over the nipples are there to tease a man.

Or rather, I do like it, but it pisses me off he got it for me. He must have picked it out and paid for it without me seeing while we were out shopping.

"I could run," I finally say.

"You could."

"I bet I can outrun you."

"I'm betting you can't—besides, how did that work out for you an hour ago?—and you sure as shit can't outrun a bullet." He pulls his gun from his lower back and leans over me and opens the door. "By all means, have a go."

"You're an asswipe, Smith. A total asswipe."

He takes hold of my chin and leans in, and my heart starts to go wild as his warm breath teases my lips. "And your hair's pretty all one color. Dark brown, is it?"

"I prefer my silver hair, thank you." I sniff as he sits back and I swing a leg out, the cool breeze licking over me. "And of course, you'd use a gun."

"Here." He puts it down, next to the driver's door. "Run."

"I bet you've got some James Bond rings on."

"James..." He stares at me as a chopper flies over us. "What? Do you think my rings shoot poison darts?"

"I think—" I stop. The helicopter's louder now as light hits the car, making me jump.

He puts a hand on my thigh and the heat of it burns up the cold from the breeze. "It's for us."

No one gets out, but before I can move, Smith is already out of the car—gun nowhere to be seen, and he slams the trunk and runs to the chopper, bent down. Another man gets out and takes the bags from Smith, then Smith comes back, slings my pack over his shoulder... some CIA agent I am, I didn't even notice him dump it on the grass in the field.

Smith motions to the helicopter and I have no option but to run with him, past the other man whom I don't really take notice of other than he's tall like Smith.

Once we're in the helicopter and in the air, I stare out as the man below gets into the car. It grows smaller and disappears as we head off away from the field.

It takes me a few moments to process everything. This isn't any kind of CIA or Army chopper. It isn't even anything I've seen in photos from secret deals made.

This is luxury, from the soundproofed inside to the buttery leather seats and carpeted floor.

And Smith, looking completely at home. What the hell is that about? He motions me over. I'm halfway up before I make myself sit again.

The man laughs. "Fucking brat. Get your hot little ass over here."

"No."

"Don't make me force you. Consequences, remember?"

I narrow my eyes and cross my arms. "What are you going to do, strip me naked and fuck me?"

"Yes. And the pilot can see everything. There's a feed to him."

"You utter prick."

But I get up and he slides a hand between my thighs and strokes my denim-covered pussy. "For show."

He's not smirking, but it's in his voice, and I want to hit him. Hard. Because my legs start to shake and my knees give way.

Smith takes advantage and pulls me down on him so I'm straddling him, and he starts to lick my throat, nibbling on my flesh, sucking where he bit me before. It sends a throb of deep, dark longing through me, right to my clit, down to the tips of my toes.

"Fuck, you taste good. It's one of the reasons I'm not throwing you out of the fucking helicopter."

I smile sweetly at him, and then I nuzzle his throat, biting him so hard he growls and rocks me on top of his erection.

"That, too." He pulls my head back and bites my chin, then kisses his way to my ear. "And you smell amazing, Calista."

"Is that a poem?"

"Please," he says, "and the rings don't have poisoned darts, but I'm wearing them for a reason."

"I knew you were a lame-ass James Bond."

"He's a problematic man," he mutters, slipping a hand under my top to fondle a breast. I want to smack him away, I really do, but he can do wicked, wild magic with his thumb.

"Where are we going?"

"France and then to the US."

I should ask why we're taking a detour, but I know he'll just lie to me anyway.

My stomach lurches. Not at going home, but I need... I need to find my agent or figure out what happened to him. I have to find out more about the Collectors, and if Trenton was one of the ones who went down. And I need to—

"If you're innocent, then you don't have to worry."

I put my hands on his face and dip my head to bite his ear. "You think I'll see the light of day, Smith?"

"Not my problem."

"You're the one kidnapping me."

"Seeing you back."

"It's a soft kidnap and we both know it."

"Which," he says, slipping inside my bra to roll a nipple and pinch it, "is why we stick together, and why you need to understand you can't escape me. I don't want to hurt you, but I will."

"Can I get off now?"

"You want to give him a show?"

I reach down and grab his dick and he just studies me.

"Be very careful what you do, Calista."

I give him a squeeze, borderline hard, and his eyes flutter half shut as he bites his bottom lip. And it makes me hot in all the ways. But I take the moment to scramble off him, and when we land somewhere in the South of France, it's a short drive to a private airfield.

There's a passport check especially for us, and our bags are taken on board, including my backpack with my computer.

Smith pulls open the doors that lead to the waiting plane. We step outside at the same time that the plane explodes into a violent storm of twisted metal and fire.

CHAPTER 11
SMITH

I throw her down and cover her as hell rains down around us. We were close enough to the explosion that the blast is a little too dangerous. The heat from the explosion a little too fucking hot.

In the chaos, I drag her up and out of harm's way. Anyone else as young as her would probably require me having to waste precious minutes coaxing back to calm. Shit, I've had to do that with freshly minted agents before. And ones I've needed to extract after they've spent years behind desks.

But Calista takes it and runs, like she's compartmentalized what just happened. Fuck, I don't know, maybe she's used to blasts. Maybe she gets off on it. But I don't think so. I think the part of her brain that makes her so good at her job gives her a place where she can operate on all cylinders when things like this happen. There's always time to fall apart later.

I can see why the CIA recruited her instead of locking her away.

I can also see why they want to get their hands on her now, this time as possible enemy number whatever the hell.

But we run, her hand gripped tight in mine.

Calista moves with me, fast, low, keeping to the edges of the building where there's cover, and she doesn't try and dart into the first door. She doesn't try and break free and run.

A feral part of me wants her to, though. I want to tackle her down and hit the pavement with her. But this time it wouldn't be to cover her from the brunt of the explosion. No. I want to cover her so I can fuck her.

I don't even question my brain's direction. Libido is just that. So's a carnal pull to someone. Doesn't mean I won't hand her over when the time comes, and doesn't mean I won't keep her with me only to throw her under whatever available bus there is the moment I'm done with her.

She's definitely sitting on something, either something she knows about or is still trying to process, and I'm going to find out before anyone else gets their hands on her.

Hence *this*.

We're traveling light without bags. People scramble around, screaming, voices shouting and emergency vehicles flying past us. We move quickly, Calista scouting the area, eyes wide.

We're almost there.

The airport car sits just outside the airstrip, and I order her into the back as I jump behind the wheel. She doesn't ask how it just so happens to sit here, very conveniently, and I don't fill her in. Instead, I take off at a brisk pace, out into the nighttime countryside of the South of France and in the direction of another airfield.

It's close, and when we get there, she only looks at me as we're hustled onto a sleek jet. My jet.

She rubs a hand down the front of her face, not saying a word as we strap in and we go through safety checks. She doesn't speak as we take off, and she ignores the whiskey I get for her from the attendant.

It's not until we're in the air and she's downed her drink that she says, "Who are you, really? And who just fucking tried to kill me?"

"Those are some heavily weighted questions." I settle back against the plush leather recliner. I know she thinks we're heading right back to the US, either Washington, DC, or New York, but we're not.

I can't let her go yet. There are things I want to know.

Like why she had the number from Estonia about the Collectors on the burner phone when she slipped her SIM card into it. Like what she knows about Bolivia and the weapon.

And I want to know the connections between all of it. Bolivia. Sex trade. Collectors. New weapon.

I know they're all connected somehow. I can smell it.

And I'm going to investigate every angle, every potential location and cell, before I give her up.

The weapon thing... unless she managed to uncover every-thing... might be a red herring, at least for me. That's CIA shit through and through, and she's either someone who fucked over her agent for money, or she stumbled onto something big and dangerous and deadly.

Could be the former, it's probably the latter.

But the Bolivian connection is too coincidental to ignore.

Right now, she's alone in the world. No computer. No evidence that isn't in an easy-to-get-to place, or so she thinks. I'm betting she has copies of her information somewhere. I know she can probably break into CIA servers, too, which is next-level espionage.

"Why do you think someone's trying to kill you?"

Calista's basically bouncing in her seat, panic evident in

her expression. "Are you crazy? Were you there? The plane fucking exploded as we were about to board."

I lean forward. "Could have been for me. Not you."

"Was it?" She stills, a small gasp escaping her lips. "Who are you?"

It's how she phrases it, like she'll keep picking until she learns everything. It's not going to happen, so I feed her nothing and the truth.

"A man with a lot of enemies, a lot of money, and a lot of power."

"Then let me go. You don't need the payout from handing me over."

I settle back in my seat and gaze at her. We've got hours of flying ahead of us, and apart from the pilots and flight attendant, we're alone. "Interesting that's what you lock on to. The money aspect."

She blows out a breath.

Calista's hair looks good. It makes her look her age, maybe a little older, more polished, like the clothes. And maybe I'm a little perverse in the fact that I miss the silver-blond and colorful hues streaking the cut.

Looking like this, like a chic, sophisticated young woman, Calista would be someone my Smith Hunt cover persona would date and even consider marrying. And then he'd likely go and fuck a whole lot of hot, available pussy, the kind that likes to be fucked in a sex club, likes to play games with them in public places.

But the real me? I don't cheat. I rarely have relationships. They come with baggage, strings, and weights. I have no need or desire for any of that shit.

But Smith Hunt, the persona who likes to fly around in a fancy fucking jet and marry shiny, young pussy that's well-behaved, is going to cheat.

The fucking punch in the gut is if I was him, I'd cheat on this woman with the hacker girl inside of her.

Because me and my alter ego want both versions of her.

Now I'm the one scraping a hand over my face.

"Feeling bad you kidnapped me?"

I flick a glance at her. "Fuck no. Feeling bad I didn't bring a gag."

"You're a real funny guy. Please," she says, deadpan, "bring some surgical tape because I'm coming apart at the seams."

"Get your ass over here."

Her eyes go hard. "I'm on a fucking plane with you. I'm here."

"No. Get over here. To me. On the floor."

She gets up, which half shocks me, taking her time to unbuckle the seat belt, and she crosses from her luxury seat opposite mine.

But she doesn't sink to her knees. Instead, she rests a hand on either side of my head and leans in. "I'm not getting on the floor."

I'm not buckled in. Grabbing her by the waist, I flip her down so I'm on top of her, nestled in against the heat of her denim-covered pussy. Deliberately, I rub up against her. "You're not real good at following instructions."

"I'm not real good at being humiliated. Or being told to suck an old cock."

I laugh, nipping her throat, making her arch up into me, her soft moan negating her words.

"That's where you're wrong. I think you'll love sucking my cock, and I didn't say anything about humiliating you."

"It's what you get off on, right?"

"Do you?"

"I just said—"

"We both know your words and your reactions are galaxies

apart." I kiss a line down her throat as I skim my hand up under her top to expose her lace-covered breast. I find that hard little pebble of a nipple, kissing my way down until I can take it in my mouth, hold it between my teeth, and run my tongue over it.

She starts to pant.

Little fucking Calista likes being bossed around. No, she likes to fight before she submits. That's the beating heart of her. She wants my games just like I want hers.

She's grinding against me with her hips, and I'm having a hard fucking time concentrating on what I'm doing. Which is deconstructing her.

I bite. Hard. Calista lets out a wobbly cry and spasms. And fuck... did she just come from me sucking and biting and teasing her nipple?

She fights me now, but I easily hold her down. "You want my old cock, admit it."

"Screw you."

"See? You want me."

The fire that flashes is worth a thousand willing pussies, a thousand naked women who crawl on the floor for me, who ride me and beg for more.

Calista suddenly breaks free, and I flip her around so she's on top of me. She takes a shuddery breath before dipping in for a violent, sharp-edged kiss. When she tries to pull away, I thread my hand in her hair and bring her in, harder and wilder. She whimpers, clawing at me.

What I want is to bury myself in her again.

What I want is for her to crawl on her hands and knees to me. To sit between my thighs and suck my cock. I want her to fucking worship it.

I don't think I've ever wanted to bend a woman to my will quite like that.

I do now.

Shit, most women love my cock. I'm popular at the sex clubs, especially O-Ring, the Knight's very own. Girls who work there who want me, others who frequent the place, too. I fuck a lot of them.

And as long as they're of age, I haven't given a damn. I prefer older, but in a club?

Young, sweet pussy is pliable to will. And the sweet, young things who get into O-Ring are the hottest out there. I'll share. I'll fuck them in front of the others if my mood takes me.

It's just when I'm on the hunt, when I choose a lover, I prefer them older. I like what experience brings. And playing primal games with a woman comes with the least amount of mess.

I'm not a fan of mess.

I'm definitely not into anything resembling a relationship, especially of the sexual variety with girls around my kid's age.

Except, apparently, this one.

Not that it's a relationship. Not that I have any intentions of pursuing one, even if that were possible. But if I was looking... no. I'm not. She's a fuck and nothing more. And a fuck with an agenda behind it. I want to know what she knows. Whether she knows it or not.

Calista might not be able to see the connections, but I'll be able to.

And this?

She tastes of all the good things wrapped in bad.

I explore her mouth in a dark, pagan way. And then as our tongues start to twirl and duel, start to dance and fuck, I push her off me.

Her hand comes up to my throat and she tries to squeeze as she climbs back on.

Everything in me explodes.

I push up into her hand, adjust her grip, help her choke me. She rears back but I hold her in place.

"You're crazy."

"If you're going to try and kill me," I say, dragging her down while keeping her hand on my throat, "you might want a weapon. I'm a bit too strong for you."

"I can kill you."

"Then try."

A beat of thick silence spreads, sucking air.

"No."

I sit up, taking her with me and let go of her hand, but pull her on my lap, right up over my hard cock, and she shudders. The heat at her pussy is enough to light fires.

"You know you'll be paying for that."

"Because I tried to choke you?"

I shake my head, beating a tattoo on her hip bone. "No. Because you didn't try at all."

"Maybe I wanted to get your attention."

"Calista, you have it."

"Who are you—?"

"Ex-government. And I take on jobs for money. You're one of them. That's all you need to know." I let her go and nod at the seat opposite. "Buckle up and rest. We'll be landing soon."

"Where?"

I look at her for a long minute. "I think you should be more concerned with who we're going to see rather than where we're going."

CHAPTER 12
CALISTA

Belize in Central America is hardly even a country. It sits in a coastal region that hits a mountain and some dry desert along with jungle. The stretch is long, the regime unstable, and it's one of those places that's always overlooked.

So why the hell we're here, in the jungle, at an abandoned mission is a mystery known to Smith only. I'm actually shocked he finally told me where we landed.

There's a small city closer to the coast, but he chose the freaking abandoned area. The abandoned area being patrolled by men with machine guns.

It's more well-known as a farming region, but really it reeks of illegal trade and militia. Or at least that's what I think.

Smith is hardly forthcoming with any bit of detail.

He changed into cargo pants and an olive-green shirt on the plane and gave me an outfit to change into that's more breathable than denim. It's daytime and we had to drive along the coast and into a jungle made up of vines and trees and strange sounds to get to our destination.

"Walk." That was his command a few hours ago, and as the heat and humidity slowly began to choke me, I just concentrated on putting one foot in front of the other. Thank God I changed my clothes on the plane because this air is oppressively hot.

My lungs and legs burned until we finally came into a clearing with cooler air. In the middle of it stands a mission, complete with its tiny chapel.

A beautiful woman takes my hand and shows me to the shower that's operated by a pump system. I also hear a groaning generator nearby. The woman, Sofia, talks in fast Spanish that I can understand, telling me about how many businesses have chosen to base themselves in other countries that are more politically stable than here.

"Instability hurts business," I say as she shows me where things are for a shower, including a change of clothes. I narrow my eyes at the skirt. We're in the jungle, so it's an odd choice, but it's clean so I don't protest.

"The city has fallen into shambles. And many girls disappear. Some say for a better life, but I don't know." And the dark expression that crosses her face hurts my heart. "Things... they happen."

She doesn't need to elaborate by saying they happen to women. Her look grows darker, and it's understood.

It's the look I've seen on people close to trafficking, when I was helping to uncover cells in the early days of my CIA career, to read through chatter and track down a man who turned out to be a low-level Collector, someone who sold women no one wanted—no one among the superrich, that is.

Sofia's expression is now full of rage and anger and pain, and that tells me it happened to someone she knew.

Henry and I might have been the illegitimate children of someone who was trafficked, left behind when our mom was taken, but we still didn't experience what she did while she was in captivity. We just dealt with the upheaval growing up, handling life with a mother who was damaged beyond repair.

"Might have been." Because we don't know for sure if we were the indirect victims of trafficking. Our grandmother's story kept changing. To protect herself or us, or our mother, I don't know. And in a way, I'm not sure I want to know.

All we know is she got out. Physically, anyway.

And we made do when our grandmother died, and Mom was... Mom.

But her fate is one I want to avenge.

Her fate is one I don't want others to go through, either directly or as a loved one left behind like Sofia likely is.

I thank her, shower, and pull on the top, flowy skirt, and boots I've been given. I leave the laundered cotton panties and wash mine. At first, I thought the skirt was a strange pick, but it actually lets my skin breathe so I'm grateful for it.

Then I go and search for Smith, scouting the area as I walk.

If it's a base for illegal operations, it's small. Three off-road vehicles and, as far as I can tell, just three men with guns and their rifles swung casually on their backs. They're clearly not planning to use them.

Or maybe this area's known for bandits. Maybe they're just protecting livestock at night. There's plenty of it, from what I can see.

The place doesn't seem lived in as a dedicated home, but it's used, so it brings me back to the fact that there might be something here to be guarded. Although, these guards don't look like the lethal type. I could steal a truck and—then what? I know I'm in Belize. But beyond that? I know nothing.

And even if I got away, where the fuck would I go?

Smith has the fake passport, and I'm assuming mine got blown up in France.

Dammit, I miss being able to slide into news and the intel behind it all.

He's also got a heavy-looking canvas pack that he pulled from the plane.

I'll need to get into it before I can go anywhere.

The little building reminds me of what I'd expect a convent to look like. Scouring the area, I look for Smith. He's nowhere to be seen, and as I step backward to take another glance around, I almost fall over a chicken and the chubby child who's chasing it.

Sofia mutters something, sweeps up the child, and hands me an empty bowl. "Please help?"

With a sigh, I follow her in to begin my foray into kitchen prep.

Not my strong suit, by the way.

Sofia is in and out of the small kitchen while I chop and prep vegetables for a stew that looks like it's going to be spicy.

"I'm sorry, Juniper," she says, chasing off after her child again. When she returns with the little boy tucked under an arm, she tries to drag the big pot onto the woodfire stove.

"Unless we're having boiled toddler," I say in Spanish as I take the pot and fill it with water, "I'll get everything going."

Because clearly this is women's work. But I don't allow myself to utter those words. Instead, I look at the vegetables and grains as Sofia insists on putting the order of things in a line for me, so I can chop and put it into the stew. I smile and nod and wait for her to finish.

She's older than me by a handful of years, and the child's clearly hers, but if she'd just leave me alone, I can think. If I'm alone, maybe I can smuggle a knife as a weapon.

When she's gone, I fall into a routine of thinking, chopping, and planning revenge against Smith. That and trying to untangle what I know.

"Nothing, that's what," I grumble.

But I must have stumbled onto something. And the CIA obviously thinks I'm behind the stolen weapon. The Bolivia connection bugs me, too.

Dammit, I haven't done anything wrong. If I can just make sense of some things, like where the hell my field agent is, like who and where are the Collectors, like what's become of the founder, Trenton, who might have raped and abused my mother... then I'll happily walk in to talk to the CIA.

With a deep, resigned breath, I concentrate on chopping.

It's not until the peacefulness is disturbed by a shift in the air that I know I'm not alone.

Smith.

"Go away."

"Is that any way to talk to your savior?"

I snort out a laugh. "More like kidnapper with a part-time hustle in side thorns."

"Pretty, and yet I can't fucking wait to hand you over. Maybe if I ask nicely, they'll let me torture you, just a little." He steals a carrot moments before I bring the knife down on the wooden chopping block. "You do know that kind of violent action gets me hot, right?"

"Well, considering you're a kidnapping son of a bitch... I'm not surprised."

I don't know why, but the needling banter lifts me, makes me want to smile.

It also turns this dangerous man into a pussycat over the feral panther I think he just might be.

Based on everything I know about him, I believe he's a man who's smart and very comfortable in his skin. But his talk of violent action, chasing me down, all that hunter and prey crap getting him hot

I don't think it's talk.

And I don't think I've seen the real Smith.

Well, actually...

I think I've seen a facet of him, a glimpse of what he wants me to see with hints of what he actually is and what he'll do. I don't mean his job, I mean him. Who he is down in the marrow of his bones, down in his soul.

This man... He's like a panther playing before his meal because, though he might want to eat, he's not hungry. The desire to kill hasn't been stroked into life.

When I say dangerous, what I've seen is a dangerous man, and that... that's the tip of the iceberg.

I take in a shaking breath.

"Why the CIA?" he asks, leaning against the chipped white sink next to me.

With a shrug, I finish the carrots and tip the board into the pot. There's a knife at the back of the workbench. It looks sharp. Maybe it's a paring knife. Hell, maybe it's for stabbing sexy, hot, dangerous men and making a run for it. I don't know, but I do know I'm going to steal it.

His gaze travels to where I just looked but he doesn't do anything about it.

"To rid the world of men like you."

"Or make money by selling secrets. It's been done."

"I'm not doing that," I snap.

"I really don't give a fuck if you are."

"Then why ask?"

He leans in. "To get a handle on who you are and what you'll do. Maybe because I never expected you to enjoy this." Smith spreads a hand.

"Cooking?"

"Line work." And the slightest smirk lifts his mouth.

"This isn't that different than writing code. The repetition, the getting it right, the looking for—" I stop. He's not interested in code or hacking. He's... poking in my brain. "I find it soothing."

"And what else do you find soothing?"

I start chopping the potato. "Kintsugi."

"What the hell is that?"

This time my cheeks burn. It's my little hobby and I never share it. Not because it's anything to be embarrassed about but because... I don't know, because it doesn't fit.

"The Japanese art of fixing broken ceramics with gold."

"Hmmm."

"Hmmm what?"

Now he shrugs. "Just hmmm."

"Just how ancient are you?"

This time his gaze catches on my mouth and I press my thighs together as slow heat builds there, because that look is like fucking. "Thirty-nine. Me and my old dick are too old for your little fantasies."

"And your daughter is twenty-three."

"Yes." He moves away and finds a bottle of what looks like golden rum and he pours two glasses. Smith puts one next to me and downs his and refills it. "I was sixteen when she was born."

"Oh."

"We don't have much of a relationship."

"Shocking. You're such a charmer. I can't imagine how you wouldn't be a doting dad, too."

He puts the bottle down with a soft click on the windowsill.

Somehow the gentleness is worse than if he slammed it down.

"You know nothing about me or my fucking life, Juniper."

I normally like my middle name, but not when he says it with that scathing touch. "You're not the only one who was recruited young. Dakota was... let's just say she was something of a very delayed surprise."

I try and think of something to say. But nothing comes.

There are questions that crowd my mind. Did her mother keep her from him? Was his kid adopted? Relationships can be repaired.

"M-my brother didn't want anything to do with Mom for a long time. I guess you've read all about us, but our grandmother raised us, and then our mom came back. She was never the same. Damaged, scarred. She was so self-destructive. And she was in and out of institutions. But they made up, created a bond before... before she died."

Death by suicide. That was the thing, but I'd had suspicions.

It doesn't matter.

I tracked down the man who led her to this horrible outcome. Maybe he's our father. Maybe not. I don't know or care.

I uncovered it two years ago in an old file. An investigation into Jon Trenton and his business dealings. The Collectors. His twisted, depraved preference for young girls.

My eyes burn hot.

"Sylvie's long dead and there's no fixing my shit. Dakota's better off without me in her life."

"Smith?"

"What?"

He softens, trails fingers down over my cheek, rubbing light on my lower lip. It's like a balm, like something I never knew I needed. The touch isn't sexual. No, this touch is... it isn't sweet, but it's tender and comforting and it makes my eyes burn hotter and my vision blur.

"Will you let me go? If I promise to turn myself in. I-I have something I need to do."

He leans in and kisses me soft and long. Then he raises his head, takes the knife from my nerveless fingers, and hurls it across the room where it embeds into the wall, the handle vibrating.

"Fuck no," he growls. "You run, you even *try* to run, and I'll fucking kill you."

CHAPTER 13
SMITH

Rodriguez is an old asset of mine. I trust him enough—about as much as I trust any non-Knight.

Throwing the knife, losing my temper like that... it's not me. I keep everything tucked up, compartmentalized. But there was something about how she got in too close to things I didn't want uncovered, or rather, how I let her. No one had a fucking gun to my head.

Dakota's normally off-limits for conversation. Jones knows enough of the story. Orion knows whatever he needs to know, as do the others. But there are some Knights who don't know a thing and I kept my relationship with Dakota fractured for a lot of reasons.

So why I even told this fucking child a thing about it is beyond me.

And then I let myself soften toward her, like I'm losing my motherfucking mind.

I'm violent, primal, a hunter with no conscience. My sex games are so much more than what Calista's ever seen. Most of the time, my kind of D/s play is wrapped up in clearly spelled-out rules.

But with her, I don't want any rules governing my actions. I want it elemental.

I want her as mine to pull apart and devour.

I grit my teeth. Like I said, I'm losing my fucking mind.

Rodriguez and Sofia are heading to their home and farm a few miles down the road. This mission is on their property but on the edges, a place where very dark things have gone down. In the next week, it'll be occupied by the militia, men waiting for a war that might not even happen.

If it doesn't, they'll move the cocoa leaf crops as planned. Some might say to just put a stop to this kind of farming altogether, but it's not my place to give a damn. If rich fucks want to snort cocaine, then let them. I'm not being paid to stop it.

But if trafficking young girls enters the picture, and it's likely that's the case, then I'm here to shut it the fuck down. One of the other Knights has an operation to stop an outpost in another region of this tiny, troubled country.

The CIA is looking into things in Central America, but they have the wrong intel. Maybe it was crafted to misguide them, either deliberately or by accident. I don't fucking know, and I need to find out. And I can't let Calista go until I can piece this whole thing together. I need to know what she knows and she'll stay with me for as long as it takes her to divulge it.

The mere mention of Belize only got the mildest of reactions back home. But the most I've seen was the expression on Calista's face after Sofia mentioned it. That's how I know I'm onto something here. And it's more proof that I can't let her go. Not just yet.

I'm gathering clues and she's my map.

"Thanks." I put my feet up on a wooden stool as I recline back in a chair outside. Narrowing my eyes at the satellite-linked laptop from Rodriguez, I shoot off a message to Jones using Harry's Fix It—the Knight's messaging system that masquerades as a boring little store. We all know the codes and what they mean but nobody else would have a clue.

Need some pipes looked at. Possible leak. This week?

It doesn't take long to get a response. *Tuesday, ten a.m.*

Sounds good, I message back. *Book it.*

"Trouble?"

"Nah, just some boring crap at home." I don't look up as I send the message. I shut down the messaging app, close the laptop lid, and hand the computer back to Rodriguez.

Jones'll have a small plane waiting for me. I can't fly my own jet since we'll be operating under the radar. I just need to tell him when and where. But now he knows my location. And if Rodriguez tries to sell me out, he'll have that information, too. The laptop was no doubt being tracked by the IP address from the second Jones got my first message.

Even if Rodriguez just looks up what I did, he'll just see a front business that handles mundane plumbing issues.

Some might say using his computer's a risk. But I prefer that to using my phone. That's for emergencies and for me to tell Jones where I am when I need the help. *If* I need the help. Using it for anything more is too big of a risk, one I'm not willing to take.

Dinner is spicy and good. My little reluctant captive is quiet, not that I blame her. The closer we get to the handoff, the more real her problems become and the tighter the noose around her neck becomes.

As I stare at her, she shifts in her seat and breaks her eyes away from mine. I don't know what she was up to back in the kitchen, but I'll find out. As the others say good night and file out, she stays put, eyes so stormy one could get lost in them and be dragged under by the volatile waves there.

THE TRUTHS THAT DECEIVE

I push away the fact I like it, the danger of the hunted getting feral. Maybe she took the knife from the wall earlier, maybe not.

There's a guard farther down the road just out of sight. I don't need to check with Rodriguez or confirm it for myself. The four-by-four sitting in the shadows speaks volumes.

What it doesn't do is tell me if we're being guarded or kept under surveillance. It doesn't matter if Rodriguez is loyal to me. In places like this, trust can be twisted and things turn on a dime.

I don't think Rodriguez is trying to make a quick buck or save his family by handing me over to an enemy. But who the hell really knows?

I trust him. But I get the conflict.

Family comes first.

He's aware I can get out of most situations. And he'll bet on me not looking for payback if he does happen to use me.

I have enemies. All Knights do. And being CIA, ex-freelance intelligence. My enemy quota's high.

I can add little Calista to that list now.

She has a glass of rum in front of her. It's rough, burns the esophagus on the way down. But I've got something else in mind for her. Smoother, guaranteed to give her sweet fucking dreams, but I leave her alone and wait until she sees the bag next to me.

I watch as her gaze skitters over to it, but she doesn't do more than stare at it like it holds her way out of here. She's thinking passport. Not her computer. I need to get into the device, but it's got a thumbprint lock.

"You know, you still haven't explained the whole thing," I say, taking a sip from my glass.

"What do you know about the Collectors?"

I hide my smile. She's trying to play me by bouncing the

question my way. But she's still too new to how this game is played.

Her interest is deep, on some kind of personal level, but I'm not sure of the connection. I don't think she's involved in that sordid industry, although it's not unheard of for women to do that. There's disgust on her face, and it makes her wild, fierce, and all the things I want to explore in her.

I shut that carnal thought down fast, just like I shut down the thoughts of her long legs, one of which she has drawn up. Her skirt pools up a little, showing thigh.

She's not wearing panties. They were drying when I used the bathroom before, tucked on a low rung of a chair just outside the room. And now... fuck yeah, I'd love to follow the line of her thigh, slip her skirt up higher, see if I can catch a glimpse of pussy, of the tattoo. See if she's wet and stroke down into the slippery heat of her.

"Enough." I could goad her but decide against it. I need her to spill information. I need to see what she knows.

If I hadn't seen that text from the Estonia number, I'd have already handed her back to the CIA—or whatever group wants her—and her head would still be spinning as I walked off to collect my fee.

But luckily, or maybe unluckily for her, she's uncovered something about the people who took my daughter.

And I don't care if this tiny trafficking cell she's found never heard of fucking Dakota Hunt; I'll destroy them anyway.

Just like in Scotland. Even if the leader there had survived, it would have been only a "long enough" scenario.

My mission is to murder every last motherfucking one of them.

Reaching into the bag, I pull out her computer and her eyes light up. "I saved this, you know."

"B-but—"

"Had it in that car to be loaded up last, and then the plane blew up." I pause. "Why?"

"Oh my God..." She gets up, rushing over to me. Cramming herself cross-legged like a kid into the chair next to me, she puts her hands out. "I can't believe it!"

But I don't hand it straight over. "Why?"

"The plane?" Calista shrugs. "Maybe in the information I have? I had threats, those low-level ones, and my agent... I..." Her cheeks turn pink. "Maybe I poked into something I shouldn't have. That's the thing, I don't know. One day I was going to work, and then there were looks and online lockouts. I could get around them, but I didn't know what I was looking at. Whoever blew the plane up could be after me for something I have no idea about."

She sounds so innocent, and I'm halfway to believing her. But I stop myself. She might be young and deskbound but she's fucking smart and they trained her.

I change tactic because yeah, I know who blew up the plane.

"Can you show me?"

"No, because—because you can't read code."

And she doesn't have it on her computer. She doesn't know what she might have seen or found, or maybe they just think she's guilty in regard to the weapon. Because it's a big deal, from what little I know. It's fucking huge.

"The Collectors? Other sex traffickers?"

"I don't know much. Just..." She opens the lid of her computer and I'm a little surprised there's no password, but all she does is open an album. It's full of photos. Her as a kid with a boy, as a teen with the same guy, now a young man. Her brother. And then there's a beautiful woman and an older version of her. I'd guess those are mom and grandmother.

I look at Calista and then her mom. She had to have been as

young as me and Sylvie, maybe younger, when she had her kids.

"Did they take her?"

Calista only shrugs. "Why don't you have a relationship with your daughter?"

Her shrug speaks volumes. It tells me she's convinced a Collector was involved with whatever happened to her mom.

And if so...

She's got information on them. A girl like her would.

So I give her a little in return.

"I didn't know I had a kid until I returned from the UK. It'd been my second trip there. I was recruited, went to college young like you, and then I trained. When I finally came back to Michigan..." I sigh, rub my face, and this time I take a swig of the rough rum from the damn bottle. Then, just before I hand it to her, I slip a small pill into it.

She takes a sip, waiting for me to finish my thought. "I discovered I had a kid. I was twenty-one at that point."

Close to Dakota's current age now.

And she's marrying—

Nope. Not going there. I can forgive some things. And Orion's one of my closest friends. She's good for him, too. Any fucker can tell. But there's no fucking place here for a heart-to-heart over my kid and her future.

I'm not ready for that.

Just like I'm not ever gonna be ready to talk to Dakota about any of this.

"Your ex didn't tell you about the baby?"

I close my eyes. The pain still festers deep in my soul. I'm not the boy who loved Sylvie. But I remember that guy. Sylvie thought that guy took off on her. In her eyes, I didn't care.

Neither one of us knew her letters to me had been intercepted. She was lied to. And she died thinking I didn't give a shit about her... That created jagged edges time can never smooth out.

"Sylvie was a good girl. Way better than I ever deserved. What can I say? We were kids, and hormones are beasts. But I did love her. It never would have lasted, but she never got to tell me anyway. Her parents were rich, stepped in to help, and then she died in a robbery before she got to see her daughter grow up. Before her daughter even reached five. She was twenty when she was killed. It fucking sucks."

"I'm sorry."

"Why?"

She shuts her computer, gets off her seat, and kneels at my feet. Then she reaches up and places a hand on my cheek. It's warm and good, and I feel like a fucking prick. I *am* a fucking prick.

"Because I am. Because death just makes pain sit with nowhere to go and heal. Time never helps. The pain just wears on."

I nod. "Time's a bitch."

"What about your daughter?"

"Fuck, she hates me with a passion. But that's okay. That hatred has protected her. She lives with a friend of mine and his daughter, her best friend Harley. We hardly see each other, but I know she's protected."

Calista bites her lip, those stormy eyes filled with softness that irritates. "I'm sorry."

"I don't really know her. Father through DNA only."

"Bullshit." She pushes away from me and grabs the bottle of rum I gave her. She takes the final swallow, and I'm almost positive when she looks at the empty thing, she's thinking about hitting me with it. "No man gets a big-ass tattoo of North and South Dakota in red if they didn't see themselves as an actual father. And you love her, even if you deny it. I know the truth."

"Calista?"

"Yes?"

"Come here."

She sways, her eyes a little glassy. And I kiss her, pulling her into my arms. She kisses me back dreamily, open-mouthed, melting against me. Seconds later, her body slumps over, the kiss dying on our lips.

I pick her up, hugging her close as I grab the laptop with my free hand. I walk into the bedroom and settle Calista onto the mattress. Then I use her hand to unlock the computer.

The drug should work for a few hours, so I take the computer and head back out.

She may claim to be innocent, but she has secrets.

And I'm about to uncover each and every one of them.

CHAPTER 14
CALISTA

"You fucking asshole, you drugged me."

Smith's dark head is bent over my computer, a frown on his face. It pisses me off that the amount of attention he gives me is about the same as he'd give a vaguely annoying fly.

Only a sliver of light peeks in through the window. A cool breeze whispers over my heated skin.

It's a clear night.

But not inside me.

I'm a furnace of barely controlled hot anger.

"I asked you something."

"No," he says, "you made a statement. There's a difference."

Those words drive home the one fact I let slip away during this trip from France.

It doesn't matter if he's nice or cruel. It doesn't matter if he saves me or holds a gun to my head.

There's a reason I keep looking for outs and ways to escape, and it isn't what waits for me at the end of this fucked-up road trip.

We're enemies.

He's my enemy.

No matter how amenable he can be, I've seen him turn on the proverbial dime into darkness, savageness. Violence. And yeah, he's made no secret of what's going to happen to me when we get back to the States. My captors will probably meet him at Dulles or Reagan National Airport for the handoff. Or, considering this is the mysterious Smith, some small governmental airfield where the CIA will be waiting with guns.

We're at the opposite ends of things.

Only he's dragging this whole thing out, hopping between countries without giving me any reasons why.

There's one fact, though.

We're enemies.

Him and me.

There's no denying that.

I put a hand in the pocket of the skirt, and it touches the smooth, now-warm steel blade I stole from the kitchen.

An ugly thought nips at my brain.

He's asked mostly about the Collectors when he's questioned me.

Not my CIA agent.

Not what I know about the weapon, which isn't much, and what I do know is disjointed.

Yet he claims the weapon and whatever I might know is the story behind why I'm being escorted back.

Story. My mind snags on that.

He's not CIA or government now. He lies when telling the truth. It's a gift. A dark one. And he does that to me. I keep asking and he keeps giving me the truth wrapped in nothing. My "who are you" questions are met with generic answers.

Meanwhile, there's someone who doesn't want me to put whatever they think I have in the right hands. Whatever that is.

I need to get away.

With a slow look around, my stomach drops. There's no way I'll get to the four-by-four outside. But I'm not waiting for whatever he's waiting for.

"Put my computer away, there's nothing on there."

To my surprise, he does just that. Closes the lid and slides it into the backpack.

"You're wrong, Calista. There's a lot on there." He links his fingers over his abs and meets my gaze, taking me in like he can see inside my soul. "I'm still deciding if it's of interest."

"I thought you were just paid to deliver me. You said you don't care about anything more."

"True, but I'm a curious kind of guy." Then he sighs. "Sit down or go back to bed."

"I'm not tired." I try not to search out a path of escape with my gaze. I'm thinking the tangle of jungle is my best bet. All through this region, according to Sofia and her chatter, are farms, little towns, and communities. The bigger city, as she calls it, is closer to the water, and I know which direction that's in. But I don't want to race down random roads where Smith can track me.

The jungle offers more hiding places.

And then what?

I don't have a passport.

Ways and means always exist, and while I don't know anyone in the region, I can do it.

Running and doing things my way seems better than waiting for a man who'd sell me on the black market if I was able to command a good price.

"Go to fucking bed. We've got an early start tomorrow."

KRISTEN LUCIANI

"Why were you on my computer?"

His grin is dark and humorless, and it sends shivers of need through me. I know I'm fucked up, because that smile shouldn't turn me on. It's a smile that tells me he'll devour me and leave nothing in his wake, not even my bones.

"A hunter likes to know what makes the prey tick."

"You're a shitbag." I glare.

"I've been called worse."

He stands and walks silently over to me, the air around me quivering with his presence. It pulls at my nerve endings.

Smith looks down at me. His overall effect should be somehow diminished now that he's out of the suit that probably cost a fortune—probably Tom Ford or some designer I've never heard of—but he isn't.

The cargo pants and boots and shirt are a dime a dozen; any good surplus store has them.

But on him, he looks like an elite hunter. The pagan god who'll hunt you down, play with you, and then sacrifice you to himself on an altar of stone.

No matter what he wears, he's deadly.

And he turns me on in every way a man shouldn't.

"Go to fucking sleep."

I swallow. "Actually, I think I will."

And I know I'm going to run.

Lying in the lumpy, hard, narrow bed is torture. But I'm biding my time.

Before, he knocked me out and I didn't even notice the discomfort. Now... sober, drug-free, and plotting his destruction—or at least my way out—it's pure misery.

118

But the mission's quiet. Just the hoots and growls and rustles from the nightlife of the jungle.

Smith's gone to bed, and I bet he took the backpack with him. And somewhere in the last hour, I've decided it's worth the risk of trying to get it. After all, I'm betting my passport, the fake one, is inside.

I get up, carrying my shoes and putting them outside so I can make a quick escape. The moonlight cuts a river of silver on the windows of the vehicle, like it's calling to me to run. But I force myself to go back inside and get the backpack.

If he finds me with it, I'll say I wanted to look at the photos... He can't deny a girl that.

Then again, it's Smith, and what little I've learned from him is yes, he can do that and would. He's into payment for actions, and this is a doozy if I'm caught and don't get away with the excuse I come up with.

The old, simple place is quiet, the floor made of worn cement or stone. It makes me wonder why. And what lies beneath it.

In countries like this, hidden tunnel systems aren't unheard of. Drugs, people, all kinds of things are kept in the earth. Secrets. Things to be smuggled. Places to hide.

But I'm not here for that, and in the dark, I don't see any entrances to anything below. Maybe there's a cellar. Or maybe it's just whatever material was chosen.

I take a breath to settle my nerves, my scattered thoughts. The fear that hammers in my veins.

What if he's lying in one of those narrow, lumpy beds, waiting?

Worse, waiting outside? Or in a room?

I push open the door to another room past the living area, something that might have once been used for prayer or meals.

Light floods in from the moonlit night beyond, and there's Smith.

Sprawled on the bed.

Boots still on. He's still dressed, and I throb at the sight of him.

A man should look small, vulnerable when passed out.

Smith doesn't.

He's big, strong, and he looks asleep.

The fucker drugged me, enough to knock me out for a few hours, and that fact disturbs me more than it should. I'm not sure why.

Like he didn't want me out for too long, so why is...?

I stop myself from completing the thought.

Does it even matter?

One hand dangles off the edge of the bed, and it rests right over the backpack.

I hold my breath and ease it out from under him, stopping every time it makes the slightest of sounds.

But I finally get it free, letting out a silent but relieved breath. I back out of the room, eyes on him, as I clutch the pack to my chest.

The urge to run beats in time with my heart, but I don't. Instead, I slip carefully back through the mission and out the front door, where I sit, shaking. Waiting.

If he gets up and I'm sitting out here, I've got a chance through it. A chance not to face his brand of retribution. I've tasted some, but not the dark stuff he claims he's partial to.

And very willing to unleash, if I give him a reason.

Smith is my enemy.

I silently repeat that mantra.

I still don't hear him, so I check the pack. Buried at the bottom are the passports, clothes, and a dead burner phone.

I'm about to close it up and get out of here when something crinkles. Paper.

Shaking, I reach into the front pocket and pull out a folded, old-fashioned map.

I really don't have time, but I can't afford not to look. I open it and my heart leaps. Belize. And I trace a path through the edge of the jungle and down to where the city is. It'll take a day, maybe two. Unless I can steal a vehicle.

I pull on my boots and tuck the map away. Then I walk slowly and carefully to the edge of the jungle. Once I step into the darkness where the pools of moonlight are splattered like paint, I wait.

Nothing.

No one.

But it's like eyes are on me, watching.

And they probably are. The jungle's full of creatures that thrive in the night. Yet, I can't shake the feeling it's more than that. I'm being hunted.

I pick up my pace, move faster, carefully, trying to stick to the shadows as I move deeper inside. There are paths all through here indicating that people do use the jungle. This place isn't wild and impenetrable, so I keep to the shadows as much as I can, trying to keep noise to a minimum.

Something crunches to my right and my heart squeezes hard, sending a shot of white-hot adrenaline through me. Like electricity, it lights up all my nerve endings.

A whisper taunts me, and I don't know if it's in my head or real.

But the sentiment is.

Run.

I do.

I dart through the jungle, heading in the direction of where the city will eventually be. My lungs burn as vines and branches slap at me, scraping at my legs. I stumble over thick roots in my haste.

A bird loudly calls out and I almost scream.

The ground's soft beneath my feet and it starts to clear, the last thing I want or need.

Frantically, I glance around and veer right, then left and dart behind a tree.

Pressing my lips together, I try and stop the harshness of my breathing, the desperate need for lungsful of air. I want that soothing balm over the burn, but I make myself take shallow, silent breaths.

I wrap my fingers around the knife in my pocket, pulling it free. My palm's slick with sweat, but I just tighten my grip on the handle, too scared to rub my hand dry.

Is someone out there? I close my eyes and strain to hear, see if I can pick out footsteps over the natural breaths and sounds of the jungle.

But there's nothing.

Crap, maybe I imagined the word "run." Maybe I conjured up the thought that someone's following me.

Surely Smith would've grabbed me back at the mission if he wanted to come after me. If he was awake.

And then, all of a sudden... everything turns cold.

The men with the rifles.

They had them for a reason.

Farmers don't carry weapons like that, and when Sofia and Rodriguez left earlier, I noticed that the chickens were locked in a coop and the goat left with the family. The men who stayed behind didn't dress like farmers. They didn't move like militia or men smuggling drugs. They were like men ready for something. Or someone. But who were they on the lookout for?

Shit.

Smith might be the least of all the evils out here.

He—

A hand slams over my mouth to stifle the scream and my eyes shoot open.

Oh. My. God.

Him.

CHAPTER 15
SMITH

The fear in her eyes is beautiful.

It's primal fear, that delicious, anticipatory vibration that startled prey puts out into the atmosphere, and I don't yet know what she'll do in response.

I tracked her the moment she stepped outside the mission. I was aware of her the moment she stood up from the bed. No, fuck no, I was aware of her the entire time, even when she woke from her drugged sleep.

"It's a stupid mistake to make, thinking I'd sleep through you coming into my room." I grin. "I caught you, fair and fucking square. The question is, what should I do with you?"

Her eyes narrow. The fear still thumps and pounds in her veins but with it, excitement and anger. They give the storm in her gaze a fierce electric current.

"You're easy to track, Calista."

And now I have her, just when she might have realized rushing out into the jungle at night was a stupid thing to do.

The blood that pounds through her veins warms her skin, gives her a vitality I want to sink my teeth into.

"Your safe word still holds," I say. "It's the only thing I'll pay attention to."

She's vibrating like she's going to run or do something. I slowly release my hand from her mouth, sliding my fingers down the front of her top, all the way down to her pussy. But I don't explore, just let my hand gently graze. Like it's by accident.

I want to see what she's going to do.

She's got a knife, the knife I left in the kitchen after she basically hung out a sign stating she wanted to stab me with it, but she doesn't raise it. Instead, she pulls away, ducking around me. Then she breaks into a run.

Wrong fucking move, little girl.

I take off after her and tackle her to the ground. Her knife falls out of her hand, but she knees me, narrowly missing my balls. Then she scrambles around, grabbing for the blade in the dirt and rotting leaves.

My heart damn near punches a hole in my chest, and I get so fucking hard when her fingers close around the handle, I let her escape just a little before pulling her back to me by her ankles. Her pussy flashes in the moonlight as her skirt twists up and her thighs part as she tries to kick me again.

Calista keeps pushing at me with her feet until I rise up over her. That's when the knife flashes and presses in against my throat.

Our gazes clash. I grab her hair with one hand and waist with the other, flipping her so she's on top of me. "Better if you wait until I sink so deep in you that you see fucking stars, Calista."

"What?" Her voice shakes and she licks her lips as she straddles me. "Wait for what?"

I move my hand from her hair to her throat. "To cut me.

But sweetheart, make sure you go for the jugular. Then you can play in the blood while you literally fuck the life out of me."

My words hang.

There's horror all over her face. Need, too. And lust.

"You're crazy," she whispers. "Batshit crazy."

"Yeah, but that all just got you hot."

"No, it didn't."

I push into the knife, the blade biting my throat, and she goes still, not sure if she wants to cut me deep, or if she wants to throw the weapon away.

"Yes, it did, and it does." I grab her hand with the knife, keeping it there as I haul her close by her throat with my other hand. "Otherwise, why aren't you running? Why are you rubbing and rocking against me? And why—" I drop the hand from her throat and push it between her thighs, into the dripping wet heat of her cunt "—are you soaked?"

"Maybe because I hate you and want you dead."

I bite her lip and pull the knife free from her fingers. I toss it aside. "But little prey, how are you going to do that when you don't have the knife?"

Then I kiss her. She locks her legs tight around me as she sucks on my tongue, her fingers buried in my hair.

"Suck my cock." I don't wait. I unwind her from me and dump her on the ground, freeing my aching dick. I need her mouth and her tongue. I need to pound the back of her throat and watch her swallow everything I give her.

I rise up on my knees and grab her by the hair, hauling her to me. "You have a word, prey."

"Fuck you," she says, sending a thrill of triumph through my bones.

"Open that pretty mouth." I take my cock with my other hand and feed it to her, and the stretch of her lips, that special sucking wetness of her mouth is fucking incredible.

It's like I already won the prize before the competition even starts.

This is perfection. Out in the middle of the fucking jungle. No rules, just one word that can stop everything.

And she doesn't use it.

Calista's a kinky little slut. I can feel the tremor, the small sounds of need as she sucks hard, her tongue managing to move on me even though I barely fit. Fuck, I haven't even begun to thrust into her, to hit the back of her throat.

She tries to go down farther, her fingers digging into my hips. I wind my other hand in her hair, and I start to skull fuck her, a brutal game of destruction and ownership.

I want to destroy whatever boundaries she might have. I want to obliterate any doubts, any lines she might have drawn in the sand.

There are no lines anymore. There's only devour and conquer. Slave and master. Hunter and prey.

Calista starts to drool and gag, but I keep driving deeper, testing her limits, pushing her past them until I'm balls deep in her mouth. I'm so hot, aching as I hold myself in her. The gag reflex massages the tip of my cock and it's so fucking good I could come from just this.

But I want more.

I start pulling out nearly all the way, only to hammer back into her, over and over, her mouth and tongue working, gag reflex massaging me. Pleasure builds inside, focuses laser bright on my cock and balls. But I control the pressure to explode, the slight pain of holding back when the over-whelming urge is to come.

This is something I need to last so I hold on, slamming into her, the sputtering sounds and the wetness that drizzles out of the sides of her mouth driving me closer and closer to the edge.

Fuck, she sucks like she wants Olympic gold. It's too much.

My balls are already tight, and the urge to release consumes me. I push down into her throat and come hard, shuddering and shaking with the violent release.

I hold her there, her throat working hard as she struggles, trying to gasp for air. So I play that dangerous, pleasurable game where I keep her mouth clamped on to me until the point where her vision must blur, until she must be lightheaded, lungs feeling like they could easily burst. I don't know her actual lung capacity, but I know how long a person can last before they pass out.

She's almost there.

I finally release her, and she falls back to the ground, taking huge, gasping breaths. Calista coughs and splutters and half rolls on the ground, her skirt totally twisted as she tries and fails to stand. She's got to be furious right now.

Good.

Tucking myself away, I wipe the blood from my self-inflicted knife wound and crouch in front of her so I can push those bloody fingers into her mouth. "I'll return the favor, Calista, but I'll tell you what..." I look around, find the knife, and give it to her. "I'll take the backpack. And you? Fucking run."

She raises her head as I stand, and in the dark, her eyes glitter with anger. There's a smear of blood and drool on her lips, some cum on her chin. She slashes the air with the knife, but I easily move away.

"If you don't run... just know that I'm not done yet, so..."

"Bastard."

And she gets up, half falling back to the ground. I stand in her way farther down the track she found in the jungle, and she runs back the way she came.

Grabbing her backpack, I take off after her.

I love this part of the game, where I'm partially satiated,

where my prey isn't sure if it's real or not, isn't sure she wants to play. It's only happened a few times, going this deep with someone. Usually, hard rules are set up.

My game with Calista only has one. If she uses the word Code, I'll stop. No matter what, I'll stop. But if she doesn't...

All bets are off.

I'm fed, but I want to be gluttonous, so I pursue her at a pace, speeding up when I want her to go hard, slowing when I feel like it. I block her at various turns until the light from the mission starts to filter in through the dark trees.

Then I pick up the pace.

I grab her at the edge of the jungle and shove her against a tree. Dipping my head, I bite her so hard on her throat she yelps and throws back her head. Then she reaches for my dick.

With the hand that holds the knife.

I take hold of her wrist and squeeze until she drops the weapon. Then I sink down, and holding her up, I lick up between her thighs and suck on her naked pussy. I alternate between nipping her plump lips and flicking her clit with my tongue. When I suck it hard, she shudders, moaning, and I can feel the pulsations of her orgasm against my mouth.

I'm not done. Fuck, I could lick and eat her all fucking night long.

"Smith..." she whispers, voice a little broken. And I wait, looking up. She sinks down. "I..."

We're eye to eye and we stare at each other. Electric sparks flare between us.

She's mine.

In this game of primal play, she's fucking mine.

"Code?"

"What? Did I use it?" she snaps, shoving me. And because of how I'm crouching I lose my balance and she pounces.

She's on top of me, her demanding fingers in my hair,

mouth close to mine. And it doesn't take much to free my cock and push into her.

Calista moans when I thrust hard into her pussy. "Yes..."

"I like when my prey fights, and you're full of teeth and claws and twists and turns," I say, flipping us so I'm on top of her, pulling out to drag her ass in the air so I can plunge back in. I push her face down into the dirt and she shudders.

"Only because you don't do it right. Oh yess..." She shudders again and she's so fucking tight and hot.

And slick.

So wet I can slide balls deep with each push. Her cunt parts for me, swallows me, and she feels so fucking good. As good as her mouth.

"Harder, Smith. Harder."

"Bossy little prey."

"Prick old-ass hunter."

I just laugh and slam hard into her, grabbing her hips to piston in deep, so deep.

She comes again, her convulsions so strong they set me off. I collapse on her, our legs giving way, and we lie in the dirt and vegetation for I don't even know how long. I don't want to pull out of her. She's warm and wet, and the tiny little spasms are a delicious tease on my now half-hard dick.

Christ. Calista isn't my type. She's too young, too mouthy, too full of secrets for a man like me. She's too... compromised.

But damn if she isn't the most phenomenal fuck I think I might have ever had.

The girl's humping back into me, but it's almost a subconscious thing. She's letting me know I conquered her, that for now, she's mine. It won't last. Of course it won't.

It's in the nature of the game.

Right now I've won, I've brought her down, had my way, destroyed defenses, devoured her.

But creatures like her, the true prey I crave, are phoenixes. She'll rise, stronger, with more fight. And she'll go for the jugular again.

If I let it happen.

I do have an agenda, one I'm deviating from because of what I didn't find on her computer. Because of the things she said about her mother. And because of that message on her phone.

Sure, I want the information she has about the weapon. I want to know if she found it or if her asset gave it to her. There's a traitor somewhere. But that's not my biggest priority. It's a bonus to get that kind of intel.

I want to know what she has on the Collectors.

The research I found on her computer about the Collectors was basic, but it's a start.

This girl has somehow uncovered information about too many classified things, and she claims she has no idea how they connect.

But someone does.

And one question burns my fucking brain.

What does the CIA really want with Calista Price?

CHAPTER 16
CALISTA

We didn't stay long on the jungle floor. And I'm...
I actually don't know what the hell I am at this moment.

But I do know some things. Like the fact that I don't like him. That he's my enemy, a man willing to hand me over for money, who doesn't give a damn about what will happen to me once he turns and walks away.

But I also can't deny I fucking love sex with him. Even thinking about it makes my stomach swoop and my toes curl.

"Shower time."

It's the first thing he's said to me since he finished ravaging me in the jungle. A shudder ripples through me when I think of what things might have found us rolling around on the jungle floor, human and otherwise. I try to convince myself the shudder is one of disgust, fear, and horror.

But it isn't.

I'm turned on.

I suck in a breath, nod, and hurry ahead of him through the clearing, snatching my arm from his hand when he grabs it.

I knew I had kinks, but that whole thing?

Jesus. It's like I lost track of who I was for those scorching hot minutes.

With that kind of no-holds-barred sex.

The hunt. The capture. The fucking fiery passion that ensnared us both.

I turn on the water faucet and stare into the spray.

I've never experienced that kind of play before. The number of sexual partners I've had could be counted easily on two hands.

I'm about to peel off my shirt when I catch the shadow that falls across the floor.

"Can I have a little privacy?" I snap, my mouth battling against what my body screams for.

More.

Smith straightens from where he leans against the door-jamb. "After that? Sweet little thing, I've seen all of you; there's nothing more for you to hide. And water's kind of scarce here, so you're not showering alone."

Smith pulls off his T-shirt and I almost stagger at the bloodstains on his chest from where I cut his throat.

Where he forced me to cut him.

"I should have cut deeper."

"I told you to try, but you were too anxious to get your tight little cunt on my dick."

This is the real him.

The beast behind the urban sophisticate.

The predator behind the indifference and money.

He's dangerous, and I hate that he turns me on.

He undoes his boots and kicks them off, then drops his pants. Naked. Perfection. And the cock's as big as I remember it feeling in my hand, my mouth, and my pussy. And God help me, I want to touch.

Smith pulls off my top and bites each nipple through my bra. The bites are sharp, bloodthirsty, and they stake all kinds of claims. Then he unclips it and lets the bra drop to the tile floor.

"Take off your boots and skirt now or I'll drag you into the water with them on. And I'm not sure you're going to like that, because I'll make you fucking wear them after."

"Be still my fucking heart."

He only smirks at that.

But I believe him and shuck the rest of my clothes off in record time. He's already under the water, soaping up as I step into the tiny enclosure.

And cold like ice hits my skin, making me yelp.

"A wimp at heart. I'd say it's almost endearing. Although, a little shocking."

I grab the soap and lather up. There's no shampoo, so I rub some in my hair, and then I snatch the washcloth from him. But he waits a second before he pushes me into the wall of the shower, soap dripping on my face in the tight cubicle.

He kisses me, a feather of warm lips on mine, and it's so sweet it breaks a piece of me apart, deep inside. "You need to learn to pick your battles, little girl. And this isn't one of them."

"Everything's a battle with you."

"Playing, yes. Otherwise, it doesn't have to be." He steps back and gently takes the soap and cloth and starts to wash me, starting with my face. The water burns patches on my skin, and the rough cloth doesn't do much to help. I must have grazed my face somehow.

Then it hits me.

From kissing him.

That's what it is.

Whisker burn.

Oh man, I haven't had that since I was years younger and

spent hours and hours kissing my first real boyfriend, the one I lost my virginity to. Funny, I can't conjure his face or his name now.

Smith and I... we didn't spend hours kissing. But the kisses were fire, and they were rough and wild and—I swallow.

He doesn't say anything, just shifts us around to run a hand through my hair, fingers against my scalp. He's halfway through washing me before a thought attacks my brain. "Is this your fucked-up version of aftercare?"

There's a telling beat of silence.

"It's called a shower and saving time."

I snatch the cloth back. "I can wash myself."

He shrugs, turns his back, and rinses off. It's a weirdly intimate jostling war for the cold spray as I finish up. And damn, dragging my eyes off his broad back with the tattoos and scars, the tight, hot ass of his, the huge cock that I'm a little too eager to catch a glimpse of, is harder that it should be.

Especially when he turns my way.

And I can see all of him. Scars. The tattoo. The washboard abs. That damn cock. The strong legs and kind of body most women would drool over.

Not to mention the mark on his throat that makes my heart lurch.

"I don't know if you're looking at me horrified you cut me or horrified you missed your chance to kill me," he says.

"Maybe both."

"Of course, that's you. I can't begin to think of a reason why you're single."

I push him. "And you? I'm pretty sure it's your winning personality and warm ways that has you—"

"Knee-deep in pussy?"

"Only knee-deep?" I say, giving him my best withering look

which is hard to do naked and cold. "And I had been about to say single."

"I'm being modest. And the women want me for my big cock."

"It's what you do with it."

He grins, rubbing up against me so I'm between him and the wall and no longer cold. Just wet.

"I know, little girl."

"You're just a walking ego."

"Sweet talk," he says. "I like it."

"I'm not..." I draw in a breath, gaze catching on his cut once more. "I really am sorry."

He frowns, then touches it. "No, you're not, and don't be boring."

"I..."

Words escape my grasp. And what the hell am I doing? Having some kind of moment with him? In a shower in Belize when he's pretty much forcing me to go back to the States to face whatever music is coming my way? And that means no computers, no information, no finding my agent or Trenton.

People have been looking for me in Germany, threatening me. It's why I went into hiding.

And then someone blew up a plane.

He went private over commercial, which means he's planning to deliver me into the hands of the CIA or whoever ordered me to be picked up.

He also thinks there's enough danger that we're here hiding out in a tiny Central American country.

"I know you're not telling me the truth."

"You're a job, nothing more. Pick you up, keep you alive. Deliver you for money. Nothing else to tell. The rest? Meaningless."

The water from the shower patters down and cold needles

hit me with the harshness of his last words. "I had threats, the vague kind. My field agent disappeared. I don't know what's going on. And anything with any sex traffickers is personal to me."

With that, I jump out, grabbing the towel and drying off. I towel dry my hair, thankful that the heaviness is gone with the undercut, the ease of the style why I chose it. Wash and run and add a little product and I'll be ready for an evening out.

Not that I do that. Haven't in months.

The shower turns off and he swings a towel over the railing before stepping out. He pulls on a T-shirt and tucks it into another pair of cargo pants.

"Clothes for you are in the bag. Put them on and be ready." Smith steals the towel I wrapped around my body.

"Great," I bite out before lunging for the towel.

He holds it out of my way, eyes roaming over me, the blue burning into my skin. I hate how my nipples get instantly hard for him and my pussy throbs.

He flashes a knowing grin.

"Don't flatter yourself. I'm cold." But I don't drop the towel I have in my hand for my hair, no matter how much I want to. "I'm not into you."

"You are, Calista. The kink connection is real. You and I click. Just don't even attempt to use it on me. I'm the wrong guy for that. I'm delivering you. End of story. Your pussy isn't enough to make me forget the job I was hired to do. Get dressed."

He walks out of the bathroom.

By the time I'm dressed in the black stretch pants and T-shirt, I can't find him, not that I look hard. The mission is mostly draped in darkness; the only lights are the one in the bathroom and one near the entrance, along with a few outside that illuminate the yard.

I can see enough in the kitchen, though. Light peeks in through the window. The cupboards contain canned food and bottled water.

The fridge is empty from today—everything, including the bread—was eaten with dinner. But I'm not hungry. There's something gnawing at me, making my insides twist and turn in on themselves.

Not wanting to steal any of the supplies, I decide to use the tap. Before I fill the glass, Smith comes inside and hands me a bottle of water from one of the cupboards.

"Seriously, put down the glass. You don't want to drink the water without boiling it first."

"Yes, sir."

"Music," he says, "to my fucking ears." He slides a clip into his Sig and puts his phone into the bag. "C'mon, Calista."

I sigh and follow him.

Smith grabs me and shoves me against the wall, just inside the door.

"What—?"

"Did you hear something?"

I frown. "No…"

But he holds a finger to his lips and hands me the pack. Shaking, I put it on. There's training and there's fieldwork, and this… something that's changed in the air.

Then I hear it.

A low voice, probably closer to the jungle than us.

I don't catch it, what's said, but he leans in.

"The fucking car wasn't there when we got back. And the men Rodriguez had here earlier don't sneak around."

"Then…" I stare at him, clenching my hands. "Smith, do you think your friend double-crossed us?"

"I don't know. Everyone has a price. Or a breaking point. Or maybe this is something else."

His low words don't hold accusation. They don't have to. There's more than enough in there. In his meaning. I'm somehow a hot commodity. After all, if he's here to deliver me for a paycheck, it stands to reasons others might want a slice of the pie.

But others on what side?

Who else wants me outside the CIA? Outside of him?

It's the ever-revolving question, the one with countless what-ifs and no answers I can see.

Smith might be my prison guard, but I shift, moving closer to him, closer to his heat and strength.

"What do we do?"

"They'll probably come in through the other door, nearer where the bedrooms are. There are a couple of lights on, but mainly to see outside."

"So we can see if someone approaches."

"That was the idea. Like the light outside the kitchen."

"Maybe they're—"

"Calista, anyone out there is considered our enemy until we know otherwise. We're going to make a break for it. Try and reach the jungle."

"Try?" I stop. "Because the lights work both ways."

"They can see us like we can see them. Ready?"

I nod.

"*Run.*"

CHAPTER 17
SMITH

Fuck.

Guns open fire as we run. More of them than I thought. The bullets fly through the air, fast and deadly, and we're out in the open with no way to reach the fucking jungle.

A bullet sings high as it narrowly misses us both, and I manage to squeeze off a shot before she cries out behind me.

Heart slamming, I turn and push Calista to the ground.

I land on top of her, holding her hands over her head on the dirt and covering her body with mine. "Are you hit?"

She shakes her head, eyes wide with fear.

There're too many gunmen to take risks. She's too fucking young and inexperienced to thwart them. And whoever they are, they waited very patiently for us to make an exit.

But they're shitty shots. Because someone less than an expert would have hit her ten times over. Maybe me, too.

Fuuuck.

There's a tracker in my ring which will provide the Knights

with our location. But that's not my first concern. It's her. Right now, I have no idea who's behind this. It could be anyone.

"Stay calm," I murmur, not daring to move as the corner of the backpack digs into me. "Just—"

"I'm not a goddamn damsel."

Her bite and the warmth of her seeps into me. The backpack is half on her, as if she was thinking to use it as a weapon if needed. I know that's what I'd do. Behind her snapped words, she sounds calm.

We lie on the dirt, the cool of night vanishing from the burn of concern for her well-being. I focus on the voices.

They're speaking accented, rapid-fire... not Spanish... Portuguese? What the fuck? As the voices ricochet off the trees, I can only pick out a few words.

Then another voice comes in. This one speaks Spanish. Male. Also accented.

"*Estoy buscando al hacker, Hendrix.*" Then he shifts. "Do you know him?"

She jerks a little and I move slightly so my legs hold her down.

The butt of a gun slams into my head, sending pain, white and hot. It explodes beneath my skin, along my nerve endings.

"Did I say move?" English is easier for this asshole. Spanish isn't his first language.

A nasty thought comes to me. We could have been followed since Germany. Hiding my trail wasn't ever a priority. We took the scenic route to give me more time with her, to get her talking, to dig into details that I should have left alone.

If I was alone, I'd have made it to the jungle.

If I was alone, I'd have fought from within the mission, escaped a different way.

If I was alone, I wouldn't be in this position.

"I'm not good at following orders," I say. "Who are you?"

"You seem to be under the mistaken idea you're in control. You are not." He bends close, hot breath stale with cigarettes on me as he traces the edge of a knife down along my cheek. "Are you Hendrix?"

Calista moves again. "Don't say—"

"What's it to you?" I ask over the top of her. And then, pushing down on her to keep her in place, I start to rise because I fucking recognize the accent. It's Bolivian, and—

Something big hits me so hard, my vision dots with black spots. A pricking sensation pinches my skin. Then the entire world turns black and pain-free.

WHEN I FINALLY WAKE UP, the crushing pain is back in force. It takes all my effort to crack open my eyes. My vision blurs and I can't focus, so I keep them closed and listen instead.

I'm not alone. There's someone with me in this dank, dark place. But it's not cool. It's humid as fuck with latent heat seeping from above. I'm guessing we're near the water since it's so damp, the air can choke me.

But what water?

Where?

Not Central America.

I can't have been out long enough to be transported by plane to any place too far away. We could be in Cuba. Maybe Jamaica or Mexico. I'm now just naming hot fucking places. What I'd really prefer is Florida. Or... maybe not. Because there are lots of places in the Everglades where you can get rid of bodies.

Shit. Same with Cuba.

My head throbs. The exact spot I got hit—fucking twice—with a gun and whatever else the Spanish and Portuguese-speaking Bolivian used.

The pain cripples me and my ability to think.

I let out a deep, quiet breath.

This isn't going the way I'd planned.

We're underground, me and my pretty cellmate who sighs and tells me everything I need to know about her safety. "How long have I been out?"

"A little longer than me."

I nod, lean back against the cool brick wall, and cross my ankles without opening my eyes again.

Because yeah, it's her. Knew it as I came to. But knowing she's okay, that she's here with me, in the same predicament.

It's a fucking relief.

I can figure a way out of this.

Whatever the fuck "this" is.

Her being here tells me she's not working with the people who took us. Not that I thought she was, but it's good to know for sure.

"Smith, I thought you..."

"Takes more than a whack on the head and some knockout drugs to kill me. Though if you thought I was fucking dead, then you need to go back to spy school. And take some basic dead or alive classes. Forget the first-aid shit. Breathing's usually an indication of life. Pulse is good too."

"You're such a dick." Her hand settles on my thigh, a burning brand I can't help but want to lean into.

"You know where we are?"

"They knocked me out, too. An injection. I..." She stops speaking and suddenly, a sharp smack explodes against my face.

I open my eyes and glare at her pretty, scared face.

"There's food and bottled water, but I didn't..."

She didn't eat it. A good rule to follow. So many things could be slipped into food or water. And she knows from experience since I drugged her back at the mission in Belize.

I look around. We're definitely underground, in a cellar with thick walls and no window to the outside world. I'm guessing we're in a town or outskirts of a city, one of those places where people can operate unnoticed, but the buildings are close together. This place has that exact feel.

The place smells like earth and brick and the mustiness of being closed in. But it's also not dirty or full of cobwebs. A clear sign that it's used.

I look around again. It's not storage, either. No chairs or boxes or marks on the floor or against the wall to indicate where things might have been kept.

A single bulb on the ceiling casts a pool of light and creeping shadows. I eye the heavy metal door. What I want is to get us the fuck out and lose myself in her.

But the getting out's an important first step.

I struggle to stand, the pain in my head throbbing with each step I take to reach a bottle of water. The label's been pulled off, so it's some brand I'd possibly recognize. Either that or they're paranoid. Maybe a bit of both.

I twist off the plastic top, take a deep swig, and go to Calista. She looks up at me and it squeezes my chest tight.

She looks impossibly young. Talk about feeling every inch the depraved and dirty old man I am for laying a finger on her. I hold out the water. "Here."

"I don't think—"

"They're not going to drug it. They want us awake and clear to answer questions."

Calista's silent for a long minute, then she takes the bottle I hold out to her. She takes a delicate sip. "How do you know?"

"Because I'm experienced."

"Because you're old?"

A half smile breaks free.

"That, and if they were going to use a truth serum or some other kind of torture—which doesn't work—they would."

I hope. Most people haven't gotten the memo about torture not working on one who doesn't want to talk.

Some torture works, a little, or when you want to work some aggression off, but... I sweep a glance over her. Apart from the fear, she looks fine.

Although looks can be deceiving. "You okay?"

She hands back the bottle, nodding, but our fingers brush and her fingers are like ice.

Strange when heat seared me at her touch earlier.

Or maybe that wasn't body heat transference. Maybe it was just the general reaction I have to her. Fuck.

It's not that I care, apart from having her in one piece to deliver so I can collect. I don't give a shit that I'm rich. Money's always good.

Scratch that. Money and secrets are always good. And she has secrets.

Maybe secrets I need.

Especially if they're about the sick fucks who wanted to do vile things to my daughter.

"You nod but..." I shrug.

She shakes her head and rubs her arms. "I said I'm okay."

"Are you?" I grab her chin and stare into her eyes. They're glassy, just a little though. The storm's receded, and right now, they're just gray. Apart from those two spots of color, she's pale.

She smacks my hand away.

"I'm not a child, Smith," Calista mutters. "This is just a little out of my wheelhouse, okay?"

"I'm aware. You're a desk jockey, not field." I rake my gaze over her, lingering on the soft invitation of her pretty mouth. "Did they say anything to you?"

"Why?"

"Because I don't really want to deal with hysterics."

Her eyes snap fire and she rises, fingers sinking into my T-shirt as she grabs it, and I let her pull me in close. "Hysterics."

"You. Female. Inexperienced. Young." Somehow, I keep the smile at bay. "Hysterics."

"I'm not hysterical." She takes a breath. "And you know it. No, they didn't say anything. You went limp, and then they stuck me with a needle and I woke up here." Calista bites her lip. "But Smith... they took the bag with the computer..."

"Hey." I draw her in, kiss her gently. At first, it's just meant to be a comforting kiss, but it deepens, twists down into something more and I wish... I draw back.

Her sweet taste is on my lips, in my mouth.

"You said there wasn't anything on the computer."

"Just the photos," she says. "But... with hacking, like with spy work, everything leaves a trace. I should have... I should have destroyed it."

I turn her words in my head, selecting the right ones.

Calista's smart. So I go for the truth. But I keep it generic.

I shrug. "I want to know. I'm nosy."

"I'm your kidnap job."

"And now we're here. Who's after you and why? And why the fuck was someone texting you from Estonia about the Collectors? They were more or less broken apart not too long ago."

"Are you going to add that you can only help me if I help you?"

"Will it get you talking?" I ask.

"No."

I smile. "Here's what I think's gonna happen. Soon one of them will come through the door and take me and then you. I'd like to know what I'm up against."

Her shoulders slump in defeat. "I don't know anything, nothing more than you. Back in Germany, my field agent said he thought something wasn't right, so I... I collected bits and pieces. But I haven't been through them. Haven't connected the dots."

They think she has something. Question is, who?

"What about the Collectors?"

She slants me a look. "I don't know."

Now that's a lie, but I keep it to myself.

"But you have suspicions," I say quietly. "About the weapon."

"I think it's more than one person trying to sell stolen blueprints." She pauses. I can feel her groping for the right thing to say. "And I think it might go deep. Bolivia's involved. I think the misdirect is to the usual suspects in the Middle East. But... until I can get my data back and go through it, I won't know."

She talks, and it's a whole lot of nothing but I'm fixated on what she let slip, 'until I get my data back.' She has it all. In one place.

I draw information from her, switching the subject, talking about her hacker days, entrepreneur sidelines, of a server in Jersey and a cloud full of nothing, and apps she hasn't released.

Any other job, and I'd let it go. I'd have taken her back right after the show at the art event. And then I wouldn't have thought of it ever again. She knows nothing about the pieces on the black market that have already been made. And the weapon is not exactly my business. Just the hefty windfall for her pretty little head.

But Bolivia and the Collectors and the sex trafficking?

Combine all that with interested parties coming into the picture along with a new weapon?

It's definitely of interest to the Obsidian Knights.

And I can't rely on them busting through that the door. What I need is a plan, and—

The door creaks open and a big, tattooed asshole in need of a shower and a shave comes inside the space. His eyes light up at the sight of Calista.

It makes my blood turn to acid.

The guy grabs her by her hair and hauls her up from the floor, making her yelp. It takes everything I have to not move. To not wrestle the gun from him and kill him for daring to touch her.

"Pretty, isn't she?" the big goon says, his hand stroking over her as he holds her tight by the hair.

Her lips are firmly pressed together, and her body vibrates with anger and fear. It's so strong I can almost smell it.

The asshole's hand grabs a tit, squeezing, making her wince. There's a fine line between pleasure and pain. Exquisite, delightful.

In game mode.

With a willing partner.

The line between good pain and bad is a fucking rift. And he's on the wrong side.

"Maybe I take her and make her talk. What do you think?" he says, his rough beard grazing against Calista's cheek as he rubs it with his own.

"I say stop touching her."

"Or what?" The guy's hand moves lower and starts to touch her cloth-covered pussy. My vision bleeds red.

I want to rip his balls off, filet his damn cock. I want to poke the fucker's eyes out and cut out his tongue. But first I want to cut off each fucking finger that touches her, that brings the gleam of tears to her eyes.

"Or," I say, trying to hold my temper, ready to take a gamble on what I'm about to say next since I don't know what the hell is even happening. "I won't give you what you want to know, because after a little chat with the girl, now *I* know where the blueprints for the weapon are."

CHAPTER 18
CALISTA

I swallow the cry of betrayal, and it's so much more painful than any agony the brute grabbing me can cause.

The flash of heat in his words is so strong, harsh, that even as I suspect he's buying time, I can't shake the feeling he just pumped me for information.

And I gave him something.

I just don't know what.

I twist, trying to get away from the asshole who mauled me.

"Okay, then." The man nods at Smith. "I'll play."

The man flings me away and I stumble, unable to keep my balance. I crash onto the floor on my hands and knees.

Smith's up and halfway to me when the guy pulls a gun.

I've got a feeling Smith would have caught me if I'd been flung near him instead of to the right and behind.

I rear up, ready to attack when the merest flicker of gaze from Smith stops me.

"What do you have? I could taken her." The guy laughs. "Questioned the shit out of her."

"She doesn't know anything. She's wet behind the ears." Smith doesn't look at me and I don't know which of them I want to punch. "I was hired to get back what she stole. And I did. I just checked with her, and she doesn't know a fucking thing."

"Really?" the guy says in his accented English, gun on Smith. "You're sweet on her enough to risk some torture?"

"Touch her and you'll know a very prolonged, very excruciating death." Smith's smile looks benign but there's poison in it. Violence. Anger. "Not sweet on her, she's in enough trouble and she's ignorant. There's no need for torture since I just volunteered."

He's not betraying me. He's protecting me.

I think.

Because I didn't give him anything.

I don't even know what I have. The only thing I hedged on, ever, is the Collectors and that's personal.

The man's deadly, a hunter. He's playing a game.

With me? Or the jackass here with us?

I want to say it's with the big guy, but maybe my idiot brain's a little soft on Smith. My body burns for him because every touch, the hot, primal games he's played with me, all make me melt.

There's a reason I haven't used the safe word.

I don't want to.

I like his brand of kink, it exhilarates me like nothing ever has before.

It doesn't mean I trust him. Or like him. Or... even if I like him, that doesn't put us on the same side.

Not that I like him, though.

The guy looks from me to Smith and back again. "Or I take her and have some fun."

"And then," Smith says, "I don't talk."

I'm not a crier, and on demand is almost impossible. But I've had guns pointed at me. A man who turns my stomach has felt me up, mauled me, and now he's threatening me with torture at best, rape at worst.

"P-please..." I have to cry, so I think of not seeing my brother, of not avenging my mom's death. And I think of Smith's daughter, the girl he clearly loves and tries to pretend doesn't mean that much, and my lip trembles. "P-please, let me go."

I then bite the inside of my cheek, hard enough the coppery taste of blood comes, and it brings home all the violence that could happen. And what the CIA might also do to me, and I manage a few tears.

Fuck it. I'm scared, beyond scared... terrified, so I bury my face in my hands as my vision blurs and I pretend I'm bawling.

The man hisses in disgust.

Outside the door someone calls out to him. It's a sharp command in, I think, Portuguese. It's not one of my languages, but from the slowness of the command, and the repeat, I don't think it's this guy's, either.

He yells back an affirmative. It's something that I understand right away. The big guy then motions to the door with the gun on Smith.

"Come on," he says. "We'll see what you know. And if you try anything, I'm tasting your sweet thing here."

Smith doesn't look at me as he's led out, the gun poking him hard in the back and I stand, dropping all attempt at tears as helplessness overcomes me. They disappear out the door, the echoing slam like some kind of bell toll at a funeral.

The moment they're gone, I look around again. I don't see any telltale lights for cameras, and besides, there's nowhere to keep them hidden.

I have no idea who is behind this. So many people might

want this weapon, and the blueprints... Johnny, my field agent, was on the trail for an important piece of the puzzle when he went MIA. Before he went dark, he told me not to trust anyone.

Then again, he might have said that because he was feeding me bad intel.

Slowly, I creep toward the door and place my ear against it. The wood's thick, very thick, maybe even reinforced.

I need to keep my eyes on the prize. Finding the fucker who raped my mom. Who used her, got her in with these people, the Collectors, or... I don't know the details, but I have to find out the truth.

Beyond the door there are muffled sounds. Voices. But I can't make anything out.

I reach for the handle and stop.

If I can even get out and there's a guard waiting, where am I going to go and what the fuck will he do to me if he catches me? The disgusting giant already gave me a taste. He also taunted a cold and furious Smith with my fate.

Smith...

I swallow, legs wobbling, tears pressing hard and hot at my eyes.

Funny how trying to cry in fear was hard work, but fear for Smith, a man I admit I crave in a sexual way but am not sure if I like, the tears want to come.

I think if the man had hurt Smith, shot him, I'd have attacked him. I'd have cried for real.

What does that say about me?

Other than I'm fucked up.

I move around, stepping over the tray with the thick-cut sandwiches and the remaining bottle of water, to see if there's some miraculous secret passage out. A giggle rises in my throat at the ridiculousness, and I swallow it down.

Like I'm going to press a brick and freedom and unicorns will be waiting to fly me the fuck out of this hellhole?

This isn't Harry fucking Potter and no one's locking us up with secret passages.

But I keep checking.

Finally, I collapse onto the floor, slumping back against the wall, wishing I had a weapon hidden. I rub a hand up under the long layer of hair that hides the undercut.

The door opens and Smith's flung in. He lands on the ground, and I'm on my feet so fast, rushing to his side, my heart thumping.

He groans and I gently touch his face. He lifts his head, his blue eyes burning into me, lip bleeding but other than that, he looks fine.

"You should see the other guy."

"You look fine," I say as he pulls me into him. I hate myself for going, for leaning into him as his mouth presses to mine. He kisses me, tongue hot, seductive, the taste of his blood, of copper and salt, it all makes a heady mix.

The taste of Smith and blood.

"Looks," he whispers, "can be deceiving. And it hurts. On the inside."

I push him to lift his shirt, but he pulls my hand away. His mouth back at mine. "They're coming to get me again. They want information on where you have the weapon shit. There's a setup with a satellite computer. The cloud you mentioned?"

The cloud? "I told you I have one, but there's nothing on it."

"Bullshit. You're under thirty, everyone has a fucking cloud. And they keep crap on it."

I've got a couple, a personal one for not overly personal things, one for backup digital photos. And... I swallow. "Where are we?"

"Best I can work out, Cuba. But none of them are Cuban. Outskirts of Havana, is my best guess."

Suddenly, I pull back. "How...?"

"Information gathering's easy with certain people. These are grunts. Hired help from various countries. I don't know who they're working for, but they want the weapon info you have."

"How...?"

"Think about it, Calista." He slips a finger down my cheek and I can't shake the feeling he's playing me as well as these people. "You got people looking for you. Your employers want you. Someone powerful wants whatever you have."

I take a shaky breath. "If you give them something, we're dead. If you don't, we're dead."

"No. I'm buying time. Time to trust me, Calista."

I narrow my eyes. "But I don't."

"Fake it."

Since I was younger, I'd store pointless stuff, things I made, code and fake info. A game I played with Henry when I was teaching him how to hack. He was only half-dedicated to coding and hacking. There was real stuff hidden there, but it wasn't useful. And I was also trying to find ways to hide information in plain sight. Make it so I could have sensitive information almost out in the open and no one would know because even if they could get past all my firewalls and protections, they'd would still need the key to unlock what it all meant.

It's something I'd been working on with the CIA. And it's also one reason why they wanted me. I could cipher cryptograms and break all sorts of codes others had tried to hide their information in.

But occasionally I'd throw something in there to test, nothing much, but always coded.

"You can give them this." I lean in and put my mouth to his ear, trying not to breathe in his intoxicating scent. Then I whisper the cloud address and the password.

He kisses me again. "Calista, I could fuck you."

"It's just a kiss."

"Then later." He rests his forehead against mine. "Whatever happ—" Smith stops. "Thank you."

He pushes himself up and then bangs on the door. "Got it."

It opens and the brute looks at me and licks his thick lips before dragging Smith out. I leap up and punch the door the moment it slams and locks.

Did he play me? Again? Or is he buying time? And how the hell are we supposed to get out of here if we give them what they think they want?

The door opens again. I stumble back and two men grab me. They're also big, and they speak the dialect of Bolivian.

At first I think they're taking me out of there, but they shove me back into the room and onto the floor. I land with a thud, pain and shock ricocheting through my ass.

One of them grins down at me, uglier than the brute, and the other kneels behind me, pulling me down.

It takes a moment before I start to struggle. A moment before I get what they plan to do next.

Then the panic and the fury bubbles and spits. I kick at the grinning one while trying to kick the other one off me.

"Let me go!" I say.

He dodges my leg and unbuckles his pants and says in English, "I don't understand."

"Bastard." I twist out of his grip, kicking again. I manage to hit him just shy of the balls. He grunts and waves a hand at his friend who has my top half pinned down.

He punches me, and for a moment everything is numb. Ringing.

Something hits my face, soft, stinking, and I shriek. The one pinning me down pulled out his dick.

Oh fuck. He's hard. It's not that huge but it's big enough, and I don't want it anywhere near me. He drops, sitting on my legs, and he reaches up to pull my pants down.

"No!" I scream and try to lift my arms so I can grab the cock that's rubbing on my face, getting harder by the millisecond. I just need to grab it and try and gouge it, twist it, cause the fucker some intense pain. But he's on my shoulders and upper arms, and I'm locked down.

Tears run down my cheeks in puddles as I try to throw them off. Pleading, angry words pour forth.

The one at my feet has his hands hooked in my pants now and has them down to my ankles.

"No, please, no," I whimper, my body locked tight against the ground with no lifeline to grasp on to.

And no one coming to save me.

CHAPTER 19
SMITH

I don't think. I don't even breathe. I just shoot.

Both the motherfuckers who are on top of Calista crumple to the floor.

The one who was trying to get into her pants—literally—is now slumped on her legs. She kicks the lifeless sack of raping shit off her and struggles to get up. I pull her to her feet, trying to check her over, needing to make sure she's okay.

"Calista—"

"Looks like Smith found a prize," Mercer says.

He's followed by Malone, Liam, Orion, the Black Widow, and Jones.

The Widow insisted on coming.

Calista takes them all in. "Smith?"

Before I can speak, the Widow shoves me out of the way and puts an arm around Calista. "Smith, you could have at least left one of them for me."

With that, she takes Calista out of the room.

I don't want to let her out of my sight, but I don't have a say in it, and to be honest, the less time spent here, the better. I glance at my fellow Knights, including the one marrying my daughter, one of my closest friends, and the one I really don't want to engage with at all anymore.

Jones lifts an eyebrow. "Plan going well?"

"You might have hurried shit up a little bit."

He ignores the dig with nothing behind it. "You get anything of interest from her? Other than that bruise on her throat?"

I ignore that.

"Enver never told me who wants her; chances are he doesn't know."

"Not what I asked, but from what he told me, it's one of those jobs where the client pays extra for delivery and no questions." He shrugs, looks around, then gazes down at the two dead assholes, their deflated cocks almost ghoulishly comical.

It's a fitting end.

"Why are there so many fucking cretins in this world?" Jones asks.

I glance at him again. "Fuck if I know. I just wish I'd been able to make them, and the big one, suffer a little bit first."

"If you'd left them to me and Mercer," says Malone, slinging an arm over my shoulders. He's sporting a beard and judging from the almost preppy look, he's either changed his ways or it's for a job. "We'd have loved to have fucked them up for you."

Liam calls him over. Malone pats my back, then leans in close. "Talk with Orion. He had to deal with the same shit when Mercer and Ivy got together. If ice and rock can communicate, you can do it, too."

I scowl at him. Ivy is Orion's sister. It's not the same thing at all. "You find a woman and you're suddenly a relationship expert?"

"Hey," he says, moving away from me, "when you meet a girl like Scarlett, you have epiphanies."

"Still can't believe she likes you."

He puts a hand to his heart. "It's a goddamn wonder of the world. And so's the fact that Calista has it bad for your old ass. Go figure."

Malone winks and disappears to talk to Liam before I can respond.

"Your question?" I say to Jones. "She has shit, but she's reluctant to spill it."

"That you know of."

"Yeah, well..." I mutter as I take in the place with new eyes. Alone, I'd have gotten out. With Calista? I was on my way when the cavalry turned up. "I appreciate the help, don't get me wrong, but I could have gotten us the fuck out."

"You definitely got yourself the fuck in."

I smile grimly. "I did. Not how I'd planned but it takes getting caught to catch the fish. Or some shit like that."

Jones shoves a body with his foot, then bends down and searches the guy. I let him conduct the search on one and then the other because I'm liable to do damage after death, and it might look a little fucked in the head.

It is fucked in the head.

"Nothing..." He shakes his head as he rises. "Weapons, but nothing of use."

"Grunts. Goons. Disposable jerks who crossed the wrong line here."

"How you getting her to talk?"

"I will, Jones," I say. "You know that."

"And if I said hand her over?"

"You're not my boss." We exchange a look. "This is about a new weapon. I'm pretty fucking sure Enver's working the angle of getting the blueprints, but I think it's in our best interest to find out how deep people in our government might be, along with others."

"She's not one of them?"

"No. This crew..." I wave a hand. "These are grunts, like I said. More than I thought, easy to manipulate. They didn't know anything. Just sent here to find the hacker and what she has."

But something isn't quite right about this whole thing, and he knows it, too.

"If this is just about the weapon," I say, taking the gun he hands me and checking the clip. "I don't think she knows what she might have. Especially since the CIA breaks up sensitive stuff like that."

And she's not technically high level enough. I say "technically" because the agency knows her skill set.

"Is that new?"

"Fucking civilian. No," I say. "Always has been and always will be. Built-in protection system."

"Or she wants you to think that. She's a master hacker." He pauses. "Devil's advocate."

I roll my eyes. "I worked for them. I know how they operate."

"When are you handing her over?"

"If it's just about the weapon, she'd have already been taken in Germany. Way before she went into hiding."

"Or they waited and watched instead. Who recruited her?"

That, I don't know. "I'll find out. But come on, you know like I fucking do that the agency has a way of doing things. They'll watch, and then if someone goes off-grid, they'll strike."

"You have her, so technically she's off-grid," Jones mutters, kicking one of the dead assholes again.

I nod. "I have her and maybe they are just watching."

We exchange another look. "This weapon," he says, lowering his voice, "it's not something we can find that much about. I've tried. All I know is it's new, in high demand, and the blueprints, once they're put together, will change the landscape of terrorism."

"That's the official word from the CIA?"

"From intel I spent a lot of time looking into."

I don't ask if this has rolled into another job, mainly because I know he won't tell me. We're Knights. Secretive, powerful above and below the law. But based on what he's saying, it makes sense why the CIA would go to such lengths to get Calista back.

But the Collectors...

We finished them. As good as we could have, anyway. We have some still in our pockets and... I'm going to have to get everything from Calista. All of it. Piece it together. And then, after whatever Jones needs is taken or uncovered—because he's definitely after something—we hand her over.

The Collectors... could this really be about them over the weapon? Because even though they're decimated, there are still some around, other cells we couldn't find and crush. Or maybe our little hacker saw something else she shouldn't have.

Because the more I think about it, the government has the team who came up with the weapon. And they still have the original information, the OG blueprints.

Gut instinct?

Calista's troubles aren't stemming from the weapon blueprints and schematics being sold to the highest bidder...

I think she's a scapegoat.

"Jones..."

"She's just another piece of a puzzle, one they want, one you'll hand over. When she's given you everything." He motions to the door. The others have left and we make our way out to the large car that's waiting. "And this? Glad we could join you for some fun, but..."

"Some of it got out of hand." A muscle twitches in my jaw. Like the men I killed who touched her. All fucking three of them. "But?"

"Don't get too caught up."

"Never. She's a commodity, nothing more."

And with that, I shut down the feeling that I'm a total fucking liar.

THE PRIVATE ISLAND in the Florida Keys, close to mainland USA and Miami by plane, is a stopover. We own it, so it's the perfect place to rest up for a few hours.

Calista's back with me. The others have scattered.

I'm fresh from my shower, buttoning a cuff link when I come out into the living area of the suite we're in. Calista's sitting on the white sofa. She looks around, then at me. "I'd ask who you are but it's going to be the same answer, isn't it? A lot of bullshit wrapped in nothing paper. Eva... your friend?"

The trip here from Cuba wasn't long and Eva, aka the Black Widow, sequestered her.

Fuck, I don't think the Widow's much older than Calista. And I'm not sure if Eva's even her real name. She's a Knight and we don't dig into each other. What we are at the tables and suites in the depths beneath O-Ring back in our New York headquarters is taken at face value.

Every single one of us has a past.

Every single one has secrets. We all earned the right to reveal those when and if we want to.

"What about her?" I switch to the other cuff link.

"She was very nice to me but was the same as you."

Yep, sounds about right. We all have a story, and it's never the truth.

"She's nice to women and girls. Men? We have to earn her respect." I lean against the doorjamb. "Your room's through there." I gesture to the main bedroom of the suite. "This is a resort so order in, but don't venture out, if you get my drift."

"And what about you?" She's avoiding what happened, the impact of her words so hard I can feel it pressing down like a weight.

"You should get some sleep and—"

"I'm not broken." She throws a cushion at me and jumps up. "I'm trained, I know—"

"Those men tried to rape you, Calista, they—"

"Don't treat me like a doll. Like a broken, fragile thing. I'm not. There are worse things than what they did, and—"

"Like death? Or like me?"

"You don't even warrant a blip on my radar. I like kinky shit. I might not like or trust you, but I like what you do."

I half smile. "Good to know. And you need to rest." I give her a gentle push toward the bedroom. "I can send someone up to talk to you."

"I'm a prisoner again?" she asks, deliberately misunderstanding me. We both know I meant a therapist. Not that there's one here, but I've got two options. Push her to see if she'll crack or hold her.

And the latter?

It's dangerous.

"You're not a prisoner, but this resort is a special kind. Like a kink sex club but also a resort. People can come and play. There are parties. Gangbangs for the lady—or gentleman— into that. Free use weekends. Orgies. And of course, primal chases, where those who want to be hunted and get down and reconnect with their more basic urges can. And yes, sometimes

THE TRUTHS THAT DECEIVE

men are hunted. Me, I'm a hunter. I know you like being prey, but that's not what this weekend is about. This weekend is general BDSM, and a lot of slaves being led around on all fours. Fed from bowls. Treated like their mistress or master's playthings."

"Not my scene."

"Didn't think so. So again, that therapist?" I leave it hanging and her eyes turn to a pure and raging storm, one that tells me she's made of strong stuff.

I don't know who wants her but I'm off to find out what I can tonight, try to bait whoever might be biting, and sell some blueprints I don't have, along with a piece of the Bolivian sex trade game. There's a club in Miami that has no rules, where there are questionable practices, that we're watching.

On the plane back to the States, I told Jones about my concerns about the Collectors and how the ones remaining might be playing in actual trafficking waters.

He didn't tell me I'm paranoid. Just to do what I need to find them.

And then hand over my little hacker.

"If you try and stick a therapist on me, I'll knife them and then you."

I nod. Slowly. "You could come to Miami. But you'll have to get changed. There's a closet of clothes to choose from."

"I prefer my clothes."

"They're in smithereens back in France, remember?"

Calista stares me. And I'm pretty fucking sure she's weighing my words. She hasn't asked about her computer, which means she either thinks it's toast or that I have it. It's the latter, but we don't exactly trust each other, so she's not asking and I'm not volunteering.

It ups the tension.

Makes it gorgeously borderline unbearable.

Just like this conversation.

"One question. How did your friends find us?"

She's trying to work out if I played her. I hold up my hand. "My ring. It has a tracker and when we didn't show at a rendezvous point, my friends came looking."

She just nods.

"One question. If I take you to this hardcore sex club in Miami, are you going to try and run away?"

"What are you going to do if I say yes?"

"Not sure yet. But just know I'll find you and hand you over immediately if not sooner."

She nods. "What if I ask you to help me uncover who's after me?"

"I might be inclined to say yes." I pause. "For a price."

"I guess I'll get changed."

She's only gone twenty minutes, and she's found the red femme fatale wig I had added to the things in here. It's easy to prepare a room in a couple of hours when you're part owner of the resort you're heading to.

The dress is black, low-cut with a split up the side and a tie at the waist. I wouldn't call it sex club attire except I suspect beneath the veneer of just respectable is a very naked woman beneath. And her heels scream "come fuck me now."

Everything about her says there's no way she can run.

But I know she's going to.

We join the others and take a small plane to the mainland. From the airfield, it's a short car ride into Miami.

We're almost at the sex club when I get a message from Reaper, who's in town. *Heard through the grapevine the people you might be interested in are a no-show for tonight.*

When's good?

Can you hang around until tomorrow?

A slow smile spreads and I send a message through to the driver about our change of location.

"This doesn't look like a sex club," Calista says in the red wig that's fucking white-hot on her.

I slant her a look as I lead her in past the line of people, the bouncers letting us in without question or delay. "You're a sex club frequent flyer?"

She trails a finger down my tie. "There's a lot you don't know about me."

"Come on, kinkmeister, I'll ply you with drinks and you can show me your tricks."

The club is smoky, clandestine. It's more underground dance club than anything else. And the beast inside me is stirring. A place like this is perfect to start a real-time chase. Over the beat of the music, I lower my mouth to her ear. "Drink?"

"Champagne."

I go to the bar for a bottle. And when I get back, she's gone.

Oh fuck, do I like a woman made of strong stuff, one who can and will run. Even if she is too young for me. I pull the phone from my pocket and open up the CCTV feed. There she is, running out of the place like a pro in the shoes. And I grin.

The chase is fucking *on*.

CHAPTER 20
CALISTA

My feet are like hot coals and knives rolled into one, but high heels, though I don't often wear them, are a superpower of mine. For some reason, I can walk and run in them. Though usually not this fast, not for so long, and definitely not ever in six-inch platform stripper heels.

But I don't dare take them off. Not until I can get somewhere I can disappear. Somewhere I can get to a computer.

On my thigh is a garter, and secured in that is a credit card I pilfered from Smith. He has a few so he won't miss it immediately.

And I know using it is like shooting fireworks up to announce my whereabouts, but I also don't intend to be free for very long. I'm just hoping its long enough to check up on the Estonian connection.

Maybe send a message to Riley, if his old private number still works.

Smith didn't take me to a sex club. He took me out, like he

doesn't think I'm okay... no, like he doesn't trust me. Which is fine by me, because that goes both ways.

The streets are crowded with partygoers and girls in bikinis and heels. There must be a nighttime pool party somewhere, but after a few people give me weird looks as I run past them, I dart around a corner, down another street, and force myself to slow to a brisk walk.

I turn onto another street, this one with colorful buildings. My senses are overwhelmed at the scents of cooking meat and the sounds of laughter and chatter while people play chess and checkers at tables on the sidewalks and in little cafés.

What I need is a place with a computer. There's salsa music floating out of one place and it's big, a café, yes, but also a place where people dance. I go in, intent on asking someone if there's an old-fashioned internet café or something like that when I spy a little closed-off area at the back.

I look behind me, but I don't see a man over six foot whatever in an expensive suit following, so I head back, taking note of the location of bathrooms and exits other than the door I came through.

Bathrooms are down a short hallway that probably leads to the kitchens and the manager's office.

Good. Places to hide and run to if I need. But I don't think Smith's following me.

"Think" being the most troubling word in the mix.

"Excuse me," I ask the waitress, "can I get a coffee and use the computers?" I point to the ancient-looking machines that probably fell off the back of a truck about ten years ago.

She nods. "Enter your credit card details on the screen."

I find the one farthest from the noise. With a clear view of the entrance, I pull out the credit card.

My café Cubano is strong and sweet, the computer slower than the dead.

I stab in the card number and dive down into the dark web to see if I can contact Senator Riley.

I call the old number over the computer and leave a cryptic voicemail stating I'll be in touch again, but if he gets the message, to call me on a number generated by the BurnEd app, one that creates untraceable temporary numbers. I link it to an app that translates and stores any voice messages as a text, and then I start to search other things.

Chatter on the weapon.

Information about Johnny.

And Trenton.

My search still comes up empty for Trenton. By all accounts, he's dead, but his wife's in New York. And a son... how did I miss this every time I've researched him?

I copy her details down and send them to my Jane Doe cloud, and then I deep dive into other things.

She did an interview over some center she opened, and even though there is no direct link between her and Trenton, I manage to connect whatever dots I have. I send all that to that cloud, too.

Then my fingers freeze over the keyboard.

There's a picture of me and Henry. It says I'm wanted for questioning.

A movement captures my eye, and I look up, eyes wide. There, at the door, is a man in a suit.

It's not Smith, but I'm so jumpy I shut everything down and slide into the darkness of the hallway.

I lock the door of the bathroom and lean against it, trying to stop the race of my pulse. I'm alone, so why—

"Because," I whisper, "he's on his way."

It's in the air. My blood. My senses.

And every second I spend in this bathroom means he's closer to getting me. He probably discovered the missing credit card. He might have had an alert set up. I don't know. All I know is I need to run.

With a breath, I unlock the door and pull it open.

And stop.

Smith blocks my way. "Hello, little girl. Going somewhere?"

"Away from you."

He doesn't touch me as he moves forward, and instead of standing my ground, I back away from him. Before I know it, he's closed the door and locked it. The dulled sound of sex-soaked salsa permeates the rickety wood of the door. He backs me against the counter with the sink.

"That's the wrong way," he murmurs, lifting me onto the ledge, his hands burning brands into my hips as he does so. "The door's behind me."

"You locked it."

"True." He kisses a trail up my throat, pausing to suck where he's bitten me before and my entire body throbs. A moan breaks free. "I expected more of a chase. But perhaps my prey wanted to get caught."

"No."

"Not 'code'? Just no?"

"I don't..."

His hands whisper over my skin, one slipping down along the split in the skirt, and I don't even understand how he has such an incredible hold on me.

I want to fight him, I do. I want to go toe to toe and show him his prey has teeth but there's a heaviness inside that tells me maybe I want to be caught, that I want to curl up for him, offer myself to him. Because I fought already. Against horrible men.

Men who weren't playing a sex-fueled game. Men who

hadn't given me a safe word. Men who wanted to hurt and intimidate in the wrong way.

Maybe I want to feel warm and wanted by someone I want, now that he's caught me.

But I'm not telling him that.

I won't ever admit it to him.

"How did you find me?"

He slides higher up my thigh, then up my body. "You should check wigs for trackers. Clothes, too."

"Asshole."

Smith kisses me and I cling to him, kissing him back, suckling on his tongue. The kiss is deep and soft, with a romantic edge, one dipped in erotic intent.

When he finally steps back, his blue eyes burn hot as he looks down. "Fuck, you're gorgeous."

A cool breeze from the air in the bathroom hits the fabric covering my nipples, the wetness between my thighs.

"You fuck."

His mouth twitches. "Is that an invitation or are you telling me where to go?" With one quick flick of his fingers, he undoes my zipper and the dress falls around me.

"What do you think?" I make no move to cover myself.

Right or wrong, I like it, the kick of adrenaline it gives me, like how it ups the desire in my blood. And yes, I fucking love that he looks at me like I'm a dream come true. What woman wouldn't get off on that?

And I need it after Cuba. Need it with a desperation I didn't know I had.

"I think your body is for sin, my sin. My pleasure. My prize. This is your chance to use your word."

"If I use it," I say, knowing the answer, "you'll stop?"

"Yes."

He leans down to lick one nipple and then the other, pleasure streaking through me. Smith raises his head. "Well?"

"Code."

He takes a step back and my chest tightens as all my nerve endings cry out in protest.

I reach out, catch his jacket, and pull him in. "Change your mind?"

"Testing the word."

His mouth twists into a smile, one that doesn't reach the blaze in his blue eyes. "Verdict?"

"I don't have to like you to want you." I lift my face to him, but he doesn't kiss me.

Instead, he moves back in.

"True." He slips his fingers over the garter and holds up his card. "Naughty."

"You're slow on the uptake."

"Who's to say I didn't notice it missing from my wallet?"

"Most people have this shit on their phones."

"I'm old."

"What are you going to do?" My voice is breathless.

I want his punishment. His touch. I want whatever he might throw at me.

"This." He sucks and bites my nipples, pulling one into his mouth to roll it with his tongue before his teeth come down and he pulls back, then he goes to the other one.

Smith shifts from nipple to nipple, back and forth, turning me into a furnace of need, of sensation, that makes me moan, makes me dig my short nails into his neck, and I'm not sure if I want to push him away or pull him to me.

Yes, I do. I'm sure. I want more. I don't want him gone.

Not that he's going anywhere, but the desperate need for more pushes, *hard*.

He kisses and nibbles down until he pushes my thighs apart, wide. And he licks a path over my slit. He sucks my lips and tongues my pussy, then shifts up to my clit as he drives two fingers into me.

I groan, raising my hips, and the sensations spread like molten heat through me. God, he's like someone with a PhD in sublime pleasure giving. He slides his fingers in and out, pumping, rubbing over my G-spot, and my head falls back as the soft-rough wet of his tongue moves over my sensitive flesh.

"You know," Smith says, looking up at me without stopping his delicious assault, "your mouth tastes sweet like sugar and strong like coffee, but your cunt... it's the mother of all fucking delicacies. I could eat you all day and night."

I gasp as an orgasm slams into me, that wild rise of pleasure hitting, and I come hard. He pulls out his fingers, pulls me off the edge of the sink, and turns me around.

I'm limp as a rag doll and I let him move me.

"But you've still been bad, stealing, running, deliberately letting yourself get caught. And this..." He fingers my asshole. "This is going to be mine."

My heart leaps and dances as behind me in the mirror, he releases himself and pumps his thick cock, then lines up.

The concentration on his face is an aphrodisiac of its own.

For a moment, I think he's going to claim my ass, and I want him to, even though my heart's a little wild at the thought of something so big in that tight hole.

But he doesn't.

He slams into my pussy, holding himself at full entry as he reaches balls deep. "And nothing, nothing will be as fucking perfect as this. Me in your cunt. Except your mouth, and I suspect that tight little asshole of yours will be my undoing."

He starts to play with it as he pulls out and slams back into me, angling himself so that his thick cock splits me open, invades deep, and rubs my G-spot as he hits all the way in and then pulls out.

Each push into me is a revelation, each withdrawal filled with anticipation of him driving home once again. Because he feels so fucking good stretching me, filling me, his cock hitting all the right parts of me.

And then... oh... God...

Smith pushes a finger into my ass, and he starts to fuck me in both holes at the same time, as he brings his other hand up to my mouth and pushes two fingers in.

"Oh fuck," he says, gazing at our pleasure-soaked reflection in the mirror. "Look at that. You're the perfect little slut of a sub, the perfect little tasty prey. But I think you want me to take your ass. Look at your face as I fuck all your holes, see how you push back to meet me, so eager, so hungry. I think you want me deep in your ass."

I try and answer, but garbled sound comes out and he half closes his eyes as he slams into me again. "But I don't think so. Not when you didn't really want the chase, when you let your-self get caught."

Oh. Fuck...

He comes, shuddering into me. And watching him own me sets me off again, and his cock seems to get bigger as he spurts. I come hard around him, spasming.

When we're done, he pulls out and turns me, walking me back into the door, kissing me hard.

"You know we can finish this here, because I think I might love you down on your knees on the tile in the bathroom, or maybe..." His eyes glitter.

"What—"

"I have a place and we can finish there—because, darling, I'm far from finished—and then?"

I narrow my eyes. There's a Smith-shaped bomb coming. "What?"

"We can talk."

Talk? For a moment I'm dumbfounded. He wants to... talk? I don't understand his game.

"What do you mean, talk?" I ask carefully.

He waits a beat. "I mean, tell me what I need to know, everything, and I don't give a fuck how classified."

"Or?"

"Or we head to Washington, and I hand you over to whoever the fuck is paying me. Your call, Calista."

CHAPTER 21
SMITH

M y place in Miami is luxurious and run by dedicated staff who keep it ready to go at a drop of the proverbial fucking hat.

There's an office. One that's got class and is locked down like Fort Knox since it's the only place where my computers and guns are kept.

My fellow Knights also use my place on occasion if they need a Miami base. But right now, those Knights who have business here have hotels or are staying elsewhere. So it's a perfect high-rise slice of luxury where once inside, Calista will have no way out. At all.

I pour a drink, offering her one. She shakes her head, perching on one of the stools in the gleaming open-plan kitchen.

I lean against the counter, glad the marble and stone island is between us.

Because what I really want is to hunt her down in the penthouse. Honestly, it wouldn't be much of a hunt, but I've already caught her once tonight. Anything else would be a bonus.

I stare down at the amber liquid as she pulls off the wig and dumps it on the island.

She looks her age when she's not wearing it. Her natural hair brings her down into her truth of experience level. Who she should be with. And that ain't me.

With the wig, she gains a whiff of femme fatale, a woman with a load of experience, and if I don't think too hard, one who could be between late twenties and early thirties.

It doesn't add years to her.

Just the illusion of a lived-in life instead of a very smart girl handpicked by the CIA for her hacking skills.

Skills that tell me she spends most of her time behind a computer.

Looking her age makes my guilt rise.

What it doesn't do is squash the need for her again. The desire to own, claim, fuck her every which way.

"I thought we weren't finished." She goes pink in the cheeks, but her chin rises defiantly. "You said we were going to finish and then talk."

Oh yeah, I said that. I really am a sleazy fuck.

She gestures, crossing her legs, showing me a whole lot of sleek, slender thigh. Knowing she's naked under the dress, all it would take is me walking over to her and pulling the tie to let it fall open.

She could take it off, too.

Fuck. I run a hand over my face. Because yeah, I really want to strip her down. Worse, I want her to do it for me.

"I changed my mind."

"What do you want to know? I told you what I have, which is nothing. At least from what I could decipher. Just encrypted, and I mean really encrypted files I haven't had a chance to try

THE TRUTHS THAT DECEIVE

and break into. Stuff I collected for Johnny, things he had stored."

Johnny, her field agent. I frown. "For him?"

"He was out with an outlier group that wanted to make money selling weapons. The CIA was trying to find out who ran it and if they had any of the weapon blueprints. Small parts of them kept showing up on the radar."

She's very clever. I take a swallow of my drink. The small snippets are truth, and maybe the rest is too. But she foreshadowed that information by telling me she hasn't yet cracked into anything substantial.

Calista's given me nothing.

I look down into my glass for a long minute and nod. "If I said this could save your brother?"

I'm still looking down, but I can see her from my periphery. Her head shoots up and she turns almost green, that shade that comes from being nearly sick and so full of absolute fear, it's debilitating.

I've seen it in others before.

When we were in Cuba and those fucking animals I killed touched her, she was angry, scared, defiant. Full of hate.

But my words right here are the things that threaten to bring her to her knees.

"If—if he is killed and you're behind it, I'll kill you."

"He's been watched by the CIA, Calista. What do you think, person of fucking interest?"

"That I need to get the fuck out of here and find my brother."

I shake my head and take another swallow, straightening up and crossing to the island, setting my glass down with a click. "You're trained but you can't take them on. I might not be able to keep you from their reach, but we can hold it off, and I can make sure your brother doesn't go down, too. If you tell me what you know, what you really know."

"You mean, work with you?"

My phone buzzes but I ignore it. Whoever it is—and it'll be a Knight—can wait. It's the phone Jones gave me.

"I'm trying to help."

Calista looks at me. "I know. I'm just not sure if it's me or yourself."

"The greater good?"

"Do you even know what that is?"

"Calista."

She sighs and slides off her stool. Then she comes around the island to grab the bottle and drink straight from it. "I told you. Johnny disappeared and said he was onto something just before that, a way of letting me know not to report him missing if that happened. Not immediately, anyway."

"When he didn't show, I started poking around, putting together more information from areas I shouldn't have been in." She lifts her head. "I hid what I found but I haven't looked at much. And I can't make heads or tails out of some of it. Blueprints, coded notes." She shrugs. "And I... I also took them after the generic threats came in. That's all."

I push a hand through my hair, then shrug off my jacket. I think she's giving me the truth, but I need more. I need to know where this stuff is. She mentioned the cloud, but I doubt she gave up the one where she stored everything. No agent worth anything—especially one who is a hacker—would do that.

Slow and steady. I'll get my hands on the data for a look before she's handed over. Before I hand her over. And if she won't give it to me, what did she say?

Every hack leaves a trace, or something like that.

I'll get someone at the Obsidian Knights headquarters to get onto it soon.

But first. "Estonia and the Collectors?"

"What about my brother?"

I don't face her. Instead, I check my message. Seems like I'm going to that sex club tonight, after all.

The gun I tucked into the back of my pants is something I can't take with me. So I pull it out and leave it on the edge of the island while I buy time and wait for her to tell me whatever it is she has.

"My brother?"

Deliberately, I shrug. "Tell me what you know."

"That they're pieces of shit and they got ripped apart. One arm of them. They make you seem nice."

I let that slide. "Why are you so interested in them?"

"A man. He's supposed to be dead, but his accounts, his secret accounts are active. And I had to dig into some dark web stuff to find that out. But his wife—widow—whatever is in New York, and I want to find her. See what she knows."

"Why?" I type back a message and tuck the phone away.

"Because I'm pretty sure he raped my mom. When she was young. M-my brother?"

With a sigh, I turn.

The gun's in her hand, pointed at me.

"What are you going to do? Shoot me?" I ask her softly.

"If I have to. Promise you'll help him."

I walk up to her slowly. "If you cooperate. And if you're going to do it, pull the trigger now."

"I will."

Calista's hand doesn't shake, I'll give her that. And she holds the gun in the proper position, a CIA girl down to the bone. What I'm not sure of is if she'll actually pull the trigger. I walk right up until the barrel presses against my chest.

Then I close my hand around hers.

"Do it, Calista. Pull the fucking trigger."

"You don't think I will?"

"I don't know. Will you?" I counter.

"If you push me."

She still doesn't shake, even now, but her eyes get wild, a little bloodthirsty and it turns me the fuck on.

So I help her. Slide my finger in over hers and she jerks, pulling the fucking trigger.

The gun clicks.

"Empty. I didn't put a clip in it. But good to know what you're capable of." I ease the gun from her hand and slide a thigh between her legs, pressing up against her pussy. I lean down to graze my mouth along her cheek and up to her ear. "There are different kinds of chases, Calista. And this one is fucking exhilarating."

"You're a sick bastard."

"You're the one who picked up my gun and threatened me."

"I..."

I kiss her, tangling a hand in her silky hair. I angle her head and slant my mouth more fully over hers, invading her depths, tasting her. The scotch and the fear. The anger and the desire. Her claws and the rivaling softness as she goes down for me, fighting as she gives it up with a whimper of need.

She's hot and wet and rubbing on my leg, her tongue fucking and twining with mine.

Her small sounds of pleasure slide down into my bones, burning the center of me. I'm hard, of course, I'm fucking rock-hard.

The kiss is the perfect precursor to sex in and of itself. And she fits. We click. There's a thing there, the chase and hunt, the defiance and submission, the delirious pleasure in catching her. That's all the kink, the deepest part of me.

But the fact our lips and tongues and bodies meet and make the other flicker works on a fundamental level.

If I had to take her, right now, we'd just have vanilla sex. Fuck, if I had to light some candles and wine and dine her to bed I would, and I think it might be just as good as the adrenaline-soaked rush of a physical chase. Just as good as the gun pointed at me and the will she, won't she pull the trigger.

Sure, I knew it wasn't loaded.

She didn't.

She didn't even check.

Right now, I want to say fuck everything, ignore what I'm planning and just enjoy the ever-loving shit out of her right up to handing her over and collecting my paycheck.

I kiss my way along her throat, her skin soft and delicate, the heat of her rapid pulse a delight on my tongue.

I don't need to do this. Dig into her secrets, find out more about the guy who's interested in sex slaves and new, classified weapons. I can just hand her to the CIA and still poke around for Jones later.

"Fuck." I break the kiss, brushing back her silky hair as her glazed eyes try to focus. I keep one hand tight on her because she's swaying a little too much. "Fuck."

"I didn't... I wouldn't..."

"Pull the trigger?" I brush her lips with mine. "Don't ruin it. I have to go."

She wrenches free, grabbing at the island. "Where—?"

"Not your business."

"Are you going to keep my brother safe? Maybe help me with this guy who—" She stops, swallows, and something cold and sticky moves down my spine at what she might not be telling me. "With the guy?"

"I need to go."

She snatches up the wig and puts it on. "The sex club? The creepy one? Is that where we're going?"

"Where I'm going, as in not you, not we. Fucking *me*."

She looks around, frowning. "If you had a knife block, I'd grab one and—"

"Hit me with the block? Stab me with a knife? Slice my neck?" I smile. "I'm honored. Two bloodthirsty threats from you in one night. You're staying the fuck here."

"I won't be here when you get back. You'll never find me."

"And how do you think you're getting out?"

She stomps off through the living room to the floor-to-ceiling glass window that reflects back a ghostly reflection, and she uses it to fix her wig. "I have my ways."

She probably does. I sigh. "Fine. Come on, but don't say I didn't fucking warn you."

I'm not her father. I'm not her protector. I'm here to make sure she gets handed over. This is a detour, and if she wants to come... Hell, she can fucking come.

But I do make contingencies. I provided a mask and private suite in case she freaks out.

The car takes us there. She's both dressed right and wrong. A rich woman who isn't sure she wants to partake. I wanted my persona to be a man who does anything. But I can make it work. And yeah, the wig and the dress with nothing beneath is still hot as fuck.

Couples fuck as we make our way down to the lower level. Some people wear masks, others don't. I grab a mask from a naked hostess with piercings in all the right places on her waxed body, piercings at her cunt set up just so her slit is open just enough to show off her swollen clit that glistens with juices.

As I fix the white lace mask, which announces she's taken,

onto Calista, I sit down on the sofa in the members' section. One man is getting a very hands-on lap dance, and another is fucking a girl's ass while another man feeds her his cock. A mistress makes her slave literally lick her boots.

"I'm not sure who this guy is," I say to her, pulling Calista onto my lap and sliding a hand up her skirt to stroke her pussy, "but this is the designated area."

Calista stills. "He's heading this way now."

I look around. "How do you know that?"

"Because," she says, something like panic and betrayal quaking her voice, "I know him."

I'm about to ask who when it dawns on me.

Right as she says it.

"It's Johnny, my missing field agent."

Fuck.

CHAPTER 22
CALISTA

P anic scrabbles little cold claws in my throat and twists my stomach.

Smith seems relaxed, he still pets my pussy like he owns it, touches me like I wish I didn't want him to.

But I know he's not. He's anything but relaxed.

I can feel the buzz of live-wire tension in him. It's vibrating, slightly heated, a different version of the hunter I know as Smith.

The sexual hunter Smith, I mean.

He's still a hunter, a deadly creature, but this vibration isn't fueled with a sexual energy. Just like the lack of interest on his face as he looked around the club earlier. I'm not saying he wasn't noticing or finding any of the explicit sex acts and extreme nakedness—that woman he got the mask from had her pussy pried open with body jewelry, for fuck's sake—hot, but he was dispassionate like he had what he needed right next to him.

Me.

That was all an act, a hunter hunting a different, nonsexual prey.

This... This is a man weighing up lightning fast any and all options.

And it's terrifying.

Because I can almost feel the tension beneath the looseness of muscle in his jaw as he works out what to do.

"Kiss me, Calista."

Startled, I lean in, my mouth on his. And he drives his tongue between my lips in a deep and primal kiss, then he licks down to my chin, and he sucks that. It takes a moment for the weird intimacy of it all to fall away and for me to realize he's talking to me.

"The average-height guy? Brown hair, facial scruff? That's Johnny?"

"Yes."

"How well does he know you?"

"We've met a bunch of times, but most of our relationship's been on the phone or online."

"He knows you," he says flatly. "He's a fucking agent."

Smith pulls his hand from between my thighs and threads it in the locks of the wig and kisses up to my ear. "I need you to stay calm and look completely into me."

"A hard ask."

"Try." His sarcasm breaks the tension a little, and I relax. "Good girl. Okay, here's the deal. There are bathrooms on the top level. Walk past them to the fancy ones, the suites. They each have their own individual locks. Go into the last one on the right—"

"You know a lot about this place."

"Jealous?"

"No." Maybe, but I don't say that.

"Been here before." Smith doesn't offer any further explanation. "Go there, lock the door, and wait for me."

"How—?"

"You'll know. And no matter what, don't take the fucking mask off. Go."

Heart beating fast, I rise and he smacks my ass. But I don't look back. I just follow orders.

I want to stay, to confront Johnny, see what the deal is, why he disappeared from Europe. But I'm not stupid. He's got to be here to sell shit he stole. He might have all of the blueprints or just some of them, but both cases suck. I gleaned from the intel I gathered that even parts could be used to create other weapons, which is one reason it could change the outcome of wars and terrorism. It's one reason things were done in parts, that anyone who worked on anything to do with the blueprints or the weapon only had tiny parts, and it was all encoded.

It didn't matter they were trying to find out who stole what or who wanted the weapon's blueprints. Shit, the whole thing can be a ruse for all I know.

My mind spins.

But deep down, I don't think it's a ruse. I think I'm a patsy.

If not one set up by Johnny, then by others.

What I don't know is why.

And if it's something simple like he's so deep under that he's here doing CIA business illegally on US soil, then why am *I* wanted? Am I actually under suspicion?

The questions whirl hard and fast enough for me to keep my head down as I move through the club and up the stairs.

Even so, I feel eyes on me, that insidious touch a man can give by just looking, by wanting to touch.

When Smith looks at me that way, delicious shivers skitter along my skin.

When other men do it, a clamminess creeps in, closes hard around me, choking me hard, and not in the good way.

For a second upstairs, I lose my way, and I'm caught in a small crush of bodies near a bar. Fingers skim my skin as they try and slide over my breasts, under my skirt.

That last hand I grab and twist, bending the finger back, and the man's cry of pain can be heard over the sensuous beat of the music.

The sign for restrooms beckons me. I navigate toward them, moving across the floor, past couples fucking, past humiliating acts like a girl being passed roughly around, her body exposed and touched like she's prime beef.

I catch her eye, and she narrows hers at me, a clear indication to move along.

Oh hell, she likes it, she likes the humiliation.

So I do. I put my instinct to dive in and try and protect—a useless instinct because I'm hopelessly outnumbered and she doesn't want it—into the back seat of my head, cramming it down low.

I turn down the wide opulent hall with restrooms on either side. But this isn't what he meant. At least I don't think so. I hesitate, and a man in a black suit appears.

His gaze hits the mask, then drops to my breasts for a nanosecond before returning to the mask.

"Miss?"

For a moment I almost scream at him, and I don't know why. It's like being alone with my field agent below, down there with Smith and even more naked girls, stretches all nerve endings thin and tight.

"I'm looking for..." I flounder. "A suite?" That's what Smith said to me. A suite.

"Did your master tell you which suite?"

Master? "I..."

"Your mask. You're here to observe, then wait for your master. Correct?" he asks, voice smooth, smarmy, and somehow soothing, all at the same time.

I touch the mask. The white thing he put on me. "The last on the right."

The man—who's handsome and trying to exude an asexual air now—nods. "This way."

Down the hall, past the restrooms, and then we turn into a darker hallway lit with small pools of amber light, and we reach the door. He opens it and gestures me in.

"Please lock the door. Your master has a key, but for your own sense of comfort, lock it," he says. "Some may not respect the mask with an open door."

He leaves and pulls the door shut. I engage the lock, then turn.

I blink.

It's like some kind of sex demon's idea of a classy boudoir. There's a bathroom off to one side. The ceiling's mirrored, and there's an oversized chaise longue.

There's a bar on a trolley with bottles of water in a corner. I take one, and then after a minute, crack the lid on a bottle of some English small batch white rum, and pour a glass. There's also a fresh bottle of scotch, which makes me think he somehow booked this.

He made calls and sent texts on our way here and...

My legs wobble.

I'm made of tough fucking stuff. But this whole place is... it's a lot. I'm not sure what to think. I get the feeling under the layer of respectably debauched sleaze is something else, something darker and a hell of a lot more sordid here.

Down where we were? No, there was another set of stairs, blocked off, a man in black standing guard. The staircase and man had been on the other side of the downstairs floor. I only saw it for a few seconds, and it occurred to me that's where the nasty shit probably happens. Girls who may not want to be there or have been coerced. The hired help. I don't know. I try to think about what else I may have seen, but nothing comes to my mind.

We didn't go near it, and I wasn't there long enough to conclude anything but eerie feelings about it.

Slowly, I sink onto the chaise and take a deep pull of the rum. The flavor surprises me, like fall air crisp with apples. The spice of vanilla and a sweet warmth that chases it down my throat.

I gulp it down, then chase it with some water. After a while, I pace around and drink some more of the rum, bored, hating being locked in without any stimulation. I could see if this was just a time-out for being too overwhelmed by everything in the club.

But I think it's more a way to create tension, to get me riled up and ready.

Because Smith's going to come through that door.

And yeah, heat curls and dances inside me at the thought, because there's unfinished business between us in the form of sex—hot, sweltering, scorching *sex*.

The hunter and his prey.

I gulp down a breath to calm my racing heart.

My libido.

My fear.

My temper.

The first and last are hard to wrangle. I feel like a damn cat in heat right now, and I bet he knows it. He loves it. He knows making me wait is effectively making me crazy.

And my God, I want to beat the hell out of him for punishing me like this.

I know he wants to keep me away from Johnny. Smith

doesn't trust anyone, and if Johnny recognizes me, there's no saying he won't tell someone where I am. And since Smith wants information about the Collectors, it buys me some time. Time I can use to get me out of the clutches of the CIA.

I drag in a breath. But I can't give Smith what I don't have, and I can't give him what I do. I can give him lip service because it's words and nothing tangible. And I've got skin in the game with regard to Trenton and my brother while Smith's very interested in the Collectors.

What I need to do is become something he likes enough to keep around. I have to worm my way in, disregard my feelings about him and focus on what makes him tick.

His daughter?

Sex?

Secrets?

Dammit, I don't know. I don't know much about him. What he likes, what his hobbies are. I know he's deadly, has a hunting, primal kink, can draw out orgasms like he's a magician, and he can make me melt with a touch.

The door opens, and I whirl around, jolted from my thoughts.

"You look..." Smith steps in before closing and locking the door.

"What?"

"Well, now you look fucking guilty. I was going to say delicious." He comes up to me, his familiar scent swirling under my nostrils. Thank God that he doesn't smell like pussy because I might be tempted to dismember him with my bare hands. He lifts the mask from my face, careful not to disturb the wig. "Maybe you're even more delicious because of that guilt. Plotting?"

"Your demise."

"Getting old, little girl. Especially when you keep giving up all the opportunities presented to you to run."

I gaze up at him. We're so close, and my entire being is pulsating heat through my veins. "You took the bullets away."

"I didn't particularly want to get shot again. It hurts. Makes a mess. Besides..." He kisses me, tongue entering my mouth for a slow, dreamy, and carnal kiss. "I took them out before we flew into Miami."

"Next time, leave them in."

"Fucking women. Crazy as bats on crack."

I toss the rum in his face. Then I throw the glass at him.

He catches it, licks his lips, and backs me into the chaise so that I'm teetering to keep my balance. "Or maybe it's just you."

The anxiousness builds, threatens to bubble over because of his words. He thought I was going to run. Fuck, should I have? "What—?"

"Calista," he says, moving closer. "you didn't run when you had the chance. Are you going to waste another opportunity to get out of here? Because if you don't take it, I can't promise what'll happen next."

CHAPTER 23
SMITH

We don't head back to the penthouse. I don't have any more business in Miami, and I need to take her to DC to hand her over.

Need to. Should do.

But... won't.

I'm not really a "do things on someone else's schedule" kinda guy.

Not that there's a schedule. Or at least one I'm privy to.

I think whoever wants her believes she won't be a problem to find.

Instead of the penthouse, we head to a jazz bar, a low-key place in the depths of Little Havana. It's dark and smoky with a different type of vibe than you'd find in New York.

"Why are we here?" she asks.

I slide my fingers around her hip, pulling her back against me where we sit in a shadowy corner. The cushions on the bench are worn and tattered along the seams, the tabletop splattered with sticky glass rings.

But from here, I can watch the door, stay mostly hidden, and try to figure out if we were followed.

I pull her onto my lap, loving the feel of her tight ass, warm and shapely in the confines of the dress. "I like the jazz scene."

She listens to the trumpet as someone starts on the sax, picking up the loose melody being created. Her nose wrinkles, spoiling her air of sophisticate and landing her in her correct age group, the era painted with techno beats, rappers, and annoying as fuck pop. "You like this?"

"Yes. Jazz is a passion, one I don't get to indulge in that often."

I don't tell her I float through one or two jazz dens in Jamaica, Queens, and on the Lower East Side.

"Really, Grandpa? You like this?"

"Yes, brat, I do. Even the open mic nights. Some of it's pretty good."

She looks at me a moment with a slightly dreamy expression that knocks me for a loop. I'm not sure what that look is or why it's suddenly appeared. Does she think she's seeing a small slice of what makes me tick?

I want to break it to her that everything she sees is me, on a certain level. She's suspicious of everything I tell her and rightly so. I'd be on my toes, too, if someone held me captive before threatening to turn me in to the authorities.

She just nods and the waitress comes over. I order Cuban rum. "For the nostalgia."

Anger flashes, replacing the dreamy look.

Shit, I'm a dick. An old, asshole of a dick, bringing up what happened there.

Calista shakes head, the red hair swishing. "I wish I could kill with my bare hands."

"This isn't a movie, Calista," I say. "There was no way you were getting out of that basement and away from those fucks."

"I wanted to see them bleed."

"I'd have paid to see you do that."

The waitress returns with the drinks, and I hand her a couple of twenties.

Calista's head tilts as she focuses on the stage where a woman in a fur stole and floor-length glittery dress joins in the instrumental ensemble with vocals.

Without looking at me, she says, "Well?"

I know what she wants. "Well, what?"

This time her head snaps around, her eyes shooting out a fiery glare. "What do you think I mean by 'well'?"

I ease her off my lap. Then I reach into my inner pocket, pull out the slender cigarette case, and light one up.

She frowns as I blow smoke into the air. The room's already got that smoky haze, the scent of cigarettes, weed, and even cigars. Calista's face is flushed with outrage and annoyance. I take another drag.

The cigarettes are for the game, smoking gives me a thing to do when watching someone and weighing them up. It occupies my hands, and I can stretch out moments while reading the room or specific people in it.

That's what I did downstairs at the club.

I'm smoking right now because I want desperately to kiss her, seduce her slowly, taking my time with her. I want to explore every inch and savor all of the newly discovered places, as well as slide into the ones I already know.

"I don't know."

Her fingers grip and jerk on her glass. "What—?"

"What I mean is, I don't know how it went. If it had been a game of chess, we'd have been in a stalemate." I blow out a stream of smoke, not really wanting the cigarette, but it makes me keep my hands to myself. "He wanted to see what I had, but more than that, wanted to know what I knew. And..." I shrug. "I don't know. Something was off. Could be he thought I was the one selling, looking to buy, and either he's still very much CIA, or he's off on his own. He's good enough that I couldn't tell."

She swallows. I watch as her delicate throat moves, watch as her chest lifts with a breath and she dances her fingers over her glass. "Maybe he is one of the good guys."

"And yet he threw you under the bus?"

I casually toss the card he gave me on the table. Lonnie Jenkins. Specialized Security. And then there's a number.

"Maybe." Calista doesn't touch it. "He could be good."

For a moment, the world shakes, and suddenly, I can't breathe. With numb fingers, I stub out the cigarette. Is she... *did* she?

But I catch the betrayal and doubt and hope on her face. There's not any indication of a broken or crushed heart. She wasn't ever into him. No, she's upset because she thinks maybe she was taken for a ride.

I don't know if she was. The man's good. Slick. Talented. And I can see them letting her cut teeth with an experienced agent because that's what her fucking Johnny CIA is. He's experienced and probably doesn't even need a handler.

I touch her shoulder as the music comes to a crescendo, and she shudders, rubbing into the small caress like a pet curling into her master.

I'm a hunter, not a man looking for a pet, human or otherwise. And then I smile. I suspect she'd gut me for thinking that.

"Whatever he's up to, I'll find out."

"Why?"

I shrug. "Curiosity. I want to help. Take your pick. I *will* need you to hand over what you have."

"I can't do that."

She can't, but she will. I know that. She's lost, scared, and wants something to cling to, to trust, and in her eyes the CIA isn't about to help. But maybe I can. Even if she's exonerated of whatever they think she did, her career there is dead in the water.

That's the best-case scenario.

Suddenly, the real reason we're here hits me hard—it was meant to be a detour to get her talking. In here, we have privacy and discretion. It's a safety net for her and she needs that if she's going to open up to me.

And I need her to. One thing I didn't expect from her agent was to get questions about sex trafficking in a club that has a reputation of high-end girls working voluntarily.

"Were you investigating trafficking?"

She goes too still, like she did when I asked about it the last time.

"The Collectors isn't a name thrown around," I add.

"I'm not sure about exactly everything they do, and no, we weren't investigating them. I didn't work in the trafficking areas."

I push. "What about Estonia?"

"I thought you read my file?"

"Most was redacted. Humor me."

She opens and closes her mouth, shifts, and I bring a hand down to rest on her thigh to settle her.

"You want to know why I'm interested?" I ask.

She wants to get beneath my layers so I'm going to let her in. Even deeper than I have before. And fuck, I hate that I'm doing it, that I'm exposing myself, but she needs to hear it.

To trust me.

"My kid, Dakota, pretty much hates me. I got someone to raise her after her grandparents died, a man named Alejandro.

She thinks of him as my friend, but the truth is, I handpicked him to protect her. He's got a daughter her age, and they both lived with him in New York."

My lips twist for this next part.

"Dakota came to Miami for a cruise and fell in with the wrong crowd. She caught the eye of a Collector and was kidnapped. They had her marked for use and abuse. Terrible things, fucking horrible things."

She claps a hand over her mouth. "Oh my God..."

"Dakota was saved by my friend, Orion, and we destroyed as much of the group as possible, but I have a vested interest in taking down whoever is left. I want to fucking bring down every last motherfucker. Did... did they..." Shit. I push the words out, even though they taste like shit on my tongue. "Touch you? Hurt you? Is that why you're so interested in finding them?"

She shakes her head. "My mother."

The words punch hard because so much makes sense to me now.

"I want..." She pauses, her fingers clenched into tight balls. "My brother and I don't know who our father is, but I've got suspicions. Henry doesn't care, but I do. Mom was groomed at fifteen, then got knocked up, had us, and..."

"Calista."

Her eyes cloud over. "After my mom had us, *he* got her back in with him, then in with others in his group. I think they were the Collectors. I don't know that much about them; there isn't much in the CIA databases. I found more on the dark web about them, and... and the trafficking." She nods at me. "Way worse than that, too. But this man... he... he dabbled with people marked as members of the Collectors. And I want him dead."

Things fall into place with alarming speed.

"According to my research, he's dead, but..."

Fuck. I try and tell myself not to get involved. But the words come before I can bite them back.

"Who is he, this supposedly dead, but maybe not dead guy? I have contacts."

"Jon Trenton."

Something in my chest tightens. I know the name but I stay silent.

"I... I saw an article about his wife opening a center in Manhattan. And I looked him up, dug into things. He's supposedly dead but he has accounts, secret accounts that only have his name as the owner. Trenton is the only person who can access them. His wife can't claim them, not without some kind of a legal blowup."

I shrug and keep my face neutral because the name, there's something about it that's familiar. Maybe because I read about the disgraced businessman's death. How he was broke at the time of his death, his business had crumbled around him. "I read that he was dead."

"People fake shit, you know that."

"I do."

"If he's linked to the Collectors, then..." She breathes in. "We're looking for the same thing. Th-that's what the Estonian thing was, a contact/hacker who supposedly had information. But I don't know what. I never got that far."

This is a way in. So I leave it where it is and don't push. Not because I care, but because too much can break someone. So instead, I let it lie.

For now.

We listen to the music, and out of the corner of my eye, as I gather her closer, I can see a man come in and stand near the bar.

He's generic.

THE TRUTHS THAT DECEIVE

And he's not looking in our direction. He's also not paying attention to the music, either.

He's here for us.

I lean down into her and kiss her ear. She makes things in my chest sing as she raises her head, lips on offer.

The dynamic between us is as thrilling as the chase. It's softness and submission, sharp bites and soothing purrs, innocence and carefully crafted moves.

"Someone's watching."

I order another round of drinks. More people will be in soon as the music changes for the late-night coked and boozed-up crowd.

"We wait?"

"Until the scene changes."

"Seems like," she says, "that's happening now."

"If he didn't recognize you, I'd rather keep it that way. Right now, I'm out with my new piece."

Her smile flirts. "So you want to drag that piece home and fuck it when it isn't moody and intimate?"

"You got it." I lean in. "You're not bad. For a piece."

"Your misogyny is showing."

I laugh. "Thank you."

"Not a compliment."

"You say that now..."

But she snuggles in, playing her part perfectly. After the drinks arrive, she says, "I know you have a heart in there, Smith, because you love your daughter. Why don't you make moves to fix the relationship?"

"I told you things weren't on good terms," I mutter.

"Yeah."

"She's marrying my friend, who wants me there, and she— I don't think she does. And I'd rather not go."

"Bullshit."

"Excuse me?"

Calista pulls back as more people pour into the place. The lighting starts to brighten, the music gets a little chirpier. "I don't buy that crap for a second."

"It isn't your business. But," I say, giving her something, "I wasn't there for her growing up. It was the safest thing for her, but I wasn't a constant in her life. I protected her by being the asshole missing father. And no, I don't think I'm going to the fucking wedding."

She stares at me, not moving. "You want to go."

"No. I don't."

"You do."

The music picks up, and I stand, dropping some cash on the table. "Come on, we have to go. Now."

It's time to leave Miami, so we head to a private airfield and board the waiting plane.

"Is this one going to blow up?" Her smart mouth makes me smile.

"Nah, I limit blown-up planes to one a week. Otherwise, it turns into a paperwork nightmare."

She rolls her eyes, then turns to climb the stairs up to the plane.

Calista curls up and falls asleep in one of the plush leather recliners almost immediately. Watching her in that state is endlessly fascinating. I let my mind wander, play over the evening to see if anything jumps out about her Johnny, but I keep returning to one thing.

What I said at the jazz club.

About Dakota.

I said it to get closer to her and gain her trust. That was the plan.

But it festers in my mind because I realize that it was the most honest I've been with anyone in a long time.

A very long time.

And it's the type of honesty I never thought I'd share again.

CHAPTER 24
CALISTA

O f all the places I expect him to take me to, the last one is a gorgeous three-story house in Brooklyn's Park Slope.

The sun's starting to spread a little light into the horizon, and even though I slept on the plane, I'm exhausted. But I'm still not exactly ready to pass out. My nerves jitter too much for that.

At least we're not in DC.

He hasn't handed me over.

Yet.

Smith shows me around the place—living area and kitchen on the first floor, study and a more informal living room on the second, a gym, and finally a top floor that houses a master bedroom with a balcony. He takes me back down to the second floor and opens a door I didn't see the first time around, one that leads to a spare room and an en suite bathroom.

"You can have this." He rubs the back of his neck. "I don't have any clothes for you."

"Is this your way of telling me you want me naked?"

"This is my way," he says, frowning, "of saying I'll have stuff delivered. Let me find you something to sleep in."

"Smith..."

He's halfway to the door when he stops and comes back over to me. I ease my aching feet out of the stupid heels. Superpower or not, it's time to turn back into Clark Kent.

"Yeah?"

"What are you planning to do?"

"Depends on you. Are you going to run?"

"I..." He's not asking about a sexual game or even about him chasing me down. It's a weird trust question. At least, I think it is. "I don't know."

"Your brother goes to school here."

My heart hammers. "I'm not about to put Henry in danger."

"Good to know."

"Are you asking me for a truce?" I ask.

The wig's off and he smooths fingers through my hair, the heat of him spiraling down into my flesh and bones.

Smith shifts the conversation. "I can work with you to see if this guy Trenton is alive, as long as you help with the information on the Collectors and any other big red flag sex traffickers."

I frown. "Aren't they all red flag?"

"You'd be surprised."

My stomach twists and turns. He smells of sin, darkness, and smoke. Just at the edges.

I don't know if his cynicism is making my defenses rise or if I'm turned on by his closeness.

Maybe both.

"And the weapon?" I ask.

"That you don't know anything about."

"Smith."

He lets out a deep sigh. "I'm not sure yet. There's interest, and..." He stops, steps back, and runs a hand through his hair. "The people I work with, they're interested, too. But the destruction or betrayal of the United States isn't exactly in our wheelhouse. This is my country and home. I'll fucking defend it with my last breath. So if you're thinking I'm going to do the wrong thing here, I say that mistrust is fired right back at you."

"I wouldn't!"

His smile is grim. "Exactly." He leans in. "I'm asking for a ceasefire between you and me, and then we can see."

I don't ask about what. I don't dare.

"And?"

"If I give you access to a computer, you'll help me with anything to do with the Collectors?"

I stare up at him. I need that help, too. Symbiosis. I get what I can find on the dark web, dig into people, and he... he can open doors. "To bring them down?"

"Fuck yes." Smith paces a moment. "And you won't run?"

I give him a slanted look. "What if I do?"

"There's a time for play, Calista, and today isn't it. Stay in."

"Where are you going?"

"Out."

~

AFTER MY SHOWER, I find a laptop lying on my bed along with some clothes. Just shorts and a T-shirt, probably used for running or the gym. They're clean but old, with small holes and worn patches in parts.

One thing I've learned about Smith is that he's meticulous. And he dresses perfectly for every occasion. If he thinks the clothes as is will stop me from running, then he doesn't have the handle on me he thinks he has.

I dress quickly and walk toward the front door. I grasp the handle, analyzing the four locks. They look easy enough to break through. An alarm system sits on the foyer's wall to the right but there's no flashing light. Maybe it's off.

I could be out of here in seconds.

It's a test, a trap.

A man like Smith wouldn't leave me in here without setting a trap.

Plus, I remind myself, there's an opportunity where I could maybe make things right. A possibility that I could destroy a monster and all of the people who had something to do with my mother's death.

Revenge is a dish best served cold. So they say, whoever the hell "they" are.

And...

"Is there anywhere to hide from him?" I mutter to myself.

Maybe, maybe not. But I can use him. The computer. So I drop my hand and head back up the stairs. I hit the gym for an hour, and then when I've worn away the aggression and anger and all the other emotions festering inside, I grab the laptop and go to the living room to work.

The very first thing I do is send Henry a message. He won't respond. It's just a post online in a freecycle site, for a book. *Scary Stories for Cool Kids.* A book that we had as kids. It's out of print, and I put up the price for it to thirty-nine dollars. Our code for safe and sound. Ninety-one is trouble, and so on. It's something we've always used. He'll see it. No one will think twice.

Henry's got a hefty collection of old books, so we decided long ago it's the perfect cover. He's always had online alerts for various books, some he just watches, wanting perfect editions. And some other ones? It became a way for us to talk without anyone else knowing.

Then I check up on Senator Riley, but there's no message. But one thing I won't dare do is open my own apps, the ones I just designed for laughs, and the ones hiding code for the things I collected on the weapon.

When I'm done, I lose myself in the dark web, so much so that I jump when the pressure changes in the room right as Smith speaks.

"Anything good?"

I set the computer down, then stand on shaky legs. "Not really. Chatter is chatter. Nothing noteworthy that I can see."

His mouth quirks but the smile doesn't reach his blue eyes. "You didn't look at what you have, did you?"

"What good is doing that? It's puzzle pieces." Some are from Johnny. Intel from him he asked me to hold on to. But the other stuff I found, poked into?

I wanted it because I like puzzles, because I'm a hacker.

I didn't think it through.

"Let me ask you something," Smith says. "Did you sell smaller blueprints that already are circulating as hardware on the market?"

"No." I shoot him a glare. "Just—"

"Just?"

"I have information that hasn't left me." My hand curls. "No one else has seen any of it."

"Like encoded blueprints probably meant for higher-ups." He shakes his head as he straightens his tie. "You fucking..."

"Idiot, yeah. I know how it looks," I say quietly, "but I didn't steal, I didn't do... the things it looks like."

"Like you took what you could to sell to the highest bidder, you and Johnny? Or that maybe you had Johnny killed? We know he's not dead, but does the CIA?"

I give him a sharp look.

Smith raises a dark brow. "I'm playing Devil's advocate. Don't look at me like I murdered your best friend."

"Did you?" I ask, swallowing.

His expression changes to curious as he goes to the small bar and pours a drink. But he just holds the glass. "Do you? Have one?"

Yes, I want to hurl at him. *My brother.* But I don't. He's my twin, my family, but he also has a life I've never had or wanted. Computers were my escape, and when I did have friends, I...

When.

A shudder passes through me. And I look down at my hands. This is stuff he could easily look up, no doubt the CIA has a full-on dossier of who I've befriended all the way back to kindergarten. "No, I... Shit, I don't have any friends, not anymore." To my horror, my lip trembles.

"Could be worse, you could have me."

A small sob breaks free. I don't know why. At all.

Smith sighs and sets down his untouched drink. "It's been a long two days. Come here."

And I do.

Why, I don't know. But he's got a hold on me. The thing inside me that keeps me separate from others, that creates the little moat around me crumbles, and I stand in front of him, gazing upward.

"Fuck," he mutters, rubbing a thumb under my eye and the tear that's probably there. "Don't. I didn't... I'm not good with kids."

I'm not wearing shoes. It doesn't stop me. I slam my foot down, hard as I can on his, and then I spring back. "I'm not a kid."

"You're twenty-four."

"And lived a life that most thirty-four-year-olds haven't, so don't patronize me, old man." I shove him for good measure. "You're not good with *people*."

Smith captures my hands. "True. But you're fucking ornery as shit."

"Asshat."

"Come here."

"Why?" I whisper. "So you can pull down my barriers and make me like you before you hand me over?"

"No, we both know you might want me, but like me? It'll never happen."

We stare at each other, and he rests his head lightly against mine.

"Maybe," he adds, "I just need to forget all the shit for a night."

"Go raid an old people's home."

"Banned."

Laughter bubbles free. "Because you're a pervert."

"I know."

We're spinning, orbiting each other, keeping away from the reality of the situation, the truth of why I'm here and what he's going to do. And that nagging voice in my head keeps barking about how he wants all my information, not just on the Collectors, but the weapons.

But right now, it's all outside the window, looking in. The questions, the fears, and heat pulsates in me, throbbing deep, sending tingling, sweeping sensations along my skin.

His fingers skim the line of my jaw and my head tips up.

Smith kisses me.

It's slow and both without reason and full of intention. It's a kiss that wants and also gives. And I sink into it, kissing him back, mouth open, tongue seeking his. They touch, dance, and a thrill slides through me.

When he lifts his head, my feet are barely touching the

ground and my heart's slamming hard against my ribs. I want to kiss him again. Right or wrong, I want more.

He's already untangling from me. And I hit the earth again. "Do you want something to eat?"

"No. I raided your kitchen earlier."

"Of course you did."

If anyone peeked in, this would seem to be a mundane moment of domestic bliss. But underneath? Wild things. "Where were you?"

Smith shakes his head. "I'm fucking tired. And you should grab another nap. We have things to do tomorrow." He stops. "I'm not handing you over. Not yet. You're helping me and I got nowhere today."

"If we have a truce—"

"I had meetings, and there are more tonight. And you? You'll continue to pretend to be my wife or sex toy, depending on where we are."

"Really," I say dryly.

"Really. You're the one insisting all hands on deck." Then he pulls a list from his pocket. "See what you can find on these names."

I take the list and spread it open.

My breath catches in my throat.

I know who some of these people are.

Collectors.

CHAPTER 25
SMITH

The list is a test. One she passes quickly. And her expression tells me she knows that's exactly what it is.

"Do you have any more meaningless tests for me?"

"Do you need them?" I counter.

Her face turns arctic, tinged with a little volcanic activity, and her hard gaze hooks into me deep.

"You need to be whipped, hung, maybe even quartered."

"Add some boiling oil and it'll be a party."

"You're a sick fuck."

"So are you," I say, dropping my voice. I place the scotch down on the desk in my study where I was just going to set up for the evening. Outside it's already getting dark, but this is New York. Things don't get started until at least nine o'clock or so.

"I think I'm just going to take my chances." She narrows her eyes. "Alone."

I'm up fast and around the desk. I capture her arm and

walk her back to the sofa. She teeters and pitches forward, but I tighten my hold. Keeping her drawn up against me, the scent of citrus and spice swirling and teasing the air.

She doesn't even wear perfume. It's just her.

"You're not going anywhere."

Her eyes get stormier, glimmering with a wild heat. "Try and stop me."

"That your fucked-up way of issuing an invitation?"

Calista lifts her chin and sways into me. "Are you looking for one?"

Earlier when I stupidly kissed her, fires were lit. All kinds of fires. Because it wasn't a kiss with an agenda. It was just a kiss that took on life and flared. It's still there, in the air, and I can feel the aftermath of it in me still, the beat of wild, carnal lust, the urge for more.

And she...

She suddenly swoops in and bites me through my shirt. Her mouth's hot and wet, teeth sharp and delicious as they sink sharply into the flesh of my chest.

"Let go, please..."

Her whisper has something in there, a note that pleads, one that begs for freedom.

I loosen my hand and she slides down the length of me, kissing her way down over my rapidly growing erection. Then she bites my thigh as she unbuttons my trousers.

"Fucking little..." Laughter rumbles up inside of me. "Sweetheart, you're the most intriguing prey I've ever met."

"Not prey."

We both know it's a lie.

She shoves me, and I go willingly onto the sofa, letting her free my now iron-hard cock.

I let her because there's something fucking powerful in a

woman who thinks she's utterly in control, who takes the chance to dive right into the den with the bigger, wilder animal.

"Well, then, Mrs. Hunter," I say, "do your best."

She slides her hands up over me, pulling on my cock and making me dig my fingers into the soft linen cushions. And then she looks up at me, eyes glittering with a feral light, one that makes me growl low in the back of my throat.

She licks me.

From my balls all the way up to the tip. And fuck, does it feel phenomenal.

My kiss earlier softened the boundaries that she winds tight around her. But this... I don't know if she thinks this will buy her time or a way out, or if she just can't help herself. Or even if it's a combination of all those things. I don't even know if it matters, because in this moment, those boundaries dissolve away.

"Swallow me down, little girl," I say.

My voice is calm, pure fucking silk. But I'm teetering on the edge, because her touch, her hands, her tongue... all of it is something I need more than the most crazed addict needs his next fix.

It's been too long. Even though it's not been that long at all.

"I'm doing what I want," she says as she starts to suck my balls into her mouth.

I almost fucking come on the spot.

I bite down on my lip to stop the words from tumbling out, just like I keep my hands digging into the sofa to stop them from guiding her, directing her, and giving myself what I need and want with her.

This is exhilarating and the suck and pull on my balls is like nothing else. It's torture and pleasure, all wrapped into one.

She releases them with a small pop and starts to lick and suck her way up my shaft, up over the top as her hand moves, giving that right amount of tension and friction and she starts all over again. Each suck, each pop, each lick and drive down of her mouth on me to the back of her throat is more intense than the last.

I can't take any more. I grab her, hand tangling in her hair as I drag her head up, and I kiss her hard. Then I take all the control, pushing her back down, guiding my cock into her mouth and I start to fuck her, the gagging music, her eager sucks pure jazz.

I'm going to come, I'm— Fuck. I explode into her mouth and she laps up everything I have to give.

"You're a dirty girl, Calista," I mutter, rising and pulling her up with me. "Why did you let me do that?"

"I wanted to."

Taking her mouth again, I drag her all the way up into my arms, and she wraps her legs around my waist. I kick off my pants and carry her toward her room. "Why?"

She takes my face in her hands. "You're hot, and I figured maybe you'd fall for me and not be able to let me go. I mean, look at me in this outfit."

Her self-deprecation makes me smile. What she doesn't get is I am fucking looking at her and she's gorgeous. I bet there's a slew of guys still masturbating into socks over her. And she has no idea they ever lusted for her in the first place.

"Yeah," I say, matching her. "I'm hotter than fuck. But you won't fall for me, obviously."

I throw her on the bed. And her little grin is worth the world. "Obviously. I don't even like you."

"And you're a pain in my ass."

"But men think with their cocks, Smith."

"Mine's got a PhD." I draw her bottom lip into my mouth

215

as I lean down over her, sucking it before letting it go. "This buys you a couple of hours."

I strip her and dive down to taste her tits, the soft, sweet flesh with those hard fucking nipples I could suck and bite all day.

It's not enough. I need to be inside of her. I roll us so she's on top because I like her thinking she's in control. Even though this is just banter, I can hear the need in her voice, and I meant what I said earlier. She's been through a lot. Maybe she needs the vanilla. And I can deal with it.

It's *her*.

She rubs her cunt up along my cock, her juices soaking down around me.

"I'll take it," she says.

I draw her down and kiss her as she grabs my cock, lining me up and sinking that tight, wet cunt down onto me. I thrust into her heat and pull her close.

The kiss is hot and turns explosive. My flesh heats, the need for more consumes me whole.

She fucks herself on me, grinding down, taking me all the way into her, rolling up and almost out, only to repeat it all. Her clit slides against my cock, and each time she comes down, it's like catching a glimpse of God.

My blood burns with each push and pull and my balls ache for release. It's almost too much, letting her have that control.

She rides me hard, trying to reach her peak, trying to come, and I can't take it a second longer. I grab her hips and circle her over me, hitting her G-spot. Her pussy quivers and quakes, her juices drowning my cock.

And I'm not going to be able to make it. I'm not—

"Oooh God..." she screams, her cunt spasms so hard on my cock that I come. Hard and deep into her as she comes, too. It's wild.

Fucking divine.

Something rare.

Addictive.

Ours.

When we come down from the euphoric high, I roll her over and give her what she needs. The kisses are soft and gentle before they get more demanding and pleading, and it's not long before we're both hungry for more.

And when I'm ready to slide into her again, I know... *I know...* for the first time that I can remember, it's going to be slow and tender and all about her.

Only about Calista.

It was a shitty thing to do, taking advantage of her.

It's been a couple of hours and I'm sliding a pod into the coffee machine in the kitchen.

I lean against the counter, rubbing a hand over my eyes. In the bedroom, she's sleeping, naked, twisted in the covers because she's a restless sleeper. Although it seems like that restlessness set in when I got up. Before that, she...

Shit. What the fuck's wrong with me, giving her an almost loving touch? Even if it's designed to do a job? I knew, regardless of what a woman likes in the realms of sex, someone younger like Calista was going to respond to that. My vanilla fucking with a gentler touch designed to tear down more barriers without her noticing.

I know how to work my prey.

Weird thing is, I didn't hate it.

I could feel the silk of her skin under my fingertips, the warmth of her as she snuggled down against me, the heat and tightness of her cunt, the way she stretched to fit my cock, the way she squeezed my dick into orgasm as she came.

Yeah, I didn't hate that at fucking all.

We're on borrowed time, because I do need to hand her over. No one's come knocking, yet. Her field agent didn't seem to recognize her in Miami, and I'm not sure what team he's playing for yet, his own or the government's. I do know he's gathering intel and he's set up meetings after checking my creds.

Interested parties want to talk, and I'm passing those along to Jones, since they're weapons related. Bolivia was mentioned, a tiny country that's somehow been involved the entire time. Although I still can't get my head around Bolivia mixed up in a new US military weapon as well as trafficking and low-rent porn with unwilling girls.

I mean, sure, the girls with fucking guns is a thing. But that's not the same as kidnapped or trafficked girls in shitty porn for fucknuts with cash, along with a side interest in illegal and highly classified blueprints for a new weapon.

Not to mention Marta's mention of some parts already having been made and sold. I make a mental note to look into that. But if I'm honest, I'm really not overly interested in the weapons angle. It'll be taken care of, and that isn't my job.

Calista's no traitor.

What I want is to use her as a way to follow my agenda. Destroy the fucks leftover from the Collectors, or whatever this new arm is.

It seems that's what Calista wants, too.

So I'm going to use that borrowed time to find out who's trafficking and using Bolivia as part of the cover. And I'm going to find out what Collectors are still operating. There are some we left, I know that. But I keep an eye on them.

This isn't *them*.

There are others.

I've showered and changed, and there's an outfit for Calista here. I have more clothes for her at my penthouse in the West Village. Because that's a better base for my next phase.

"Plotting?"

She comes into the kitchen, wearing my shirt. Only my shirt.

And my fucking pants start getting tight.

"Kind of," I say. "There's an event tonight. If you want to come."

She goes still.

"You're not handing me over?"

"Not yet."

We circle each other, wary.

"So we have a truce?" she asks. "What about Johnny?"

"What about my list?"

She frowns, picks at the edge of the clean kitchen island, then shrugs. "Most are dead or have clipped wings. It's clear they're watched and on good behavior. They're too clean. But there are others."

Her glaze flickers at me before she disappears to grab the computer. She walks back into the kitchen just as the scent of coffee fills the air. She takes my cup, so I make another and stare at the screen.

Names and activities and... shit.

Our gazes meet. "Why the fuck are these names showing up as building things in Bolivia?"

There are four. They've all got affiliations to the Collectors —tenuous but there—and now they're in New York. Two are on the list for the event tonight.

The opening of a new office building for a nonprofit.

One of those boring places where all kinds of deals go down.

"I don't know," she says. "What's on tonight?"

"Have you heard of Senator Aaron Riley?"

Her eyes widen. "Yes. He's in town?"

"Yeah. Opening a nonprofit." I look at her. "Want to go?"

A flush of color stains her cheeks. "Just try and stop me."

CHAPTER 26
CALISTA

My blood bubbles as I stare at the senator. He's as good-looking and respectable as always.

I try not to fiddle with the rings Smith gave me on the car ride from Brooklyn.

Smith never asked me why I basically jumped him.

Maybe he knows I'm trying to ingratiate myself on a faux intimate level to slow down the inevitable handoff.

Riley could be my downfall or no help at all. As it is, he looked at me once and didn't even blink or acknowledge me. The building we're at could be any high-end luxurious and discreet business. The brass plate on the outside reads Grey and Associates. It looks like a law firm or an arm of some kind of moneymaker that needs a tax write-off.

A perfect cover for all sorts of illegal goings-on. One of those impossibly monied nonprofits that are layered in so much gauze that whoever they help changes on the daily, and the real nuts and bolts of the true business are hidden.

I'd need to get hold of their computer servers to find out more.

"But that isn't your job," I mutter, trying not to jump every time someone looks my way.

Rich people stuff is nearly always dipped in shady practices. Or worse.

Smith catches my eye. He's talking to one of the names he gave me from that list, or rather, an associate of that person. The only reason the name Jean Wentworth stands out is because she's linked to Trenton. On paper and in passing. But still. There's information there.

Her ties to Bobby Moore, a man with money in Bolivia and relationships with the Collectors, is stronger. She used to be his secretary before leaving to start her own business.

I sip the wine in my glass.

I'm no field agent, but I can hold my own. I just don't like exposure, and people looking at me makes me incredibly paranoid. It's probably why my hair's usually wild like my clothes; people look at that and don't see *me*.

But not now.

Now they look.

Except Riley, who—

I stop and frown. Wait, where is he? I turn and take a canapé from a passing waiter as I search the room. Over to the right and down a darkened hall, I can see him in his dark-blue suit with a man I don't recognize.

Slowly, I make my way over, weaving through people. Light music plays in the background.

I can't help but do the rookie thing and look back for Smith. I hold my breath until I see that he's not there. A wave of relief passes through me. Not relief that I can run, because I'm not an idiot, but relief that I can focus, maybe do something, find a way out.

I slip into the hall.

I have a story. I am looking for the bathrooms. I know

damn well they're in the other direction. We're about twelve stories up, on the executive floor. As I follow down the hall with voices leading my way, I hear the ding of an elevator and the senator's smooth tones of, "I'll see what I can do."

When the doors slide closed, I step into the hallway. Riley stands there, the back of his head bent as he stares at the screen of his phone. "Aaron?"

He whirls to face me and a muscle tics in his jaw. "Who—"

"You know who I am."

His gaze darts around, and then he hurries over and grabs my arm. "My silence was a hint, Calista. You're wanted and there's not much I can do to help."

The unsaid part is so loud it makes me want to slap hands over my ears.

"Unless you give me information, help expose—"

Those are the words left hanging in the air between us.

"You're the one with a missing agent and stolen blueprints. If you'd sent them to me, I could have helped." Riley pulls me in close and it takes everything to keep my face as neutral as I can. I asked him for help. He knows something. I can feel it. But he moved into politics and...

Fear bites cold and deep.

And this is an indicator of just how much trouble I'm in.

Because he hasn't lifted a finger to help. And now he knows I'm here.

Fuck.

"Where did you hide all the information? Right now, it looks like you've committed treason. I can't help without you helping me. Who else did you get involved? Last I heard, you were in Germany, on the run. If you give me the hard drive or thumb drive with everything I need, I'll help. And that will also help your brother."

It'd be so easy. I trust Riley. He saved me from a life either behind bars or so stripped back, I might as well have been imprisoned. He recruited me, became my mentor. He's way more trustworthy than Smith.

So why is the fear chewing on my bones, making them numb?

And why am I not giving him even a crumb of information?

His phone screen lights up and I can see it's a text before he has a chance to pull it away. Bolivia jumps out at me, and the entire text is in that Balto-Slavic language.

Riley pockets the phone. "Who are you here with?"

"I came looking for you. I read... I saw you were here, and I thought I'd come to ask for your help. Can I get your card?"

His gaze catches on my finger with the rings on it but he doesn't respond. I need to get out of this before he calls for backup, before he takes down my chance... Smith. I force myself to breathe slow and steady. "Card, Aaron? A number to reach you on."

He reaches into his pocket and my heart's slamming against my ribs so hard I worry he'll hear. But all he does is hand me a heavy card made of high-grade cotton. "I need those blueprints."

"We'll talk."

"I'm only here until tomorrow. Call by seven in the morning."

And before I can say anything, he hits the Down button, and when it arrives, he steps inside. I look forward, long after the doors shut.

"Ten out of ten for composure, sweetheart."

My legs wobble at the low, deep tones of Smith, that smoky, dark jazz of him winding around me. I know it's dangerous, but right now, he's comfort, and when he touches me, I melt into the arms that close around me.

His mouth brushes the top of my head. "He asked for the blueprints, huh?"

"Aaron was—"

"CIA. Not in any of the areas I worked, so I don't think he knows me, and I've been out a long time."

"Yes, but I meant he was my mentor. He recruited me and... Smith?"

I raise my head as he drops a kiss on my lips. It's for show but I take it, hold it close because I need the magic of that caress, even if it's not genuine, even if it's a lie.

"On his phone? I saw the word Bolivia. And it was in that language."

His fingers rub over my hand, touching the card I've got clenched in it. "You're not meeting him."

"He wants blueprints."

"Of course he does. I'll tie you up if you even think of meeting him."

"He knows I'm here," I whisper, pulling back. "That means time is—"

"Not to be wasted on panic. We spend a little more time in here, and then we're going out."

"Where?"

"O-Ring."

I just stare at him. Anything with that as a name has to be some kind of sex club. And he grins slowly. It's a feral grin. One that drips with promises and intent. "Like the thing used in sex? Is this another sex club?"

"Smart girl," he says, spinning me and pinning me to the wall like lovers, but he's not anywhere near that to me. "I've got some meetings scheduled. I need to make an appearance."

"Smith—"

"Calista." His gaze rakes my features as one leg slides up between my thighs. I'm wearing a slinky black dress that's sexy, simple, and when he does what he's doing, he shows just how thin the material is, how with a touch he can make me feel naked and exposed.

Or maybe that's just him. And my God, I want to rub myself against him. All over him.

"Fuck, I can feel the heat of your sweet pussy, and I'm betting you're wet. Ever think of taking up sweet femme fatale as a side hustle?"

"I don't think that's a thing," I say. "And why are we at some stupid boring party instead of—?"

I stop before the words leave my mouth.

But he picks up the slack as he shifts his leg, lifting it to rub against me. "Fucking wet. I can feel you." He drops his head to my throat, lips skimming my flesh, his tongue shifting over a spot where he's bitten, making me way too aware of all the things we've done. "Instead of running? Instead of finding out about who's responsible for the weapons? What's your game? Because you know what the end is here."

"I told you. I want to bring down the bastard who raped my mother."

"The bastard who might be your father? The bastard who might be dead?"

"The bastard who might be alive," I correct. "And if we do that, if I can find the wife and then him, and you promise to make sure my brother's okay, then you can have all the stuff I have. Whatever it all is."

Some of it's the blueprints, some of it might be a coded buyers' list. I don't know. I'm not sure I want to know. Because I can almost hear his next words before he says them.

"I've got eyes on your brother. Protection," he says. "Whatever you have's worth money. And taking people down with the stuff you have is gonna take more time than you have."

The first and last lines tell me everything I need to know.

His fingers slip under my chin as he raises it. "You hear me, right? I'll make sure your brother's okay, but we don't have time to solve a mystery of the weapons buyer and save you. It's got to be one or the other, Calista."

My heart stops. The breath rushes out.

"What are you saying?"

"That if you help me with the Collectors, give me all you have as payment, I just might help you get out of this alive."

My knees buckle and he slips a hand around my waist. "Come on."

I want to ask. A billion questions crowd my brain.

But in pure Smith form, he doesn't let me. Instead, he moves us down the hall, back to the party. He hands me a scotch after taking two glasses from a passing tray. I sip it gratefully, preferring the leathery smoke of the hard liquor to the sour bubbles of the champagne.

He loops an arm around me, pulling me against the hard lines of him. "I know you feel like you're spinning your wheels when danger creeps in. You want to do something. Run, seek it out, hide, pick a fight. Shit, any and all the above, but none of that's going to help from getting in deeper than you already are."

"I don't know if I can stop it all." My voice trembles and I hate that he can see through me.

"What were you doing in Germany?" He pauses. "Unless you were planning to sell to the highest bidder, which I doubt, you were spinning your wheels as you got information on your maybe father, Trenton. Now you're closer so it all seems to be pushing at your door, but let me work my magic so we can move forward. The CIA wants, but they haven't pushed in and ripped everything down for you. What does that say?"

"They're either watching or I'm not high on their list. Or

they're confident they'll eventually get me." I take a shuddering breath. "I'm going to the bathroom."

I don't give him a chance to say anything. I down my drink and move toward the restrooms.

When I find the big, opulent room, I lock myself in a stall, sink down on the toilet, and put my feet up against the door. My eyes float closed, my breathing slow.

Maybe the CIA isn't coming after me, guns blazing, because they know who has me.

That one leaves a bitter taste. And that's the problem. I don't trust Smith.

But... I want to.

I just want to curl up and sleep without worry, to feel his body there next to me, knowing he has my back. But only one person has that. Me.

Smith...

He's got his own agenda, and we're both playing each other. That tires me to the core.

If I could play sex games, have him chase me down, fuck him wherever, whenever, however we want, I would. No holds. No strings. Just hot, twisted sex that borders on controlled... I don't know what to call the real deep primal games. It's not nonconsensual, it's not dubious. It's a careful setup of rules and safe words, and then exploration of dark desires in perimeters.

Letting go with someone like Smith in that would be incredible. I've had a taste and yeah, I want more. Just like—God help me—I want that dark and sweet vanilla sex we had.

I want it all.

And if I could just indulge, I would.

But the strings are thin and strong and tangled. The strings and agendas we both have as we play each other make me want to scrub the sordid off.

And I don't even mean the sex.

I mean the nasty little mind games of fake trust. He under-estimates me because of my age and I... I'm still trying to work out what I underestimate about him.

Maybe I'm afraid to find out because it'll turn out that I underestimated how little he cares about me, and how far he'll go to get what he wants.

I'm playing with pure poison and it's dangerously addictive.

The door to the bathroom opens.

"No. I'll be there," a female voice says sharply "I have the payment... I want this dealt with, too."

Water flows from the sink faucet, then stops. The door opens and closes again. I push open the stall door. Whoever it was is gone. I hurry out of the ladies' room because I want to see who it was. I can't explain it, I just need to find her.

It's not until I step foot in the hall that a woman in mid-discussion with a man looks right at me. The shock on her face tells me everything, and it matches my own.

She turns on her heel and takes off down the hall.

It has to be the woman from the bathroom. I don't wait. I run after her, and when the elevator closes on her, I hit the stairs because I know who it is.

Felicity Trenton.

Jon Trenton's wife.

CHAPTER 27

SMITH

Her flight down the stairs is thrilling, unexpected. And I wait, counting seconds, giving her the time to think she's lost me when what she's done sinks into her pretty little brain.

Calista's run and unintentional invitation beats in my veins. The rings have trackers, but I don't open them. I'm aware of her, my senses heightened whenever she's near.

This isn't a run from me, she's after Trenton's widow.

For answers.

But it doesn't look like Trenton's wife is willing to dish them out judging by the way she moves.

Jones is waiting at the Obsidian Knight headquarters, but any meetings aren't planned to start just yet. He has, through Reaper, a copy of some of the blueprints. They're probably the pieces that have hit the market. Jones can turn the smallest thing into nuggets of vied-for gold. Even if I didn't make it to the meeting, I highly doubt it would matter.

I will.

But right now, I have this to deal with.

My blood's bubbling, and I'm ready to hunt down my meal.

I head for the private elevator that's tucked away and take it down to the ground floor, just beating the main one, just beating her. I want to cut it close, to watch where she goes. This time, I'll trust instinct over tracker.

She's about half a street ahead of me. Moving fast but carefully. Different than Berlin, but I can pick her style.

Calista's trained. She can tail. But the rest of it, what makes her so good is an innate need for anonymity. It's why she hides behind a computer. She likes to find things, track things, do things without being seen. It's security, and it offers her different ways of peering into other lives.

She's too pretty to vanish, and to me she's a fucking beacon of light that draws the eye, sets all instincts quivering.

More than once, I need to move deeper into the shadows as I follow her. More than once she turns a corner and I have to trust my instincts.

She's closing in on Trenton's widow. And she is his widow. A quiet word with Mercer earlier today, and he confirmed that the man's dead.

"I killed him," he'd said.

And I believe him. There was no need for him to lie.

So now I'm intrigued about those accounts.

On paper, his widow changed her last name and runs a few centers for recovery, yoga, all that new age fucking shit. And she comes from her own money.

Mercer decimated the dead man's accounts. I didn't ask why. I can surmise, though, and I already know from Orion the guy was a friend of his and Ivy's family. Not hard to put it all together.

Mercer killed the guy because the man did something to Ivy.

And now Calista's tailing his widow in hopes she'll find the prick who raped her mother, the dead prick who's more than likely her father.

The woman turns onto Greene Street. At this time of night, SoHo's quiet, the shoppers gone. Not much nightlife here. An older, distinguished man comes out of a building.

Calista physically gasps and I can see her body quake like she got a shock.

We both know who the man is, and if I let her do what I think she's going to do, she'll crash and burn whatever's going on.

I move fast.

Swooping in, I grab her, haul her up into my arms, and I kiss her, spinning her until we're against the recessed door of a fancy store. I pin her hands behind her back, dropping the other from her waist to slide between her legs where I stroke up and over the seam of her pussy.

The lace is wet, and it doesn't take much to push aside, even less to shove two fingers into her. Then I press the heel of my hand against her clit.

"What the fuck are you doing, sweetheart?"

"Get off me."

"Not what you were saying earlier when you were licking my cock like it was your favorite lollipop. Remind me to buy you one. Or maybe some flavored lube. Toys?" Shit. Focus! "What the fuck are you doing?"

She moans low and half pushes me away, half pulls me to her, and I'm betting myself she's fighting herself over her safe word. Calista both wants to use it and wants to ask for more.

I curl my fingers inside of her and start a slow stroke that hits her G-spot as I slide out and push back in, keeping the movements steady, changing pressure with the rhythm of her breathing.

It takes everything I have to concentrate on my surroundings, to use every fucking piece of training.

Only problem is, no training can prepare a man for the power of Calista.

But I do it, and the shadow passes by us without a look.

It's only then my body relaxes, and I lean into the stroke of her velvet insides, the squeeze of that tight pussy. The heat. Her wetness and then I breathe her in, letting the intoxicating scent of sex weave its spell.

Her hips move into each slide of my fingers.

"I'm waiting, Calista."

"Stop." Her hips rock into me, fingers bite my arms.

"Not the right word."

"I hate you."

"That's three and boring to boot. What did you think you'd accomplish with confronting—"

"She's Jon Trenton's wife."

"Widow. Changed her name to Everton. I think it's her maiden name."

She gasps and clutches at my arm, and so I slow because she's tight, getting tighter as blood rushes and makes her sensitive walls swell. I don't want her to come.

I want her to stay on the cusp.

I want to toy with my pretty, delicious prey.

The intimate chase shifts and twists into something new. I'm taunting her, leading her to me and holding everything she wants just out of reach. Her orgasm is mine, and I dangle it, playing with her.

"Confronting her," I whisper as I lick her earlobe, "will get you nowhere. She thinks he's dead. What are you going to do? Announce who you are?"

"She... oh fuck... she was with..."

I lick just inside her ear and her cunt spasms once, twice, I pull back and let the peak slide back down to a simmer. "With the senator. Your mentor. And you thought what? Confront them both with one stone? We both know what he wants, don't we?"

She looks up at me, so close that her breath bleeds heat onto my skin, and the faint scent of scotch tickles my senses. Her silence is a damning yes.

And she's caught, tangled in everything.

"Why does he know her?" Calista asks, not answering. "He might know where her husband is."

"Sweetheart..." I stop, stroke her into, shifting my fingers so I've also got her ass involved, and she thrusts against them at both ends, slowly coming apart.

Her damn husband's dead. But I don't push it. "Riley's got a noose, and he wants to see how well you're going to fit it on yourself for him. Because you walk up to him in front of someone else and he'll wrap it right around your neck. You're a fucking gift. If he brings you in..."

"No, he wouldn't do that."

I'm not so fucking sure. But I just shift, pressing against her as her hips move, my erection something she can't ignore as I slowly work my fingers. She gasps and bites my shoulder.

"Oh my God."

"You're spinning wheels. Besides, you've got other issues, and I'm going to fuck you so hard you'll lose the ability to speak."

"Smith..."

I work her, pumping into her, stretching both holes and she's teetering, losing herself. "Were you going to blow up everything by telling this woman who you are?"

She's slipping, drowning in sensation. Her fingers loosen and she's pushing and pumping, grinding with her hips.

But from somewhere, she finds herself, her strength, and her head snaps up.

"Code!"

I almost laugh because she really is something amazing.

She did, however, use her safe word.

I pull free and step back to lean on the other side of the door, facing Calista. "I'm not touching. Just listening. Well? Were you?"

"I don't know. I needed to do something."

"What do you think that would do?"

"Maybe she knows—"

"Where he is? If he's alive..." I almost tell her what Mercer told me, but at the last minute I don't. It gives me a bargaining chip, something to play with. "I'll help you, but otherwise..."

"What?"

"Spin your wheels until it's time for us to make a move. Tonight's info gathering, okay?"

"I still don't trust you, Smith. But right now, you're all I have."

She suddenly grabs my tie and pulls me to her and kisses me, and then she turns and runs, heels clacking.

And I laugh.

Oh fuck. I know the prize tonight. And it's going to be worth the wait.

I count to five, and then I take off after her. It's madness. I should be sitting down across from Jones and playing the part of intermediary between him and the people interested in the weapons. I should be sitting this young woman down and making her get me everything on every last fuck who's had a tie with the Collectors.

The setup, for me, of letting some go, isn't enough. I want them all to burn. Any who thought of touching my kid. Any who's done something to underage girls or destroyed someone for pleasure.

And then I should be handing her in to the CIA contact with money and a need to win points with the agency and letting them do what the fuck they want.

I should do all of that, kill who needs to be killed and walk the fuck away.

Yet my blood's on fucking fire. I want to deep dive into her, take all I want, everything she has to offer for me. And I'm going to. Right before she gets handed over.

I catch sight of her at the edge of Prince Street, just past Broadway. My phone buzzes and I check the message.

What I want to do is take her somewhere, bend her over, and fuck her senseless. I want to claim that sweet ass I had my finger buried in.

But not yet. I've got a meeting to get to.

I send a text to Reaper, and I follow her, right up until she's about to go into a wine bar. Then, sliding a hand beneath her arm, I steer her fighting, melting body away. Fighting because she wants to run, melting because she wants to flow into me and get the orgasm I taunted her with.

She glares at me. "Smith—"

"Calista." I hold out my phone a moment. "Just got word. The senator's gone to the sex club."

As much as I want to, I don't see a way out for her.

I need what she has.

For Jones.

I need everything about the Collectors.

For me.

But Calista?

She's either going to a CIA black site prison or she's going to die.

And there won't be anything I can do to stop it, no matter how much I want to.

CHAPTER 28
CALISTA

He told me to trust him... right after telling me he has a meeting with the senator and "others."

Trust. Not very likely, buddy.

I look around the opulent room, the thick smoke winding in the air, and the rich men with impossibly beautiful women at their sides.

Or on top of them.

The hidden pocket of my dress is heavy. I slide my fingers in, over the slick, flat surface of the phone I lifted off the girl in the elevator. A gorgeous brunette in a short, elegant dress that left little to the imagination.

Getting the phone from her beaded evening bag was easy enough, especially since she was too busy fawning over the fat, sixty-plus-year-old man she was with.

The girl looked twenty-one at most.

I'd feel for her, but I saw the desire to be part of the wealthy elite burning bright. She likes how he treats her and the money he no doubt showers on her.

The two of them disappear, which makes me having her

contraband phone easier. Smith isn't here, he palmed me off. And the man he handed me off to is scary. Big and handsome, with a scar on his face, and the kind of angled jaw women swoon over. Yet his eyes, dark and almost black, are hard and emotionless.

The eyes of a killer.

What's his story? His angle? I study him and those eyes bore into me.

"Don't even think of trying your baby girl version of seduction on me," he says, basically manhandling me into a seat.

I roll my eyes, touch the phone once more before making myself put my hands on the table. "Also, Smith might kill you. I'm not sure he's into sharing."

The guy grins. "You'd be surprised."

Heat burns in my veins. And I meet that cold stare dead-on. "I don't think he wants to share me. And you aren't all that. Now, I'll have a scotch."

He pulls out a leather chair and sits, curling his hand around my wrist and pulling me to him. "You're not what I expected. But don't fucking play me. He might like you. I don't give a fuck."

A cold bolt of fear snakes through me. This isn't spinning wheels. This isn't trust. This is... I don't know what it is... I stop, narrow my eyes, and take a breath. Then I relax into his hold. "Scotch. Please."

He's about to say something when the other ginormous man, one of the men who came to our rescue in Cuba, drops next to me. "Play fucking nice, Reaper."

Then Reaper, that's what the killer holding me is called, looks at him and smiles slowly as he takes in the honey-blonde woman standing near the other big man.

"That's Smith's kid," Reaper says, hooking a thumb through the air at the blonde. "This is her fiancé, Orion. Fuck, I wish I could hang for the fireworks of the wedding, Orion, but..." He shrugs. "Got things to do."

The honey-blonde pretends not to be interested. Orion just looks hard, bored, annoyed. Reaper's got nasty delight all over his face.

"This is Smith's piece, girls and boys. Hendrix."

And then the asshole saunters off to the bar.

"Calista," I manage to push out. "My name's Calista."

Orion gives me a look but doesn't say anything. Instead, he goes after Reaper as he motions to the blonde to sit.

For a moment it disgusts me, the dynamic. Like, Smith's daughter is his to boss around, even without words, because she just nods sweetly and looks down, doing as ordered.

But I catch the proprietary gleam in his eye, and something blinding hot that's passion and love and adoration. It's so apparent for a sliver of a moment that I hurt inside because...

Because it's special.

And Smith's daughter... Dakota... her little smile is excitement and love, the gleam in her is just as bright.

It dawns on me right then that they play their own sex game. Some kind of D/s. And while they're both into it, she... she loves it.

Then her gaze hits me hard and it all shuts down. "So your Smith's latest? Normally I don't meet them. Is he that desperate? God, he's pathetic."

I squeeze a hand tight. "Desperate?"

"Not you, just bringing you here. Are you my age?"

"I'm older than I look."

"He's not a good guy," Dakota says, anger burning the edges of her words.

"Really?" The two men are at the bar, talking, and I'm damn sure I won't even make it near the exit before I'm shoved back down. Though I don't know where I'd go anyway.

Sure, Smith's here somewhere in the building, but he's with the senator and whoever else is involved in the game about the blueprints.

The ones I'm pretty sure I have.

But I don't get why the CIA is so hot for me. They could have grabbed me in Germany. Instead, they hired Smith.

Or someone did, anyway.

Then again, if I have the blueprints, so do others, and everything is on the databases. I just took stuff to decode, to play with, because I could.

Except for what Johnny asked me to hold.

Stuff I haven't even opened.

My stomach sinks. Is that it? Is it to do with that—

"...and a failure. He only cares about himself."

Dakota sinks back in her chair, arms folded.

I wasn't listening, not to her words. But I go over the cadence of her voice. It's not cold. There's anger, yes, and hurt. And a big fat dose of denial that comes from Smith's DNA. I can see him in her, but I'm betting she looks a lot like her mother.

Funny how I'm not jealous of the only woman he's ever mentioned caring for. Then again, they were kids, and I just like to fuck him. I don't like or love him.

So I don't know why I even care about his relationship with his daughter.

Maybe because her anger and hurt remind me of Henry and how he feels about our dead mom. He sounds exactly the same.

Dakota opens her mouth and I turn to her. "I don't know you, and I don't know Smith that well. But we've talked... and maybe you want to sit down and get facts straight. He's adamant you don't want him at your wedding."

"I don't." That sounds exactly like Henry, and if I'm honest, me. With him, it's about Mom, with me...? I'm more intro-

241

verted than him. Walls up, rejecting everyone before anyone can reject me.

Dakota doesn't strike me as introverted, but the sentiment is so familiar. I'd like to be more a part of things, which the job gave me, all while keeping my distance. Henry pushes things about Mom into hate because he's hurt. Dakota rejects her father because he, in her eyes, rejected her. She wants him at her wedding, no matter what she says.

"I think you should talk to him because I got the picture of a man who might sell me down the river but will do anything to keep you safe, even have you hate him. He gave up a lot for you. Maybe the world? His world."

"You think he'll love you for this?" she asks. It's not spiteful, it's curious, like she sees more in me, too, and it makes me shift on the chair like I'm in the hot seat.

I rise. "I don't think he loves anyone other than you, Dakota. He's your father. And he didn't know about you until... well, until your mother was gone. He decided, because of his lifestyle, to give you up, give up a real relationship, to make sure you grew up safe and stable and happy. And if his sacrifice isn't love, I don't know what is."

Taking a deep, shuddery breath, I step away and walk around the table to her side. "Talk to him."

With that, I straighten and cross to Reaper and Orion. I take the scotch from Reaper and down it. "I'm going to the bathroom."

"Two minutes."

I don't respond, I just take off so I can break into the phone and get onto my cloud in private.

The bathrooms put the opulence of the ones from the earlier party to shame. Dark rusts and delicate ivory orchids with onyx fixtures make it into something glamorous and chic, something I could imagine for a photo shoot.

If you're into that kind of kinky shit.

I drop onto on the velvet bench. It doesn't take much to get it open, her password is just zeros. I shake my head. Such brilliance.

From there, I can get into my stuff on the cloud.

My heart leaps. There's a message. It's voice to text.

Call me. Aaron.

Fingers shaking, I memorize the cell number, and I'm about to call when something stops me. Maybe it's him seeing Felicity, which makes no sense. Although moneyed people know moneyed people, and Riley made money when he moved into the private sector.

So I back trace it. Could be that Riley changed his mind after seeing me, but this message... it was left before then. Between leaving Brooklyn and the opening.

And it looks to have come from DC.

I close the phone and pocket it, then open the door and almost scream.

Smith glowers at me.

Everything in me goes into free fall and I half expect him to push me back inside and ravage me.

Instead, he grabs my hand. "We need to go."

"Wait—"

"No, we move now. And fast."

We race down the hall, past the bathrooms and through another door marked management. I expect it to be an office, but it's a small room with an elevator. He hits the button and the door slides open.

Smith pushes me inside.

"I thought this was an exclusive club with a restaurant and a night club with a sex club downstairs. Your depraved all in one."

He laughs. "That and it's also headquarters for billionaire criminals."

I almost laugh when I catch his eyes. They're serious. Deadly, dark-blue pools of very deep secrets.

"You're a billionaire?"

"No, I just like to squat upmarket and sneak on private planes."

The door dings at the floor marked *G*. I expect to step into a lobby, but instead we're in an underground garage with low lighting and expensive cars. Taking my hand, he leads me through the cars to a back exit that is covered by armed guards.

Whatever this place is, it's fortified, protected, and they know Smith.

There's a black car waiting on the narrow street where we exit.

The back door opens and he gives me a gentle shove. I slide inside, and the moment he closes the door, the driver takes off.

I'm not sure where we're going, but it's not to any of the places we've already been to tonight. The windows are tinted so I can't see much. We cross a bridge and we're in a crisscross of streets that are mainly industrial and bars, some strip joints and old-school diners.

And we keep going.

Finally, we pull up to a curb in front of a warehouse.

When we step inside, he says, "Welcome to your new abode."

I step in, and lights burst to life. Outside there aren't any windows, and it looks like it's unused, or if it is, used for long-term storage. But inside...

Wow, it's gorgeous. State of the art. Luxury in a hidden box. And, I'm betting, complete with security camera feeds.

There are safe houses, and then there's this. Oh, it's a safe house for sure. The street is void of people and even cars, and the other warehouses probably just sit, unused. Blend in and be seen.

But this is something else.

"No barebones safe house for you," I mutter as the door closes and locks behind us.

"I like to impress."

Smith takes me by the shoulder and crowds me up against the door. His hands skim down the length of my body, setting off all kinds of fires. I shift into him, craving his touch, needing for him to finish what he started earlier.

Instead, he pulls the phone from my dress pocket and holds it up. "Explain."

CHAPTER 29
SMITH

It's hard fucking work not feeling her up, not taking her right here and now. Not fighting for the prize of her ass, of her whole being. Not starting the chase like I fucking want.

But she's stolen a phone.

"I'm waiting, Calista."

The storm turns electric in her gaze. "You cut me off; I turned myself back on. What are you going to do? Hand me over?"

I lean into her, my mouth not even an inch from hers. Her breath is warm, moist on my lips, and I swear to fucking all that's unholy I'm being pulled to her by some invisible magnet. "Maybe I will."

"It's not much of a threat, Smith, considering that's the end game."

And I turn cruel, twisting the knife with exquisite care. "Maybe if you play it right, I'll let you go."

It's there, a brief flare, a weakening, a sliver of hope.

Then she crushes it down and something in my chest

hurts. Like she fucking reached in and sliced into my insides deep.

"No, you won't."

"I can try."

Everything goes still. Those aren't the words I meant. It's like I dropped the knife and offered her a key to a secret fucking door.

For the first time in my life, I step down. The hunter almost kneels, almost bows to her.

Almost, but not quite. I step down, yes. To get my bearings. "I can try, Calista. Why do you think we're here?"

It's a safe house, abandoned on the outside, the epitome of old warehouses in industrial Queens, and luxury on the inside. I fucking hate this place. Because all I can think about is where my daughter could have died, here in Queens.

Not the same street or the same area, but it's still... I drag in a breath, trying to reset myself. I'm a fucking Dom, a man in control, one who likes to feed his base instincts. I like blood and breath play. I like taking down the girl to her bare bones and basic, animalistic needs. Sex and pain and pleasure.

And instead, I give her a soft chase in SoHo. I fuck her vanilla-style. I hold her.

Calista Juniper Price.

A fucking conundrum if ever I've met one.

The thing is, I like my submissive with fangs and claws; I like the prey who can fight to the death, bleed and draw blood in equal measures.

In short, I fucking like her.

She comes up to me, keeping the space between us minimal. "How did you find me?"

"How the fuck do you think? Reaper told me. Orion told me."

"Did you speak to Dakota?" She frowns.

"No. I came for *you*, not a relationship beyond redemption." I pause to rephrase my words. "We're as good as we need to be and my father-daughter mess isn't your concern."

Her mouth turns up in a cynical smile. "Why was I there? To parade in front of your kid? Because last thing you said about who I needed to be was either a fake wife or fake sex toy. You know, the usual."

I don't laugh, even though I want to.

"If I knew you'd want that, I'd have made other plans."

"We weren't there long."

I breathe out, slip a hand around her waist, sliding down to her ass. "Because I was done when I was done."

"Doing what?"

"Meeting your senator, making sure introductions that your other friend Johnny set up went smoothly." I lean in, waggle the phone in the air. "And trying to glean anything at all about a connection between stolen weapons sales and the sex trade."

"You don't strike me as a guy with a subscription to *Girls With Big Guns*."

I slide up close a moment, letting her feel my hard cock. "I prefer *Mouthy Prey Monthly*."

"You would."

Calista shifts, rubs against me. Then I step back.

"Along," I murmur, "with *Primal Sacrifice*."

"Sounds positively pagan."

"You have no fucking idea." I slip my thumb along her bottom lip, the phone in my other hand. And she sighs softly.

"I've had sex with you, I think I might."

"We're just dipping toes in."

"You're not the big bad wolf," she says, sucking my thumb into her mouth.

The stroke of her tongue and the wetness shoots straight

and hot to my cock. "More like a panther. I like to hunt. I like to play." Fuck, I pull my thumb free and step back, waving the phone. "Why do you have this?"

Calista snatches the phone from me. "Wrong question. It should be 'what did you find, Calista?'"

"What the fuck did you find, sweetheart?"

Her smile is small, but there, and her fingers fly over the screen. It lights up and she holds it out.

"Call me. Aaron." I lift my gaze. "I didn't know you were that close."

She spins free, darting past me, and throws the phone. I catch it easily. "We're not, dickwad. At least not anymore. Look at the time stamp."

I do, and now I frown. "So, I guess the question is, who the fuck sent this?"

"I need a computer, some hardware to scramble the signal, and a booster if this isn't wired."

"Don't ask for much, do you?"

Her gaze shifts to me and she coils fingers around my tie, pulling herself into me. "All I want is the people who used and hurt my mother until she was dead, and for my brother to have a good life."

"Fuck, Calista, I hate it when you sound like a murderous do-gooder."

"No, I think you like it. That's your guilt."

I toss her the phone and she pushes farther in to look around.

I shoot a text to Jones. "I'll get some things delivered, but it'll take a couple of hours."

The place is one floor, open-plan kitchen, dining and living area, with a partition that leads to a bedroom, bathroom, and a study area.

She puts a hand on the leather sofa and kicks off her heels.

Then she slides her dress off, revealing that sweet flesh to me. The pale blue of her lace panties is deeper blue where her desire has soaked them, and her nipples poke through the bra's delicate lace.

I want to feast, but I make myself wait, drinking her in, from those lush fucking tits down over her taut stomach to the very top edge of her tattoo.

"Trying to buy your freedom?"

"Maybe I want a last meal."

I growl low because her over-the-top statement is a lightning bolt to my elemental bones. The twisted freak in me loves her reminder of the danger, the inevitable end where she winds up in the hands of the authorities, ones that when they choose, have no real checks and balances.

Do I want her to fucking suffer? No. But her talk, damn... it heightens the moment and makes my dick throb and push against my pants a little more. Thicker, harder, my cock wants release. Needs it.

"You know what I think?"

"What, Smith?"

"That you're wearing too many fucking clothes."

I reach into my jacket's inner pocket, and I pull out a switchblade. I walk up to her and in front of her face, close enough that she can feel the whisper of the blade as it disturbs the air, I flick it open.

My Calista doesn't even flinch.

And my prick aches.

I slice up through the center of the bra. Then I cut the strap on each shoulder, and I step back as it falls to the floor.

"Spread your legs."

I strip off my jacket and toss it, not caring where it lands. Then I come in close once again.

With a light stroke, I run the blade down her breast plate,

down over her stomach, and then between her legs, turning it so the blade's flat as I hold it there, pressed light against her pussy.

Her breathing starts to come in pants and her eyes are bright, feverish. "Word?"

"Fuck you."

I dip my head, running my lips along her throat, stopping here and there for a taste, a lick, wanting the salt and that particular sweetness of her skin. She moans.

I drop my hand, moving the knife through the air. She's too wet to let it glide over the panties. "Give me your mouth."

"Make me."

I grab her hair with my free hand and yank her head back so her lips are mine for the taking. She's ready for me to plunder, so I tease. Tiny sips along her lips, sliding my tongue in to flirt, and then, still holding her, I lift my head, and look down at the tremors of her stomach. I bring the blade up against her skin and along the line of her panties, I run it, scratching her.

She yelps. I press in, just a bit and the moan is loud. Orgasmic. I let her go and drop it so I can lick and suck her blood, the few drops I drew. I thumb her pulsing clit and the orgasm hits harder. But I don't let her have it all, I pull away.

With a vicious slice, back edge of the blade against her skin, I slice through one side of her panties and then the other, pulling them free.

I lick her, suck her clit, and bite her. She shrieks as a whole-body spasm passes through her.

"Monster."

"You love it," I say, getting up, still holding the knife. I point it at her. "On your knees."

She does that and without asking, without waiting to be told, she frees me, and I let her greedily suck me into that divine and magical mouth of hers. My body jerks, balls high, and the ache is threatening to turn into an unstoppable urge to find release, so I push her away, knocking her off-balance. She tumbles to the floorboards.

"Now that's a fucking view." I run the knife over her ass, the back of the blade, loving how it makes her shiver. Then I set it down. "Use your safe word if you need it."

I slide my fingers over her, between her cheeks, her sweet asshole calling to me, but first I dip into her cunt. She moans again as I push into her, stretching her with my fingers, rubbing her G-spot until the noise she makes reaches a higher pitch.

She's so fucking wet she's ready to come, and me?

I'm almost fucking delirious with the need for her.

I remove my fingers and plunge into her wet heat, and the sigh in the air is a perfect moment. I feel it, the coming home, and Calista's soft, satisfied smile as I stay, balls deep, burns itself into me.

Then I pull out, and shove back in, and the wetness coats my way like lube. I dip a finger into her and she jerks. "Word?"

"Keep fucking going. You've been teasing me. I need... I need to come. I need to come big... So fuck me. Make it hurt."

I grab her hips and start to hammer into her, hitting bottom every fucking time. Hard enough she'd slide if I didn't have hold of her, and she pushes back into me over and over.

This isn't enough. Not this time. Not this fuck.

I need to own her, all over. Stamp her as mine. I want to ruin her for future lovers.

But stopping is hard. Because her cunt wraps tight, and though it stretches for me, and her moans blanket me in more want, it still feels like she's trying to take my cock off.

It feels like she was made just for me.

And I need more.

I lean over her as she rocks back on me and I fuck her in

short, deep stabs that make her start growling, start grinding on me hard like she can't get enough.

Grabbing her hair, I put my mouth to her ear and bite down on her lobe. I'm rewarded by a spasm of her cunt, and it almost makes me come.

"Like that, little girl?"

"More."

"Not what I asked. Do you like me fucking you like this, like I want to climb inside you and wreck you from the inside out?"

"Yes." Her fingers claw at the floor. She's on her elbows and I want her ass higher, head and upper torso pressed to the boards. "I fucking love it, you dick."

"Here's what I'm gonna do. I'm gonna pull out, line up, and fuck the ever-loving Christ out of that pretty little asshole, okay?"

"Do it!" Her voice wobbles. "*Now.*"

And I lose more of myself again... except this time, there's a small part of me that's afraid I won't ever get it back.

CHAPTER 30
CALISTA

I'm shimmering with sweat. His body heat burns into my skin.

I think... I think I've lost my mind for demanding him to do this thing that both scares and excites me.

Smith pulls out of my pussy and smacks my ass hard, making me cry out. Not from pain because he knows how to do it so that I get a pleasing sting that rushes with pleasure and makes everything sing. No, I cry out because I'm so fucking empty and I need him to fill me.

We should be talking, strategizing. But my God, I want this.

Even as I hate being the weaker one, the prey, I love it, too. I want him to own me, to overwhelm. And I want to both fight and give in to him. I want him to make me do all sorts of sordid things with him. And more than that, I want his cock in my ass.

He paints my asshole with my juices and then slowly pushes two fingers in.

The invasion makes me whimper.

"Oh shit. Wait..."

God. His fingers stretch me open, wide, and there's a little pain as I clench.

These are just fingers.

They feel huge.

His cock actually is huge. Big, thick, hard, and fucking steel. How the hell...? I gulp. "Wait... I changed my mind."

Smith actually stops.

He doesn't pull out, but he stays where he is. "We don't need to do this," he says to me like he's talking about changing the channel. "Do you want me to stop?"

I squeeze my eyes shut. "You're so big."

"Is that *code*?"

Is it? I gulp. I...

"No," I whisper. "I'm just... you're so big."

There's silence. And my heart slams against my ribs, hard.

Then he starts to slowly move his fingers in me, his other hand coming around my stomach so he can stroke my clit.

"Your ass is mine, sweetheart," he says, "but the only time I'll hurt you is when you ask for it. And it'll always be a good hurt."

A shiver of need races through me, and I moan. "You have your prey. What are you waiting for?"

My words hang in the air, and he scissors his fingers before pulling out. He grabs my hips, pulling them higher, and then the thick head of his cock starts to push into me.

Lungs burning because I don't dare breathe, I wait. He keeps going, agonizingly slow, stretching me open and there's pain but not too much. He pushes in with something that feels like borderline reverence.

"Not much farther."

Suddenly he's in. All the way. All the fucking way and I let out my breath in jagged puffs.

"I feel so—"

"Mine," he says.

And a flare of something sweet and hot lights me up.

"Yours."

It's sex talk, I know. It's weird, a little uncomfortable, and when he starts to move I'm not sure how I feel.

But the weirdness starts to shift, and each withdrawal and push back into me makes my body hum. Smith moves harder, faster. And I groan and push back into him because he's rubbing against something and it feels good. Better than good.

I start to chant.

"More, more, oh God, harder. Harder."

"Fuck, yeah." He starts to slam into me, and the rising pleasure in me bursts into an orgasm but he doesn't stop.

He keeps fucking me, hard and fast. Smith slides a hand under me, and he starts to rub and pull and twist my clit. And I scream. "Yessss."

It shouldn't work, what he's doing to my clit, but it's building, and this time my vision wavers and my whole body is hit by wave after wave of violent, gorgeous contractions and I come. I can feel it, warm everywhere. He pulls his hand away and holds my hips tight and starts to slam so hard and deep we both start to move on the floor.

He yells out. "Fuck, Calista. Fuck!"

And then he comes. Inside of me, painting my insides, and his cock twitches. He half collapses on me, then catches himself and rolls me so I'm on him, the hardness of his cock against me.

Smith wraps his strong arms around me, his cock taking its time to deflate.

"Fuck, you're like the human version of Viagra. You keep a man rock-hard. Jesus."

He guides my mouth to his and kisses me. Then he slowly rolls us up.

"There are some clothes in the bedroom," he says, tweaking my hard nipples.

I stand, legs wobbly as he jumps up and throws me over his shoulder. Then he carries me into the bedroom and tosses me on the bed. He tucks himself away and is about to speak when a phone rings in the other room.

"Wait here."

I glare at his back as he crosses to the door. "Like I can go anywhere?"

Smith doesn't answer, just disappears out of the room. Soon, I hear him talking, and it hits me that I can also hear another voice.

That wasn't a phone, it was some kind of weird-ass doorbell.

Someone's at the door.

I quickly get off the bed and dress in black sweats from inside the closet. They're way too big, so I kick off the pants and let the long T-shirt fall to my thighs as I rush to listen.

The door is open a crack, but he's on the other side and I can't make anything out, at least beyond the words *tickets* and *tomorrow*. Heart beating fast, I press closer... something about an explosion? Nothing after that.

Then loud as day, Smith says, "Learn anything?"

I scowl as I push the door open. An array of packages in plain shopping bags is on the floor. Smith is bent down, behind the sofa. He flips back the rug and rises.

"Should I have?"

"I got you the shit you asked for," he says, ignoring my question as he crosses back over to the bags. "Clothes, computer shit. Everything that can make a little hacker's heart beat fast."

"Internet?"

"Yep." He tosses me two bags. I catch one, the other falls, spilling dark denim and black cotton.

I look into the one I caught. Hoodies, shirts. Underwear of the cotton variety. Socks and shoes. And I touch one of the sneakers. "Thank fuck, no heels."

His gaze runs up over me. "I like you in heels. You run like a gazelle in heels. Hot as fuck."

"Thank you?"

I pull out a variety of clothes and duck back into the bedroom to pull on underwear, slightly too big jeans, a top, and an oversize hoodie.

Smith turns as I come back, and his gaze slides over me, an upturn to that mouth I might crave, and I open the other things. He's right, my heart's in overdrive and I am practically gooey inside.

Other girls like rings, flowers. Give me a computer and a modem and I'm in love.

"Everything you could want." He watches as I set up. "Router, drives, computer... This isn't my jam. I know some things, but..."

For the first time since leaving Germany, I'm in my element. When I'm done, and I know my signal's about as untraceable as I can make it on the fly with the VPN and what he's got—which is pretty fucking sweet—I sit on the sofa, feet on the oak coffee table, and get to work. First, I want to know where that message came from. And from whom.

Aaron's no rookie and the message he supposedly sent was a rookie move.

In the background, the deep and low and soothing timbre of Smith's voice washes over me like soft waves. He's on his phone and I look up to find him leaning on the kitchen counter, back to me, pouring golden liquid into a glass. Scotch, probably.

For a moment I let my gaze linger on the lean, muscular form of him, the narrow hips and long legs, the broad, muscled back. He pushes a hand through his hair as he nods, then drops his hand to the counter, only to push a finger along the rim of his glass.

He's a conundrum. Soft at times when he should be hard-core and brutal. When he took me, he could have just fucked into me, taken me hard after working me open. Claimed that victory like he could claim a beating heart from a chest.

But he didn't.

Instead, he waited, went soft, broke his stalker, predatory character. For me, to make sure I felt safe.

I get using a word instead of "no" so I can explore with him the wilds of sex, the taboo, and play in rough games of him taking what I pretend I don't want to give. It's a freedom, it's sweet. And something that needs trust on both sides.

That stops me.

I trust him.

At least on a base level. And sex is as bare-bones as it comes.

I don't know what it all means. Except it means something.

My computer beeps and I look back at the screen, shooting straight up. After a minute of furious typing, I look at him. "Smith."

He comes over. "What is it?"

My breath's caught, and I turn my computer. "I know where the message came from. It's supposed to have been sent from DC, but we know Riley was here. I... I think someone might be using him. Because..."

He frowns. "Eric T. Brown?"

I pull up another page.

"Remember when I said that Trenton has a son? *T* for Trenton. This guy's here, and look... he's got links to Jon Trenton's offshore accounts. The last name here doesn't matter, his activity does. Because look."

I point to another account he has, and the donations made from it.

"They're accounts in Bolivia. A few are bigger, where if you trace the money, it shows whoever that person is—there are a bunch of different people. It's a network, so sometimes the money gets hard to trace—this money goes to a film company in Bolivia. Shipping, and—"

"Rare Birds, Inc." He shakes his head. "What can you find about them?"

I open up the account for Rare Birds.

It seems on the up-and-up, lots of big and small donations, money going everywhere, but soon I'm deep diving into names, aliases, organizations, companies. And finally, I look at him.

"How did you know?"

He spins the computer. "I didn't. We'll call it a hunch and look... These are names of Collectors, their companies, and even shipments of bird cages."

I swallow.

Did they keep my mother in a cage?

"Can you copy that?" he asks. "If this guy's in on it, a kid of a Collector who developed a taste, and one who works for the senator up close, then this Eric might be the key. The one that's hidden under everything."

I pull up Eric T. Brown's file from DC. The private one. "It says she had him very young. It's not a secret, but he went to private school in Canada and was raised by an aunt and uncle?"

"Your Riley might be guilty. He's in New York, his mom just got remarried, and that might all be coincidence. I need to look into him. In person. With the senator." But he doesn't move.

"On the bottom of the clothes bag is a phone. Make sure it's on. And all that stuff you have? The files and code you collected, the things Johnny sent you? I need a copy of everything. Now."

"If I don't?"

"Then they probably get away with everything, and I will hand you over because otherwise, they'll hunt you down."

I breathe out. "If I do—"

"Then," he says, saying words made of magic, "I will do everything I can to get you out of it. I promise. But you need to trust more than just yourself. This is your last chance."

CHAPTER 31
SMITH

Calista stares up at me, confusion and mistrust on her face. "I don't know..."

"We both want the last of the Collectors gone."

"I want to ruin them financially, hit them where it hurts," she says.

Her and me and the Knights. "Work with me, then. Jon Trenton's dead. I know who killed him and this guy, Mercer, he doesn't fuck things up. He delivers... always. But we can still take down the son. We can take down all the ones he's in bed with. He's sneaking around, probably hiding behind his mom, Felicity, and—"

"No."

She steps back.

"No?" I ask.

"No. I mean..." Her tits under the big, boxy hoodie rise and fall quickly. She looks so young right now, her hair still dark, face makeup-free, and those stormy eyes wary.

I should feel guilt scraping at my senses.

Guilt for fucking her, for wanting her, for wanting to do it again. And worse, I should feel deep, gutting guilt at being the one who's going to lie and manipulate to get what he wants.

She's too fucking naïve and too innocent for her life to end up where it's going. Under lock and key. It doesn't matter if they put her somewhere nice; she's too gifted for the CIA to let her live freely somewhere. She's way too good at what she does to work for anyone but them.

I don't need the money for the job of bringing her in. I just fucking like money. And I could have just used the information she gave me as a way to shut down a flow of money into the Collectors and their nasty, twisted little schemes. Close down another avenue of theirs.

She's already handed me a way to connect this group, the ones who are using Bolivia to move girls and indulge in depravity by helping to move and sell stolen blueprints and new weapons parts.

But I got even more than all that. I saw something she missed.

Her agent Johnny didn't skip town. He's here, watching, waiting, teasing leads.

There was a dinner from two nights ago, just a receipt on a deep dive electronic list, but I recognized the company name. It's the fake one Johnny used in Miami.

He went out with Trenton Jr.

And she didn't connect those dots.

I lift my gaze back to her face.

If Johnny's here, wining and dining, then he knows she is, too.

To me, it explains why the CIA hasn't come looking for her. He disappeared, set her up, and now they're waiting.

Until the big fish are reeled in.

And my girl goes down for her incidental part.

I'm filling in blanks, but I spent enough of my life tethered to the CIA, enough of it in the wilds of intelligence outside the CIA, and now within the walls of the Obsidian Knights to make these connections with confidence.

"I mean," she says again, "it's treason."

"You're right, but I can get that to the right authorities."

"But you're handing me in to the CIA. Or to the someone who hired you."

"Actually, they hired a friend who passed the job to me, but," I say, "I see your point. You found the connection, Calista. Between the sex traffickers and the people trying to sell the weapon. I need the information. I need your trust. And I can make heads roll."

"By getting it all to the CIA."

"Partly." I send a text to Jones and one to Reaper. "But what if I could make it so you disappear, along with your freedom?"

She doesn't say anything for a long time. I don't know what I expect... scorn, excitement? What I don't expect is the blank look on her face and it twists a knife, ice-cold, in my stomach.

"I'd ask for the hidden agenda. The clauses that draw blood."

The knife twists harder. Even as I said the words, she knows I'm feeding her a lie. And fuck, I would change her course in a heartbeat if I could.

Smart, funny Calista with a razor-sharp bite and a soft, sumptuousness that goes beyond flesh can't be saved.

She takes a breath and nods. "I wanted... I wanted to avenge my mother's death but the asshole who raped her or groomed her or whatever it was, he knocked her up, sent her off to have his little bastards, and then lured her back in for fun and games with other men until they were done and threw her out with the trash."

She sits on the sofa, drawing her knees up beneath her chin.

"She never recovered. Never got to be a good mom. Henry hated her because he mourned her loss, and hate's just easier. And... When I got that text in Germany, it gave me purpose. Like I might actually find the guilty and make them pay."

Fuck me. I rub the palm of my hand between my ribs, where that cold pain's moved toward. But I push it down because this is it, and the best I can offer. A lie wrapped in truth.

She's funny, fucking smart, and she's got skill. I know why they want her in. Skill like hers is dangerous.

For the first time in my life, first time since being an adult, I don't know what to do.

"I just... I just want to destroy the pricks and now?"

"If you give me that info, you'll get the chance."

Calista rubs her cheek against her knee, then looks up. "We both know I had no chances since before I met you. Me escaping, me living free, it's not an option. They have my brother."

"Actually, I put Reaper on your brother. No doubt he's got people who can disappear him if it comes to that."

Her eyes narrow. "You better mean disappear as in a new identity. The CIA would do it very differently."

She doesn't need to say I used the exact same threat on her.

"Calista, I need that stuff. Whatever you have. If I can use it, then I'll bring down the sex traffickers. I'm sorry the ones directly involved with your mother are gone or lost to us. But I can bring the rest down and make it look like you were a hero. Maybe I can barter your freedom."

"Maybe."

I know she doesn't believe me, but she does something. She holds out her hand, palm up and open. "I'm assuming you've got a thumb drive."

"Calista—"

"Let's pretend I believe you. Maybe I can pretend I'm on the job. Just... just promise I can see my brother. Please?"

"I promise."

It's a lie.

She rubs her hand over her face, then puts her feet on the ground and picks up the computer. It takes five minutes, but she finally finishes and hands me the drive. "You can check. It's the real deal. The unreleased apps I hid things in, the cloud I actually stored things in."

"I'm going to have to believe you, too," I say, realizing that's true. "Because I wouldn't be able to tell."

"You won't, but the CIA? That's a different story, and I'd rather be handed over and not be hung for treason. This way... if you let them know I gave it to you to give to them..." She cocks her head. "Is that naïve? It sounds like it, but... you have power."

"I work with powerful people. I can do that."

"Like I have a choice, which is why I choose to be naïve and pretend to believe you."

"It's the truth. Stay here, I'll be back."

And I lean in over the computer and kiss her hard.

It's another lie. I kiss her like it's not a last kiss but a prelude when we both know exactly what it is.

I head for the door and as it closes, I hear her voice behind me, and I think it actually breaks my heart.

"Where would I go, Smith? I've got nothing at all now."

Fuck.

∼

"WHAT THE HELL are you doing here?"

Johnny's good, a CIA veteran, but he's not me, and the

surprise blows apart his cover in little ways he doesn't even notice.

I hold up the thumb drive from Calista just out of his reach. Not that he goes for it.

I sit down in the desk chair and nod at the group of men with the girls we hired on the screens behind him.

Johnny's brown hair is mussed and he looks seedy, like he hasn't slept in a week. I suspect only part of that is the act for his job at hand.

"Sit."

He does, and he looks around briefly, maybe for our little Calista, to see if she's hiding, but he then focuses for a few seconds on the screen.

Finally, he looks back at me.

"The only one who's missing back there is Eric Brown." I point at the screen. "But his boss, the not-so-good CIA agent turned Senator Riley, is having a great time."

The man on screen is balls deep in the ass of a twenty-two-year-old seasoned veteran, a girl we rescued who liked the money and dick as long as that dick paid her.

And the beauty of the young girl is she's also a vengeful creature. She'll fuck and then let us knife someone to death if they trade in girls.

I don't think her moans are fake, though. I think she actually likes the senator.

I've got my eye on one guy in particular, a rich asshole tugging his small cock as he watches two girls dressed as schoolgirls make out and finger each other. He's a Collector. One who showed up on the intel Calista found. One who didn't make the island party that my daughter was lured to, but who I found out wanted to destroy Dakota once he got his hands on her.

Regrettably, I'm not going to get to cut the tiny-dicked man's cock off slice by slice.

Orion's in the wings.

Waiting.

And I'm just happy they'll finally be taken out.

None of them touched Calista. So I'm okay with others killing them.

"Good or not-so-good's sometimes about perspective," the man says.

I shift my gaze to Johnny.

"I'm guessing you've worked out I'm not who I said I was, Johnny CIA."

The guy says nothing.

I turn the computer toward him and bring up some of the extra things Calista dug up. Mainly on Eric Brown. "Down there on the screen behind you are most of the people you want. Sex trade assholes and gunrunners. I assume you want the shit you gave to Hendrix. You know, the reason why she hasn't been taken and locked up yet?"

"She's smart." He shifts. "I knew if there was pressure, she'd find the missing pieces."

"I have those now." I flash him the thumb drive again.

And fuck. It's killing me. Keeping up this façade as a sex club owner and power player is perfect for a lot of the Knights' work so we're keeping the place as is. But sitting in this chair, acting like I've got the power when... fuck.

When I don't. Not where it counts.

Somewhere between leaving Queens and landing here, I realized something.

I like Calista. Too much, maybe. And enough I want her to live, to be happy.

So I'm going to bargain, something I never fucking do.

"What's it worth to you?" I ask.

"Her life, you mean?"

"Calista's worth fighting for. Begging for. Bargaining for."

"She ran."

"She uncovered something huge. Bigger than what you know. She uncovered an underbelly of vile sex trade that's hiding in the shadows. And we'll destroy it. This arm of it." I pause, tapping the drive on the desk. "It *is* brilliant, using the cover of the weapons. Everyone's looking at the weapons, and when the gun sellers and mercenaries fall, no one's digging into some smutty porn. She found the connections. The ones everyone else would have missed. And more than that, she found names you weren't even after. Like the senator."

I slide the drive into the laptop and show him what we have, then I pull it out.

"Calista's brilliant," he says quietly. "But the senator... that's different."

He's either telling me they have a deal, or I got it wrong about Riley's guilt. But that doesn't concern me at fucking all.

Calista concerns me. Calista and her freedom.

"Consider the senator yours," I say. "You're going to go down there, sign your deals, and when they leave, they're all quietly going down. Let me guess, something small, FBI arrests, and then..."

"They'll do deals, flee, and we'll get them the moment they leave US soil," Johnny says.

"And Riley?"

"He'll be wanted in DC."

Yeah. I don't ask about that one.

"Calista's saved your ass. Let her go."

"Wish I could." Johnny nods and his hand closes over the drive. "She'll get a nice place to live."

"But no freedom."

"She poked at it, didn't break into the important stuff,

didn't decode it. And you helping us to catch some of the more slippery actors in this? It'll help get her a nice place and work—"

"Under lock and key."

"Better than a black site. It's all I can do."

I want to kill him.

"She's just a cog?"

"Collateral damage." Johnny stands. "She'll be under the CIA until she dies."

And I watch him go.

Until she dies.

I switch off the feed as Jones comes out of the side room and hands me a glass of whiskey. He drops into the chair.

What happens with those people, the ones the CIA wants, is out of our hands. Anyone who is left will wish they died quickly.

"You know," he says, "the girl of yours is a find. She's not just good, she's phenomenal."

"Yeah, except the CIA's going to rob her."

"Unless she dies." He looks at me and sets down his glass. "It's the only way."

The only way.

I'd hoped... It doesn't matter what I'd hoped. I nod. Then I pick up my whiskey and drain the glass.

In a perfect world, she'd have real freedom. But...

"I'll set it up," he mutters. "Unless you have a problem."

"No. We agree," I say to Jones. "She has to die."

CHAPTER 32
CALISTA

M y computer. That's what's under the rug, beneath the floorboards. In a simple safe I crack with ease. I don't know where Smith is, but I'm glad he's not here right now.

My fucking computer, all my shit. Passport. And on top are two tickets to DC.

He lied.

I guess I should be shocked. But I'm not because I can see on the computer he gave me what he'd poked into. I can hack most things. Like his phone, like all of Eric's social media accounts as well as his mother's, their credit card usage. Hell, I can even get into the CCTV around the office that the senator's using in Lower Manhattan.

"You sick fuck," I mutter at a photo I found on a dark web profile. Eric likes young girls.

Fourteen, fifteen, the explicit photos don't lie.

And... fuck it. I flip back to the curated social media page of his mom. It's perfect. Cool and calming centers, waterfalls, her at elite events. Just always left of center and shadowed, as if she's not the intended subject. It's clever. It makes her the focus but not in your face.

Put her in a lineup, and even I'd be hard-pressed to pick her out.

If he's in that office... Jesus.

And his mother just posted a picture of him a day ago, her comments about what good he's doing and how she's now off for her honeymoon.

Then she has this to say: *The first to arrive and the last to leave, always with time to listen to any concern from anyone, a real honest American.*

What a bunch of bullshit.

"So honest you're into trafficking," I mutter at the man's smiling photo.

If he's the first to arrive and the senator's heading back in the next day, then he's probably already there.

"Perfect," I announce to the screen.

I snap the computer shut, go back to the safe, and pull out a Glock. There's also a round with the pile of stuff. I load the gun and tuck it beneath my hoodie. And then I dig around in my old backpack. I have a stun gun buried down at the bottom. I pull it out and make sure it still has juice.

It crackles in the air and I grin.

The mini stun gun is purple and looks like a sex toy. I tuck that away, too.

Next, I load the phone he gave me with a card I have for emergencies. I head out into the predawn air. It's cloudy, and using the slight chill as an excuse, I pull the hood over my head and follow maps to the nearest subway.

When the train finally arrives, I'm still early enough that it's only moderately crowded. It's about five a.m., so there aren't a lot of people waiting on the platform. I ride the F train to Second Avenue and at Chrystie Street, I book an Uber. It's there in minutes. Black.

For a moment, my heart beats hard. But I'm being stupid. Because there are lots of black cars. I start to cross over to it so I can check out the license plate when something big hits me from behind. I crumple to the pavement right as the car explodes.

My ears ring and vision blurs like the world's dissolving around me. I'm dragged up and half carried away, then thrown into another car.

I kick the man and go for my gun, but he fights me, pinning me down against the seat. I manage to knee him in the balls, and he starts to swear.

"For fuck's sake. Do a buddy a favor and blow up a fucking car, not to mention save the spitfire he's got a hard-on for, and she tries to take out your fucking junk. Sit the fuck down," he growls.

I stare, sitting up, breathing hard. "Reaper."

"Yeah, you're just lucky your idiot boyfriend wants you alive. You were supposed to stay in the damn safe house. I tracked you. And if I can, anyone can."

"Let me go. I've an asshole to stop."

The man rolls his flat, hard, dark eyes. "Gotta be more specific. What kind of asshole?"

"Eric T. Brown."

He grins. "Good thing I stopped you from blowing up. I'll take you right to him."

Reaper turns to say something to the driver.

That's when I move fast. I grab my stun gun and hit him right in the nuts.

The man howls and I double over and throw open the door, then hit the pavement at a run.

I dodge through the people on the street, round a corner, then dart over Houston Street to a slew of horns and tire squeals. A bus narrowly misses me. But I make it to the other side and race down the street to Forsythe, then turn onto Stanton.

Luck comes my way with a cab, and I wave it down. Leaning forward, I give the address.

"You on the run?"

Shit, I'm breathing hard. "Jogging."

The cab driver just turns on his radio and Madonna sings about being frozen, but I barely listen to the old song. Everything burns but I can relate, because I feel like ice inside.

I just sent a bolt of electricity into a man's balls.

A man who's not just a friend of Smith's, but one I'm pretty sure is a stone-cold killer. The car—I can't think about that explosion. The driver's talking again but I offer monosyllabic answers, and I catch something about a 'car bomb' and this 'damn fuckin' city.'

Smith... If Reaper knew where I was, so will Smith. And now I've got the CIA and Reaper out for my blood. And Smith?

I don't know.

That's the God's honest truth.

In a different world, without my fate prewritten, nailed in the wall above my head, I'd want to get to know him more. I'm not sure we'd be enemies. Not by personality clash, and not by virtue of what's going on.

I'd want to know the handsome, older man. Explore kink and filth and my limits with him. I'd want him to take me hard and fast. I'd like to fight with him, see who could draw blood first. Have him choke me until I'm hazy and a sea of base emotions.

He's witty, extremely smart, maybe as smart as me, which is a thrill of its own. And he's got a kindness hidden in that callousness he likes to exude.

I'm not talking about the charm he turns into advantage, charm he treats like a weapon. No, I mean that softness, like when in the middle of hard sex play, he took time to make sure I wanted anal. And then he eased in slow when we both know he didn't have to.

He did that for me.

I want to do normal things with him like go out for romantic dinners, wake up next to him, help him in his job, play chess with him.

I want to know all the tiny things that make him up. Favorite foods and movies and books. Preferred weapons.

I want—

"We're here."

The cab driver's words jolt me out of my daydream. I pay him with the card on the phone and then get out. The office Riley is using is in an old pre-war building. Since it's early, I make my way around the back and down the alley between buildings. There I find the open door for the maintenance staff. It's easy enough to go in through there, and knowing Riley, he'll be on the first floor.

I take the stairs.

His office is big, and I slip inside, past where a receptionist would sit.

Voices freeze me.

"You're going down, you prick," Riley snarls.

"C'mon, I skimmed off the top, fed some of my fantasies, then set up some deals for you about the blueprints I got." That must be Eric.

I sidle up closer to the door.

"Blueprints that you implicated me in," Riley says. "And the fucking sex trade? I trusted you. And I'm not burning for you. I just dealt with the fucking FBI—"

"You were banging young whores. Which I can set you up with. We go over to Bolivia—"

"What the fuck? I'm not going anywhere, but you are." There's a knowing note in his voice, like Riley's going through motions, eager to just get rid of this man.

Did—?

The door opens and I'm face-to-face with my old mentor.

"Who's the cunt?" Eric mutters, coming up behind Riley.

"The cunt," he says, "is CIA."

"Well, fuck," Eric says. "Guess you two can have a shootout because I'm not going down for this."

I don't see it coming. One minute Riley's turning to him, the next minute he hits the floor, brains and blood all over my sneakers and the carpet. The loud bang of the gun still rings between my ears, and now that weapon's pointed at me.

My blood moves, cold, sluggish in my veins as my stomach does a sickening lurch into my bloody shoes.

Behind me a door bangs and I know who it is before he steps into the room.

"Put down the fucking gun, Brown," Smith snarls. "You just shot an unarmed man."

I start to reach for the gun, but Eric stabs the gun through the air. "Hands up, bitch. I'm going to blame the cunt here. Right after I kill her. Or maybe I'll shoot you and have you bleed out while I fuck her up. Taste the cunt's cunt with my cock and gun, maybe something nasty, like—"

"I will fucking feed you your own dick if you hurt her. Mark my fucking words." Smith takes a step forward. He doesn't have a gun. His hands are open at his sides. And...

Fear lacerates me.

No way he'd come in without a weapon. I look at him, his jacket. There, at the back, a small bulge where he hastily tucked it.

I swallow past the burning, searing lump.

"Smith... please," I whisper. "Go. I don't have a life anyway, not anymore."

"Shut the fuck up."

"Aw... how sweet, trying to protect her. Who the fuck are you? I'm hazy on the who's who here. I came to make sure the senator didn't live to tell the tale of any of this. A break-in, whatever. I'm good at that shit. Besides, I've got a ticket out of here in a few hours, so... Who wants to die first?"

Smith's going to do something insane. And he'll die for it.

A tiny sob escapes and I push past him. It's the wrong thing to do. Eric's eyes narrow and his arm jerks. We both see it. I'm in the line of sight.

It all happens in slow motion.

Eric pulls the trigger as his arm jerks and it's pointed right at me. The gun goes off.

An anguished roar, Smith's shout, full of anguish, rage, fills the air, my blood.

The bullet comes at me... right at the same time Smith leaps. I see him fly in the air and he hits me so hard, I fall to the floor.

But as I fall, the bullet hits flesh. Not mine.

Smith's.

It rips into him, blood spurting in the air.

He goes down.

Hard.

And his gun clatters on the floor next to him.

CHAPTER 33
SMITH

It hurts like a bitch, the agony spreading fast through my arm and upper chest. But through the pain, I don't miss the choked cry from Calista.

She rushes the guy who shot me. I struggle to pull myself up off the floor, just in time to see her with what looks like some kind of vibrator in her hand. She skids across the smooth desktop, kicking his arm that holds the gun. A second bullet goes wide as the thing in her hand makes contact with balls and then his chest.

Oh fuck.

It's a stun gun.

It cracks and sings, and by the time I'm on my feet, Eric's on his back. She fires at his nuts, doesn't stop until another scream bursts from her lips, one so loud it smothers his. Then she pulls out an actual gun—I recognize it—and she shoots him, point fucking blank.

"You killed him. You killed Smith! You fuck—"

"Calista?"

She shrieks, drops the gun, and turns. A sob, ugly and big,

breaks free. She flings the stun gun and rushes at me as the room fills with the other Knights.

I'm pretty fucking sure I'm bleeding all over the place, more blood than I'd expect from a clean shot.

But before I can say anything, the world wavers as Calista throws her arms around me and kisses me.

I stagger like I can't hold any weight, like standing is treacherous. My legs wobble.

My arm is wet and so's my side. And she's talking, along with the others, but their voices are far away, like I'm hearing them from the inside of a tunnel.

The room starts to spin and go gray.

Everything gets dim and turns black as I crumple down to the floor once again.

"Calista's okay. Not a scratch, she..."

I shoot fucking Jones a look, trying not to wince at the pain in my side. "Can I finish bleeding to death in peace?"

"You're not bleeding to death. Not anymore. The bullet nicked an artery. You're sewn up and on bed rest."

I nod. "The bodies?"

"They'll be found in the wreckage of the car. According to Forensics, the investigation is finished, they'll have four bodies. One they can't place, and..."

He doesn't need to say it. We both know who it'll be.

Johnny's off to Washington, news of the explosion no doubt reaching him. But he's gone. And Jones informed me he called to say all of our conclusions checked out. They'd wanted to question Riley, Brown, and the others in the car, but you can't ask the dead and expect an answer.

Shit. I lie back, the pain's throb setting in now that the drugs they gave me for the stitches wears off.

I don't mind the pain.

It's confirmation that I saved Calista's life.

But fuck. I didn't want her anywhere near there. What we'd learned is that this guy was greedy, depraved, and working the senator. Maybe it was the other way around because yeah, CIA goes bad, all the fucking time. Agents both retired and active can be corrupt. Like people anywhere.

But Johnny CIA turned out to be one of the good ones, and maybe even Riley is too.

Not fucking Eric T. Brown. That bastard, a man I've never met before, was the pin holding everything together.

And I regret his death.

Not that he's dead, though.

How it happened. The fucker should have suffered slowly, in agony, by my hand for calling Calista a cunt, by threatening to brutally rape and kill her. If I'd been able to, I'd have taken him down and skinned him alive with a goddamn mandolin, done things to him that would make Reaper both impressed and a little jealous.

I'd have made the fucker last, screaming to his bitter end.

Instead, he pulled the fucking trigger, and I only had time to shove Calista out of the way.

"She killed him."

"Yeah, I know." I open an eye and look at Jones. "Get the fuck out."

"I'm going to talk to the doctor, then I'll be back. Don't be an asshole."

Closing my eyes again, I try to place the weird emptiness in me that writhes with unease.

Calista killed someone.

Yeah, I know. She's CIA. She's trained. Maybe not to go and

zap a man in the balls for so long and hard, followed by an assault on the chest and then a shot to the head when he was already down, but she did. And I know why.

For me.

She did it for me.

And that's something she's going to have to live with. In her living 'death,' she's going to have to fucking live with it.

But even knowing all of that doesn't stop me from the carnal thoughts about her that always seem to fog up my brain. Maybe it's the drugs. Maybe it's something more.

What I'd really like is to have her ride me. And I'm not going to lie. There's a part that wants her in a hot little nurse outfit while she takes care of my whims on the road to recovery.

I'd start that with her deep throating me, sucking my balls. Maybe keep her snuggled next to me, her scent in my nose, soothing me, her heat warming me. Fuck, and we could argue and flirt, and I could take the time to learn more about her, the things that a dossier can never hold.

The things I haven't discovered yet that make her tick. What her favorite food is, her favorite song. Her favorite band. She seems like an *Einstürzende Neubauten* girl to me, rocking out to complex industrial German music. Yeah, *Collapsing New Buildings* is even her when I translate it. A facet of her. Of us. She—

My eyes snap open.

What the actual fuck?

Inside my chest, my heart starts to throb and ache, and a vise tightens on my head.

How did a sex fantasy turn into mush?

No.

No fucking way.

She's too young.

She's not my type—okay, in essence she's exactly my type, but she's too fucking young. And I'm sending her as far away as I can.

"You can go home tomorrow."

"I'm not a fucking baby," I yell at Jones. "The shot went right through."

"And it hit an artery. You lost a shit ton of blood. And fuck if I'm going to go and find another person to replace you in the Knighthood. It's too much work."

"For fuck's sake."

Jones sits on the chair opposite me. "She's out there. Where are you sending her?"

"A long way from here."

He rubs a hand over his eyes. "Do you think it's that easy? I've been working on the stolen weapons shit for a few months. Not for the same reasons the CIA was. But there's a guy I wanted and..." He shrugs. "Calista had an electronic trail turn up. A fluke, in the whole list of stuff you showed me. I saw that he went to a titty bar in Vietnam with a well-known Bolivian porn guy. Never would have found that link without her digging."

"Let me guess. The guy's run trafficked women to Rare Birds, Inc. and to the Collectors." I pause. "And no, I don't think it'll be easy to send her away. She'll miss her brother..."

I trail off because he's staring at me.

"I meant breaking down the Collectors and all their subsidiaries," he says with a lifted eyebrow. "We knew when we rescued Dakota that we wouldn't get them all, and leaving some around to be watched helps us track more of them. But the more we uncover—"

"The more of them pop up. I'm fucking aware."

"Loose strands everywhere." I laugh, but neither of us

mistake it for humor. "We need a super database to keep track of all of this."

Jones rises. "Interesting you say that."

"Why?" I narrow my eyes at him.

"Remember what you had to do to blow up her life?"

"Yeah?"

"Well, why not take it further?"

I don't speak. I don't think I trust Jones right now.

"I've got a proposal," he says. "If you're willing to listen."

CHAPTER 34
CALISTA

My head swims. Scarlett and Ivy came to hold my hand. I don't know them, but if I ever get the chance to make friends in my dim and dark future, I'd choose them.

Ivy is sweet, and Scarlett... she's got a lot of sass. I can tell in the way she deals with Malone, how she pushed him off even though he backed her out of the room for a few minutes, their giggles and laughter and long silences all making Ivy blush.

Her guy, Mercer... now he's interesting as well. Mercer is cold and hard, elegance and killer rolled into one. The complete opposite of her but I can see them fit together. His eyes never left her even as he stood talking to someone else.

But they only stayed a short while.

And now...

I wait.

For word on Smith. In this private hospital that looks like it sprang from a rich person's retreat. I might as well be in prison.

There's no future for me. None at all.

I can hear Smith, bellowing at someone like a crotchety old man. One who slays dragons and fights Nazis and can get up and argue after nearly dying, but scratch him? He's a cranky baby.

A giggle rises in my throat, but I swallow it down because I know it's born from hysteria and if I let it take flight, I'll be lost. I'll try to run. I'll curl up on the floor. Go on a murderous spree.

Actually, it'll be a "blow up everyone's lives by hacking them" spree. Because I'm not a murderer. Not unless it's life and death for me or someone I love.

"I killed that son of a bitch."

Not for my mother.

Not for what that asshole did to me and my brother.

Not for the girls he hurt and raped.

Honestly, I wish it was for one of those reasons. Two and a half of them are noble.

I shiver in the cool air of the private, exclusive hospital, ignoring the cold coffee sitting on the table in front of me. Ignoring the hard glare of the other man I stun gunned in the balls.

No. I did it for Smith.

Because... Because...

Shit.

I know I did it for someone I loved. For him.

At some point between when he bumped into me and planted that tracker on me in Germany to now, with me killing a man I'd never met until tonight, I might have fallen for him.

Now I'm waiting to see Smith, to make sure he's good after he passed out, covered in so much blood.

Because I thought Eric had killed him. And when Smith went down the second time, I lost it.

From across the room, keeping his distance, eyeing me like I'm a thorn in his balls, Reaper appears. "He wants to see you."

"Should I zap you again?"

Reaper raises a brow as he holds up the stun gun. "Mine."

But there's a hint of amusement in his voice, and as I pass him, he mutters something.

I turn. "What was that?"

"I said Smith's finally met his match." Then he leans in. "Not that you'll get the chance, where you're going, but... don't go around fucking trying to sterilize men who're trying to help you."

"And here I was, thinking a man like you doesn't want kids."

He snorts and leads the way to a room where he shoves open the door. "I don't. But options, y'know."

My heart starts to go crazy as I step into the room on wobbly legs and catch sight of Smith. "You're all right. I thought you'd died."

"Twice? I'm not that easy to kill, sweetheart." He stretches out on what looks like the world's most comfortable hospital bed. "He likes you."

"Who?"

"The psychotic killer who just brought you in."

"I think he likes getting zapped in the balls."

We're lying to each other again, being giddy, almost airy with words, like this is just a fun day, and death and carnage and my end aren't waiting around the corner.

Not a real end, but my freedom.

The CIA's not ever letting me go.

"I'd get you too, but he took my stun gun."

Smith closes his eyes and sighs, and with that soft sound, the laughter drains away and a heaviness settles.

"I'm sorry about Riley. He..."

"He was what?"

"I really don't know. But he might have been on our side."

"Guess it doesn't really matter, does it? He's dead." I swallow hard. "W-when's Johnny coming to get me? Is it him? Do you think I can see Henry before I go?"

"No one's coming. Shit, I should have just done this when I had the plane blown—"

"What?"

I go completely still as heat sears up the back of my head to plug into my temples, making them unbearably tight.

"That plane, I might have had it blown up."

"That's insane." I stumble to his side and sit on the chair. "I honestly don't know what to be mad at. The damn tickets to DC or that, or... I don't know, what else did you do?"

My voice is rising because I don't want this. I want him to grab me and kiss me. For him to tell me he loves me—which is just never happening—and that we're running off together.

"You can't see your brother."

I push up from the seat. "No. I'm going to be locked away. And I don't care how nice it is, how good they make it, I won't have a lick of freedom. I'll be forced to work for them until I actually die for real, and you're saying I'll never get to see my twin?"

"Calista—"

"No!" I hold up a hand to stop him as I look wildly around. "No, don't you dare tell me I'm overreacting or that it's not that bad. I helped the CIA, I helped you and your merry band of killer hot men, so I don't think it's unreasonable to want to see my brother. Did you know Felicity Trenton took down all her social media? And those bank accounts I told you about are drained? What—?"

"Calista," he says. "Of course she did, and I believe we did that to the accounts. We have ways."

Smith sits up a little, and apart from the drip and the bandage on his arm, he looks utterly delicious. So close and so far, and—

"Thing is, you can't see your brother, not for a while." He sighs. It's so soft, so full of heartbreak I want to cry. And I know whatever he's going to say won't hold a happy ending for me. Not the one I secretly want, that new shiny delicate thing. "You're not going with the CIA."

I stare at him.

"As far as they're concerned, you died in the car explosion with Riley and Brown."

Maybe there is happiness in reach, that special secret one. Maybe—

"And you and me?"

"I've got a life, Calista," he says, not looking at me. "It'll take a week, so you'll have to lay low, but you'll stay with Eva, or at least at her place. Once you know where you want to live, where you want to be, we'll get you a new ID, a new history, name. Any country, anywhere."

"Do... do you have any feelings for me?" I blurt, trying not to let my voice tremble. Trying not to let the lump in my throat morph up into tears.

He still doesn't look at me. "Live your life."

The anger flares and snaps. Not for the plane and his manipulations to get me to do what he needed, but this. I'm fucking furious and hurt, and—

"You're a coward, Smith. A no-good coward."

I squeeze my eyes against the sudden blur and burn, willing myself not to cry.

And then I turn.

I walk out.

Eva from Cuba is waiting, and I don't speak to her. I just keep going, out the door.

The sooner I have my new everything, my broken heart and I can move on.

And never see him again.

The lying fuck.

CHAPTER 35
SMITH

She's dead.

Calista Juniper Price is dead.

On paper.

I sigh and pace my Manhattan penthouse, waiting... waiting... not for Calista, because she's with Jones. Learning all about her death, about how her life as she knows it, is over.

It's been a week and my heart hasn't stopped aching.

Fuck me, I'm falling apart.

It's been a week and I went shopping for a fucking wedding gift to send Orion and my kid and came back with other... things. One, in particular.

Probably the ache and the weird shopping shit is lack of constructive things to do, people to kill.

I need an assignment, something good, hard, dangerous. I need to go and get fucking laid.

Only problem with that last one is there's no one I want.

All my fantasies seem to have become particular. They all sound and feel and smell like Calista.

I know what she was asking in that hospital room, when she asked about her and me.

She wanted to know if we could ever work. Shit, I saw her face after I got shot, before I collapsed. And it was bright with fear and fierce with love. Love she had no idea about.

"The girl's twenty-four."

Calling her a girl should make me feel better about the decision to push her away, to pretend I don't crave her, want her, need her. But it doesn't. What it does is make me feel old and perverted.

Which, I guess, I am.

She just deserves better. She deserves a life.

With me, even with Jones's proposal, it's another prison. New York's big, but she'd be stuck with me and the Knights.

For her, it isn't a life.

She's leaving at the end of next week. Norway, apparently. I'm not sure why, but she chose it. I know because everyone's falling over their fucking selves to let me know what Calista does and exactly when she does it.

I check my watch. It's almost time.

Blowing out a breath, I stop, stand in front of the CCTV feed from the street. There she is. Girl of the hour.

She buzzes the intercom, and I let her in. I switch to the elevator feed that'll take her to my apartment.

Normally I don't watch people in my elevator, as I'm not that voyeuristic. But this is an unusual event. And each second's a special kind of agony.

I want it to take forever. I don't want it at all.

But the elevator dings and swishes open.

"Hey."

"Smith..." My daughter runs her fingers down the front of her jeans, and she looks about as thrilled by this as I feel. "I..."

Dakota looks around, then at me. "Jaxson's waiting downstairs."

"I'd be disappointed if he wasn't."

"Where is she?" Again, she glances around the apartment.

I frown. "Who?"

"Your girlfriend."

"I don't have a girlfriend."

She ignores me and moves past, into the kitchen where she helps herself to some cold water from the fridge.

"Then you're the idiot I always thought you were. Look." She stops, her defiant, almost arrogant tone is ruined by the need, the uncertainty on her face, and I'm hit by a rush of love so strong I almost fall.

This is my kid and over twenty years are gone. Wasted. Lost.

"We're never going to be close," I say, feeling like this is an echo of other conversations we've had. "And I get it if you don't want me at the wedding, but..."

"You want to come to my wedding?" Her eyes are big, cornflower-blue pools of need, of mistrust, of wishes scattered and broken. And hope. I can see a tiny bit of hope in the depths.

I don't cross over to her. As much as I want to. "Dakota, I did this to us, and I'd do it again. Because by keeping you at a distance, I kept you safe."

"Not enough."

I flinch. "No. And I wish to fuck I could change you being taken, but I can't."

"That wasn't fair," she whispers. "What was Mom like?"

"Almost as beautiful as you, sweet and kind and funny. We were kids, but she loved you, and I'm betting she would have been the best mom ever to you."

A small smile breaks out. "Jaxson tells me that things aren't always as they seem. Maybe he's right. Maybe you're not so bad."

"You turned out all right."

Her smile grows a bit. "We'll never be a conventional dad and daughter. We weren't close, but maybe we can work on it. Your girlfriend—"

"Not my girlfriend."

"—spoke to me the other week. Told me about what you did, your sacrifices. H-how you put me and my safety ahead of a chance to be a real dad."

Fuck me. I run a hand over my face. "My job's always been dangerous, Dakota. I did what I needed to make sure people wouldn't figure out that you're mine. And if they did... you'd be fine. I'm only sorry I hurt you, but I'd sacrifice the world for you."

She sucks in a breath and blinks rapidly. "I... please come to the wedding."

"I'd love to." A tentative smile comes to me, too.

"But one condition."

I wait as she crosses to me and puts a hand on my good arm.

"What's that?" I ask.

"Bring Calista."

Long after she's gone, Dakota's words ring through my head.

Bring Calista.

She'll be here. I could.

But I'm not going to. I don't need to go... fuck, Dakota's not going to miss me. I already bought them something outrageously expensive. That should cushion the blow.

I know if I invite Calista, she'll get the wrong idea. Worse, I will. I don't get attached, but she's the exception making the fucking rule. Two seconds with her and I'm ready to throw around heart-shaped words and sentiments and offer to jump in front of all the bullets for her.

Like with my kid, I'd sacrifice everything to give Calista freedom, her safety. Happiness. A chance.

Unlike my kid, if Calista sticks around, I might go and fuck that up.

No, scratch that. I'll definitely fuck it up.

I walk to the kitchen, grab Dakota's empty glass, and pour in a healthy shot of scotch. Then I down it, the heat sliding through me, doing nothing to make me feel better.

Better's the point. She's better off without me. End of fucking story.

But...

I want her, not just for sex, but her, in my life, and that's the most selfish thing I've ever wanted. I'm not giving in.

Jesus, I can't. Right?

I almost jump at the buzzer. As I head to the door, I glance around, for whatever my daughter might have left.

But there's nothing, and... Fuck. It's not her. It's Calista.

Her image is a hard punch to my gut.

I'm barely able to stand still as she rides the elevator up. When it opens, she's even more beautiful than ever. She's in a short black skirt with black over-the-knee socks, and she's wearing a black blazer and a tie.

And her hair is back to its techno rainbow over silver and now red.

I want to kiss the living fuck out of her, drop down and go to town on her pretty cunt. I want to just fucking hold her like an idiot.

"You look like some schoolgirl nightmare ninja mafia girl."

She snaps her fingers. "You got it." Then she glares. "I'm

not leaving until I yell at you. You're an ass, a pig, a moron. At that fancy hospital, you acted like you didn't want me."

Things start to crumble. "Maybe I don't."

"And at first I just figured you'd had your fun, but then I started thinking of how you took a bullet for me," she says, ignoring me. "You could have died."

"I'm alive."

"You must have some feelings for me. I shot the fuck out of that guy. And do you know why? Because I love you. I hate that I fell in love with you, but I did, and I went crazy. And you—"

"Calista."

"What?"

"You know I took that bullet for you. You wanna know why? Because I couldn't bear to be in a world without you. I wasn't going to let him hurt you. My regret is not making him suffer."

Things like resolve crumble. Hard.

She closes the gap between us and puts her hand on my cheek. "But you made me suffer."

"I..." Fuck. "I didn't mean to but come on, you deserve better than me. You deserve a life."

"I deserve to make that choice. And I—" She shakes her head. "I said what I needed to. I should go."

She drops her hand and turns, and she crosses to the elevator. She's almost there when I crack.

"Don't."

"Don't what?"

"Go."

"Why should I stay?" she whispers.

Why fucking indeed. Because I'm a selfish prick.

"Fuck, I thought I could do this, not be selfish, but... no, I don't want you to go."

"Why?" Her gray eyes narrow, like she's challenging me to say the right thing, the thing she needs to hear.

But I don't know if I can.

"I'd like you to stay. If you want, you can stay. My group, we need someone with your skills. It's the only way you can stay here in New York. In the States. Work with us." I hold my breath. Jesus, I don't think I can fuck this up any worse than I am right now.

I've handled all kinds of intricate, delicate situations.

This should be the easiest thing in the world.

Instead, it's the hardest thing I've ever done.

"As soon as we can make sure it's safe, you can see your brother. Let him know you're okay. He can be trusted, right?"

She narrows her eyes. "Yes."

"Good." I stop, then push out the words dancing on my tongue. "We can be together, because I think you want that, too. What do you say, sweetheart? We can play nasty little sex games, maybe get married."

She just stares at me, her jaw damn nearly hitting the floor. I know she loves me. She said she does, and she has to know I love her, too.

Because I've been fighting it since before I got shot.

I'm going for nonchalance but man, do I suck at it.

"What do you think, Calista?"

Her eyes flash with anger, nostrils flaring.

"Fuck you, Smith."

CHAPTER 36
CALISTA

"You're fucked up, Smith."

He looks at me like I'm the crazy one and he points at himself with his good arm. Not that the one where he got shot is bad. I mean, the bullet hit the brachial artery, and he could have bled out, but it was a clean shot, right through, no bone. So I refuse to soften toward him and his weird-ass, pigheaded, stupid hunter ways.

Even hunters should show some level of... softness. Skill. Pretty, comforting words.

And this is a sophisticated man.

But he's acting like he's in grade school, like he doesn't know how to tell the girl he's crushing on he likes her.

"Me?"

I cross my arms. "You."

"I got shot for you. How am I wrong here?"

"Most men," I say, "when they propose, mention love, you asshole."

"I'm not most men. I'm a dickwad, a jerk, and whatever else you've called me since we met."

A sudden rush of anxiety consumes me. And I take half a step to him. "That was a real proposal, right? I mean, my life's in fucking shreds right now."

"No, you don't have one. You're dead, remember?"

He closes the gap between us and tucks a strand of hair behind my ear.

"I know."

He doesn't say anything more, doesn't back it up with the word I want, and pain lances me.

"I guess..." I take a breath. "I guess I misunderstood."

He goes utterly silent and wipes a finger beneath my eye. I can feel the stupid, wet slide of the tear as he goes.

"No, Calista, you didn't. And it was real. But I'm not the roses and pretty bouquets kind of guy."

"Do I look like a woman who wants that?"

"You look like a woman who'd cut me if she got a chance, jump me and fuck me if she got half a one, and then run, taunting me into chasing her down to show her just who she belongs to and who's boss."

"Me. I'm boss."

He kisses me. "I'm your fucking master, sweetheart."

"So was that a proposal?"

"Calista, to blow up your life, I blew up mine. On paper, I no longer exist. I went down with you in that car. We don't exist."

The words hit. For the first time, they sink in deep. We're out of water, except he already has money, and he no doubt has various aliases. I don't have money; it's going to take me a while to set something up. And...

"Oh shit. Smith, I can't get a job, even with a fake name. If they see me, then... How do I make money?"

"Sweetheart, you know I'm a billionaire and I'm very good at making money."

"Yes, but—"

"I'm not asking you to pay your fucking way if you're with me."

"Let's go back to the flower thing," I say. "I'm not a housewife."

"Thank fuck for that. Like I said, the people I work for, they could use someone like you."

"Really?" I chew my bottom lip. "I thought you were just saying that to throw out your horribly pathetic proposal."

He groans. "I'm sorry. It's not how I meant it to come out. But if we get married, you can sidestep a lot of the red tape involved in passing all their tests and vows of secrecy."

"This isn't *Fight Club*, is it?"

"What? No. I'm saying getting married cuts the tape."

"Is that all it'll do?" I ask the question, holding my breath to hear his answer. Because I don't want to become his wife out of convenience. I want him to want me in that way, to cherish me in *his* way.

"Fuck. I want to marry you, Calista. How is this so fucking hard?"

My mouth twitches as my heart soars. I know he did it again, proposed in a lame way, but Smith's only getting on one knee if he's going to fuck me in a really interesting position.

Because maybe he's not the "I love you" type of guy. Maybe this is it.

But I don't know if it's enough.

"Are you sure, Smith? Because I fell in love with you, and I'd like to think you might love me back."

"About that." He slides around me, walks into the kitchen, and opens a drawer. "I fell in love with you, too."

My knees shake, but I stay with my back to him because I don't want to think I just made that up in my mind. I need it to be real.

"Calista?"

I slowly turn.

Smith's standing there.

"Dakota came to see me. She wants me to go to the wedding. As long as I bring you."

I can't stop the smile. "Does she like me?"

"Who wouldn't? You're a pain in the ass, you don't stay down as a sub, you fight me just the way I like, and I can't think of anyone else I'd rather be with. Apparently, my kid agrees. Not the sex shit. But about you."

"We don't need to get married," I say. "It's a big step. But there's no way I'm sticking around unless you can say the words, Smith. I put myself out there. I risked rejection and felt it at the hospital and every day since." My pulse hammers against my throat, voice shaky. "I deserve to feel cherished, and I know that's not the guy you are, but it's what I want. And I won't settle, not even for—"

"Calista."

"Yes?"

The corners of his lips quirk upward, and he sinks to one knee.

Holy shit.

He's just done the unthinkable.

"You had me hooked from the second I cornered you in Germany. I can't even fucking have sex fantasies without thinking of how good you feel in my arms. I want to explore with you, go on jobs with you. Shit, I want to hit Whole Foods and see what you think makes a good meal. I want to introduce you to all the jazz joints in this crazy city, and I'm even intrigued by breaking pottery to glue back together with gold. I want to fight and make up with you and learn all the parts of you for the rest of my life. If that isn't being in love, then love doesn't fucking exist."

He opens the box he's holding, and in it's a ring, an oval black diamond.

I don't know where he got it from or when, but I love it. I almost swoon.

"Smith..."

"Marry me. Not because of any of that lame shit I said. Marry me because I'm crazy in love with you. I'd die for you, Calista. And I'll live with you for the rest of my life, making you feel happy and cherished the way you deserve if you say yes. I love you, more than I can even begin to put into words."

I choke on a gasp, then I drop to the floor too. I take his face in my hands and kiss him, long and slow and deep. "Yes. I want all that too. I want your forevers, your every days. I want it all. So yes. A million yesses."

He kisses me again and whispers words of love against my lips.

In that moment, I've finally come home.

To him.

To love.

I hope you loves Smith and Calista's story! And if you're desperately craving more dark and sexy mafia men, then get ready for the Corsano Mafia Series! The Mafia Enemy's Bride is a dark mafia romance with a twisted as heck masked man, enemies to lovers, and arranged marriage tropes that will have you gripping the edge of your seat.

Read it on Amazon —>

Check out the sneak peek below—>

Chapter One
Ava

Sweat beads on the back of my neck as I pace the length of my living room. I run my fingers over the top of the sofa, my fingertips sinking into the soft, supple leather. I grit my teeth, remembering the day we bought it.

Motherfucker.

I bring a hand to the back of my neck and swipe the perspiration away.

One phone call is all it would take to cancel this whole fucking thing.

I suck in a breath, trying to calm my racing heart.

It's not too late to change my mind and forget any of this was supposed to happen.

My eyes drop to the Cartier watch on my wrist, the soft overhead light making the diamond-encrusted bezel glitter. Anger bubbles in my chest. High heels click on the polished marble tiles beneath my feet as I storm around the perimeter of the massive space. The sound of my shoes clicking and clacking echoes, reverberating between the walls and bouncing into the high cathedral ceiling.

I did what I was supposed to do. Got suckered into this whole fucking ruse because it was expected of me and I'm a laughing stock. A hot flush floods my cheeks and I ball my fingers into tight fists.

Nobody knows that I know, especially not him.

I could have done so many things...painful things. Deadly things.

But I didn't. I decided there was a better, more gratifying way to get my revenge.

Except it's totally unlike anything I'd ever do...or have ever done before.

I squeeze my eyes shut, letting out a shaky breath.

Oh my God, what the hell was I thinking?

I can't do this!

My knees wobble as I catch a glimpse of myself in a decorative mirror. I run a hand through my hair, the huge diamond solitaire on my ring finger catching the light. It sparkles so brightly, so blindingly, like it could completely mesmerize and deter me from what I'm about to do.

And it pisses me the fuck off, like that bright and shiny friend who is always wearing a façade, smiling and insisting her life is magic when behind closed doors it's actually *tragic*.

It's an antagonizing reminder of what deep down I knew I could never have but hoped for regardless.

All in the name of fucking family.

I pull off the ring and hold it up to my face, glaring at it with all of the hatred I can muster. All it does is smirk at me.

The biggest bullshit façade of all.

With a garbled scream, I hurl it at the mirror. It hits against the side of the glass, tiny cracks spreading into the polished surface.

Basically what happened to me a week ago.

I look at the cracked mirror and a sharp laugh pierces the still air. I never liked the damn thing, anyway. It was a wedding gift...the something old from his grandmother who's probably seen more sham marriages in her lifetime that she can count, all in the name of power and empire building.

I walk to the mirror and run my fingers over the shattered glass, tracing each of the indentations.

Empowerment. That's what this is all about. Nothing else.

I'm taking back what that bastard stripped me of.

The doorbell rings and I choke on a gasp.

Holy shit.

This is really happening.

I walk on unsteady legs to the front door, slowly and cautiously as if I'm headed down a one-way rabbit hole of complete and total uncertainty.

Which I kind of am.

White noise fills my ears, muffling the music floating from the speakers around the house. As if it could actually soothe me.

I wipe my sweaty palms on the front of my black dress.

It falls a bit above my knee, the neckline just deep enough to tempt and tease.

The effect was supposed to be classy and respectable but let's face it. Once that door opens, all shreds of my self-respect will be swept away like last night's dinner crumbs.

This isn't me. I have to stop this now.

I clutch the brass door handle.

No, no, no! Screw that. I'm not some pathetic damsel.

I'm the one running the show now. The one who will not be humiliated. The one who will reclaim her power and strength, things I should never have let go of for a second, for anyone!

Before my mind can scream out another syllable, I pull open the door and tilt my head upward as my jaw threatens to drop.

Oh.My.God.

I can't do this...

Chapter Two
Nick

I drag my eyes over her curves, the luscious tits practically popping out of the top of her dress, the way the material hugs her hips and gives me a view of the long, toned legs that I can almost feel wrapped tight around my head when I tongue fuck her.

When being the key word.

"Ava Solitano."

There's no question. It's more of an acknowledgement than anything else.

And I don't miss the look of panic that settles into her expression when I say her name.

We both know why I'm here.

We both know the rules of the game.

And we both know—

"Yeah, um, look I'm really sorry but there's been a mistake." Her cheeks flush a deep red color. "I should have called earlier to save you the trip."

I stare at her, big blue eyes shimmering with fear. She twists a strand of streaked blonde hair around her finger then tugs it as her gaze falls everywhere but on me.

I'm used to this type of reaction. Welcome it, actually.

Makes them so much more fun to play with.

See, all of these scorned women have delusions of getting revenge on their cheating bastard husbands and fiancés. And they think the best way to get it is to do him just as dirty as he did them.

So they call my private security firm and make arrangements to meet with me, a side business I created by word of mouth after arranging private security for a lonely and largely ignored wife. I fucked her senseless, which was exactly what she needed and wanted.

And I got something in return beyond money.

I got payback. Turns out her scumbag husband was a guy who'd screwed around with the wrong people. The wrong people being my family.

So after I threw her the best fuck of her life, I used it as a way to get access into his private office. Turns out, he'd stolen from us and arranged a deal to unload the goods to one of our rivals for a fuck ton cheaper than we'd paid for them.

I stopped the deal. Took back our goods. Use your imagination for the rest.

When all was said and done, I fucked his wife again for good measure before giving her all the accounts and passwords to his offshore accounts I found in his safe after I broke into it.

Well, almost all. I might've kept something for myself. Call it a grievance charge or whatever the fuck.

You don't mess with the Corsano family and expect to get away with it.

When you work private security, you learn to be observant and become a really good listener. And it wasn't long until I realized that I could help my family more under an alias than with the threat of my actual name hanging over our enemies.

I also wear a mask for any special "jobs" I take, just for added protection. And judging by the look of shock and fear on Ava's face, she's never been hunted and fucked by a masked man before.

But she's gonna get comfortable with it real fast. I laid the groundwork for this tryst and I'm not leaving without getting what I came for.

I'd heard Solitano got himself a hot new wife but her past is pretty murky at best. She's got no family to speak of so it fascinated me that he'd pick up with her in the first place, but hey. He's a guy and thinks with his dick, so that kinda explains it.

I made sure the right people gave her my number when she got fed up with his bullshit. Poor kid. She actually believed his vows translated to forever.

And her loss is about to become my gain.

I just need access to the motherfucker's safe. And after I'm finished with her, she'll be passed out for the night, giving me full reign to do my real job.

"I don't have a cancellation policy." I move closer toward her, letting her fresh, clean scent fill my lungs. "No refunds."

"I don't care about the money." She backs away from me like scared prey, slipping on the shiny tiles. "I just can't go through with it. Okay? It was a mistake to call you."

My cock gets hard just watching the conflict on her face. I see her looking at me, her pulse throbbing against her throat, the color rising in her neck. Her lips quiver, her knuckles cracking.

I allow my lips to lift into a smirk. "You're afraid."

Her chin lifts in defiance. "Don't flatter yourself. I just decided not to let some thug of a security guard put his beefy paws on me to get revenge on my cheating husband. I'm a lady, not some whore who has something to prove."

"You want me to leave?"

I close the space between us and bring a hand up the back of her spine stopping at the base of her skull. I massage the back of her neck and she practically melts in my hand like a fucking handful of M&Ms on a hot day.

"Y-yes," she moans, her eyes floating closed, her lips parting.

I lean close, my lips grazing her ear. "Too bad, princess. That's not how this works."

Read The Mafia Enemy's Bride on Amazon —>

MEET KRISTEN

Kristen Luciani is a *USA Today* bestselling author of steamy and suspense-filled romance. She's addicted to kickboxing, Starburst jelly beans, and swooning over dark, broken anti-heroes. Kristen is happily married to her own real-life hero of over 20 years.

In addition to penning spicy stories, she also has a part-time job as her three kids' personal Uber driver, which she manages to successfully juggle along with her other tasks: laundry, cleaning, laundry, cooking, laundry, and caring for her adorable Boston Terrier puppy. Mafia romance is her passion...and her poison.

Join Me On Patreon
https://www.patreon.com/kristenluciani

Follow for Giveaways
http://on.fb.me/1Y87KjV

Private Reader Group
http://bit.ly/2iQBr5V

Complete Works On Amazon
https://amzn.to/3HgM5y1

VIP Newsletter
https://dl.bookfunnel.com/28e0amc80q

Feedback Or Suggestions For New Books?
Email Me! KRISTEN@KRISTENLUCIANI.COM

Want To Join My ARC Team?
https://www.facebook.com/groups/316777206096987

Want A FREE Book?
https://bit.ly/2Jubp8h

TikTok
https://rb.gy/uhxgdj

Instagram
http://instagram.com/kristen_luciani

BookBub
https://bit.ly/2FIcoP1

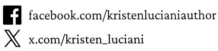

facebook.com/kristenlucianiauthor
x.com/kristen_luciani
instagram.com/kristen_luciani

Made in United States
North Haven, CT
23 January 2025

64592559R00188